NASCAR star Lan making an impres

There it was again, that look—disappointment. Disgust. Dismay. Lord, but the woman was an open book.

It fascinated him.

Lance didn't know why, but suddenly he found himself studying her face. It wasn't a particularly beautiful face. He would venture to say she was even plain, with her brown hair and brown eyes. But there was something pleasantly endearing about it. She was cute in a sweet-faced kind of way. And maybe that was what fascinated him. That sweet face didn't go at all with her hot, hot body, one perfectly outlined by her red tank top and pretty floral skirt.

...but not literally with his car

Sarah figured the man wasn't going to do something crazy, like abduct her, and so she got into the car with him. Besides, she was in no condition to walk—not yet, at least.

It was bad enough to be hit by a car, but for that car to be driven by God's gift to women was the icing on the cake. Even now she couldn't resist sneaking glances at him. He was wearing a beige polo shirt that hugged his bulging strongman arms, and she had a feeling this pretty speed demon was *ve-ry* popular with his female roadkill.

REVIEWERS AND READERS
LOVE PAMELA BRITTON!

Praise for *Dangerous Curves*

"Even if you are not a fan of racing, if you enjoy reading a
romance featuring a couple with chemistry…you'll like this one."
—*All About Romance*

"Wow! The tension and sexual excitement in this novel
are as hot and smoking as race car tires on takeoff."
—Dawn Myers, *Writers Unlimited*

Raves for *Scandal*

"A fairy tale that succeeds."
—*Publishers Weekly*

"Sexy, lively, and irresistible.…Britton strikes gold."
—*Romantic Times BOOKclub* (Top Pick)

Cheers for *Tempted*

"Passion and humor are a potent combination,
and in her historical romance *Tempted,* author Pamela Britton
comes up with the perfect blend and does everything right."
—*The Oakland Press*

"Much more than just great winter cruise reading. This is the kind of
book that romance fans will read and reread on gloomy days."
—*Publishers Weekly*

"This nonstop read has it all—sizzling sexuality,
unforgettable characters, poignancy, a delightful plot
and a well-crafted backdrop."
—*Romantic Times BOOKclub* (Top Pick)

Applause for *Seduced*

"It isn't easy to write a tale that makes the reader laugh and cry,
but Britton succeeds, thanks to her great characters."
—*Booklist* (starred review)

"The kind of wonderfully romantic, sexy,
witty historical romance that readers dream of discovering…
headed for your keeper shelf!"
—Amanda Quick, *New York Times* bestselling author

PAMELA BRITTON

in the *groove*

HQN™

If you purchased this book without a cover you should be aware
that this book is stolen property. It was reported as "unsold and
destroyed" to the publisher, and neither the author nor the
publisher has received any payment for this "stripped book."

ISBN 0-373-77098-7

IN THE GROOVE

Copyright © 2006 by Pamela Britton

NASCAR® is a registered trademark of the
NATIONAL ASSOCIATION FOR STOCK CAR AUTO RACING.

All rights reserved. Except for use in any review, the reproduction or
utilization of this work in whole or in part in any form by any electronic,
mechanical or other means, now known or hereafter invented, including
xerography, photocopying and recording, or in any information storage
or retrieval system, is forbidden without the written permission of the
publisher, Harlequin Enterprises Limited, 225 Duncan Mill Road,
Don Mills, Ontario M3B 3K9, Canada.

All characters in this book have no existence outside the imagination of
the author and have no relation whatsoever to anyone bearing the same
name or names. They are not even distantly inspired by any individual
known or unknown to the author, and all incidents are pure invention.

This edition published by arrangement with Harlequin Books S.A.

® and TM are trademarks of the publisher. Trademarks indicated with
® are registered in the United States Patent and Trademark Office, the
Canadian Trade Marks Office and in other countries.

www.HQNBooks.com

Printed in U.S.A.

For Stevie Waltrip, who always told me to keep the faith.
It finally happened, Stevie, and her name is Codi;
and for Evelyn Richmond, who was the second person
to insist I write about NASCAR. Evelyn,
I only wish you were still with us.

Also by Pamela Britton

On the Edge
Dangerous Curves
Cowboy Trouble
Scandal
Tempted
Seduced
Cowboy Lessons
Enchanted by Your Kisses
My Fallen Angel

And look for these upcoming titles!

Lord Shameless
Lord Notorious
Lord Brazen

Daytona

Legends and the Fall
Q&A with Lance Cooper
By Rick Stevenson, Sports Editor

There are certain names in motor sports that are, in some people's eyes at least, nearly as sacred as certain Popes. Names like Earnhardt, Petty, and Johnson. Men like the late Davey Allison and Fireball Roberts.

It used to be people spoke about Lance Cooper in such hushed tones, but not so much anymore. I caught up with Lance Cooper at the start of this year's racing season when he was testing at Daytona. I asked some hard-hitting questions that for the most part Lance was kind enough to answer.

RS: Lance, you used to be the man everybody talked about, but now some people have written you off as a "has-been." Can you fill us in on why they think your days as one of racing's brightest stars are over?

LC: A has-been? Come on, man. That's what you call those older guys. I'm not even thirty yet—I've got a lot of years ahead of me, as many of my longtime fans will tell you.

RS: Yes, but you've got to admit, it's been awhile since you've won a race. Care to tell us why you think that is?

LC: Heck, Rick, I *wish* I knew what it was, but the truth is I can't say it's any one thing. Certainly our engine program needs a bit of work. A few of these teams have an engine program that puts them at the top of the field week after week. Also, we've got some new people going over the wall and so that's a factor. And, too, part of it's my fault. I need to focus better. Keep my mind in the game. Avoid distractions.

RS: And you think you can fix all that this year?

LC: Without a doubt.

CHAPTER ONE

IT WAS THE WORST DAY of her life, and that was saying a lot.

Sunshine dappled the blacktop that Sarah Tingle walked upon, causing heat to radiate up through the soles of her sandals. It was late June, so walking on a narrow, two-lane road in North Carolina wasn't a good idea. But thanks to her continuing streak of rotten luck, her car had broken down a half mile back, and in the latest episode of "Sarah Tingle's Life Goes to Hell," said road appeared to be deserted. She'd stood by the side of her car for almost an hour and nobody, absolutely *nobody* had come by.

No cars. No trucks. Not even a cyclist.

That was probably a good thing because right about now she'd tackle a four-year-old for his tricycle. Instead she pulled her red tank top away from her body (the hue no doubt matching the color of her flushed, sunburnt face), using her other hand to clutch her ankle-length skirt as she fanned the material in an attempt to get some air flowing to her lower regions. Didn't help.

How had it happened? she asked herself, dropping her skirt when all she'd managed to do was entice more gnats into dive-bombing her body. How had her life spiraled so out of control? A week ago she'd been on top of the world—dating a good guy, enjoying a great teaching job, a nice apartment, and now... nothing.

She closed her eyes, ostensibly against the sunspots, but in reality against the sting in her eyes.

No time to cry, she told herself, resolutely prying her lids open. She had to deal with the fact that her car, everything she owned stuffed into the back of it, had died a splendid and dramatic death involving a loud clank, lots of noise, and clouds and clouds of smelly black smoke. Right now what she needed to do was find the address she'd been looking for. Too bad she couldn't seem to locate it, which meant she might have been better off walking back toward the main road instead of hoping for her new boss's house to appear between the tall pines, Lake Norman sparkling in the distance.

Her new boss's house.

Sarah Tingle, bus driver. She still couldn't believe she wouldn't be walking into her kindergarten classroom next week. And as she recalled the twenty precious little faces she used to teach every day, Sarah felt like closing her eyes all over again. Instead she pushed on, shoving her curly auburn hair over one shoulder as determination set in.

A half-hour later she was determined to throw herself into the lake. She'd even made a deal with herself that if there wasn't a house around the next bend she'd do exactly that.

God must have finished torturing her for the moment because right at the sharpest edge of the turn stood a mailbox, sunlight spotlighting the thing like a biblical tablet. She ground to a halt, feeling almost giddy upon recognizing the address. Two brick pillars stood to the right, an elaborate wrought-iron gate between them.

A gate with the cutout of a black race car in the middle of it.

She'd arrived. Finally.

She walked forward a few more steps—well, limped, actually; her big toe had a blister on it—so excited that she didn't look left or right as she stepped into the road, just blithely assumed no one was coming (because, really, no one had in the forty-five minutes she'd been walking).

Tires cried out in protest, their screech loud and long. Sarah looked left just in time to see the front end of a silver car coming toward her. She leapt. The car kept coming. She went airborne, then landed, rolling up the hood of a car.

It took a moment to realize she'd come to a stop.

She opened her eyes. Her head—still attached to her body, miraculously—had come to rest against something hard and cool. A windshield, she realized.

Her cheek and the front of her body pressed against the glass.

Oh, great.

She was now a human bug. How appropriate.

LANCE COOPER SAW cleavage—and that was all—a large valley of flesh where moments before there had only been open road.

What the…?

He jerked on the door, knowing full well what had happened. He'd hit somebody.

"Am I alive?" he heard the woman mumble.

Relief made his shoulders slump. "You are." *For now,* he silently added, because if she turned out to be okay, he was going to kill her.

The woman shifted, rolling away from the window like a mummy unfurled from bindings. Damn crazy race fans, he thought, trying not to panic. What'd she been doing in the middle of the road like that?

"I think I broke a rib."

She deserved a broken rib. He'd had women do some strange things to get his attention, but this took the cake.

"Don't move," he ordered, figuring he better get her to a doctor before he had a lawsuit on his hands.

"No," he thought he heard her murmur. "No doctor."

Lance reached for his cell phone before remembering service was spotty this far off the beaten path. Sure enough, no bars. "Damn," he murmured.

"No, that would be *damned*," she groaned. "As in *I'm* damned. I can't believe you just hit me."

He bit back a sarcastic retort. "Let me go call an ambulance."

"Because why should I get off with just my car breaking down?" she continued. "Why not add getting struck by a car to the list?"

"Look, don't move. I'll go call 911—"

"No," she said, sitting up and groaning.

"Hey," he cried in irritation. "I told you not to move." And wasn't it ironic to be the one saying that when most of the time it was *him* getting yelled at by rescue crews.

"Don't call 911," she said, ignoring him, which made Lance instantly angry all over again—another irony given the fact that he always tried to refuse infield care, too.

"Lady, I just hit you with my car. I'd be an idiot not to call 911."

"I'm fine," she said, swiveling on her butt ever so slowly so that their gazes met.

Lance froze.

She'd managed to shock him.

Not a speck of makeup covered her face. Usually fans were a little more overt in their attention-getting techniques—bared midriff, strategically located body piercings, even a tattoo or two. This woman didn't have any of that. Zero. Zip. Zilch.

She slid off his fender, wincing as she did so.

"Look, I'd appreciate it if you'd hold still for a moment."

"I'm fine," she said, swiping reddish-brown hair out of her face.

"You don't look fine," he said, steadying her with his hand, a hand that landed in a mass of abundant curls too soft to be fake, or permed, or heated into submission.

"I am," she reassured him, straightening. "Believe me, this doesn't feel any worse than the time Peter Pritchert ran me down."

"You've been hit before?"

"No, not like that," she said, wincing again, her flat vowels proclaiming she was from out of state, probably California. "Peter is—*was* one of my students." And he could have sworn her brown eyes dimmed for a moment, something he wouldn't have noticed if he hadn't been observing her so closely. "He had the stomach flu," she added, "and I didn't get out of his way fast enough."

"You're a teacher?" And as her words penetrated, something else she'd said earlier also sank in: *broken car.* Lord, that was her hunk of junk he'd passed a mile or two back. She *wasn't* some crazy out-of-state fan.

"I was," she said, rolling her shoulder a bit. "I recently underwent a change of career." She straightened, giving him a brave, everything's-all-right smile. "You're looking at Lance Cooper's newest bus driver—well, motor coach driver. I'm supposed to bring his fancy new RV to Daytona for him."

For the second time that day, she managed to shock him. She was his new driver. *And she didn't know who he was.*

"I was supposed to have a meeting with him, actually, which means I should probably get going before a meteor lands atop my head."

"A meteor?"

"Sure, why not?" she asked. "I mean, everything else has gone wrong today. Why not a meteor, or a swarm of locusts or a plague?"

He almost smiled. Obviously, she was hanging on by a thread. "Look," he said, deciding to hold off telling her who he was for the moment. "I think you should see a doctor. I have a friend—"

"No doctor," she said impatiently.

"Why not?"

"Because I don't have health insurance."

And there it was again, that look. Disgust. Disappointment. Dismay. Lord, but the woman was an open book.

It fascinated him.

He didn't know why, but suddenly he found himself studying her face. It wasn't a particularly beautiful face. He would venture to say she was even plain with her reddish brown hair and brown eyes. But there was something pleasantly endearing about it. She was cute in a sweet-faced kind of way. And maybe that was what fascinated him. That sweet face didn't go at all with her hot, *hot* body, one perfectly outlined by her red tank top and pretty floral skirt.

"Don't worry about the health insurance," he said. "I'm sure my car insurance will cover it."

"No, thanks. Mr. Cooper's waiting for me."

He opened his mouth to tell her *he* was Mr. Cooper, only something stopped him. He had a feeling if he told her *he* was Lance Cooper it might just be enough to push her over the edge.

"C'mon," he said. "I'll give you a ride. That's a long drive."

"Is it?" she asked, looking puzzled, as well she should because you couldn't see his house from the road and so there was no way to know that, unless...

"I've been there before," he said.

"You have?"

"Lots of times."

"You're friends with Lance Cooper?"

Okay, time to confess who he was. "I'm his pool boy."

Now what the heck did you go and say that for?

"You're his *pool boy.*"

Because he had a feeling when she realized who he was, humiliation just might make her do something crazy—like run off shrieking, hands flailing. He almost smiled at the image.

And then he saw her glance at his car—a top-of-the-line Cobra, and one of only seven thousand, not that she would know. Her brows lifted. "Wow," she said. "Cleaning pools must pay better than I thought."

SARAH FIGURED the man wasn't going to do something crazy like abduct her, and so she got in the car with him. Besides, she was in no condition to walk.

Run over by a car. If she didn't hurt so much she'd laugh—granted, it'd be hysterical laughter, but she'd be cackling nonetheless. Instead she slid into the interior of the car, her rayon-clad rear zooming across the smooth leather seat.

"You're not dizzy or anything, are you?" the man who hit her asked after getting in on his side, his southern voice smooth and oddly comforting.

"No. I'm fine." The only time she'd been dizzy was when she'd caught her first glimpse of him.

Jeez.

It was bad enough to be hit by a car, but for that car to be driven by God's gift to women was the icing on the cake. Even now she couldn't resist peeking glances at him. In a beige polo shirt that hugged his bulging, strongman-arms, she had a feeling this pretty pool boy was very popular with his female clients.

I wonder if they make him wear a Speedo, she mused to herself, watching him punch in the code she'd given him, his shoulder muscles flexing.

She'd never seen a man with muscles along the back of his neck, but this pool boy sure had them, his short-cropped blond hair curling around his nape.

"What's wrong?" he asked, and Sarah realized she'd sighed.

She looked away. "Nothing."

"You know I really would feel better if I took you to the hos—"

"No," she cut him off. "There's no need. It didn't feel like you hit me all that hard."

"Well, I wasn't going all that fast. I'd slowed down to turn into the driveway."

"See? And I jumped up onto the hood of your car, so I really wasn't hit. Just…shoved. I'm fine." And she was. The only thing that hurt was her pride. And her elbow. And maybe her knees. She rubbed at one knee now, feeling a bump and the sting of what could only be scraped skin. She bent forward, lifting her skirt.

"Ouch," she heard him drawl.

She dropped the skirt over her knee, feeling suddenly self-conscious. "Just a scrape."

"It'll need some antibiotic lotion."

"I'll ask Mr. Cooper if he has some." Which made her glance in front of her, just in time to spy the driveway open up before them, Lance Cooper's home coming into view.

"Oh, wow," she said.

"Not bad, huh?"

Not bad at all.

The massive stone home jutted from the landscape like a pop-up castle in a book. That's what it looked like, she thought in amazement, sunlight glinting off the windshield as they passed beneath trees. She shielded her eyes with her hands, taking note of the leaded windows, a few of which were colored by stained glass. Give it a few turrets and a drawbridge and Cinderella could move right in.

Apparently race-car drivers made good money.

"I wonder if he's home," she murmured.

"Doesn't look like it."

"Great," she said, dropping her hand back to her lap at the same time she blew a hank of hair out of her eyes. "The man must have thought I stood him up."

"I'm sure he figured something happened."

But for Sarah, it was suddenly all too much. "I just can't catch a break," she found herself saying, her hands digging into her skirt. Her nose was starting to clog—never a good sign—and her throat suddenly constricted. But she wasn't going to cry. Not in front of— "I don't even know your name," she said in a voice that sounded on the verge of tears, even to her own ears.

"Lance," he said softly, even the way he said his name sounding southern—*Lay-yance.* She almost sighed again.

But then she straightened in surprise. "Lance?" she asked. "You have the same name as the guy that owns this place?"

"Uh, yeah."

Later, much later, Sarah would look back at that moment and call herself the world's biggest, most bimbonic fool (if bimbonic was really a word). But right then she was barely hanging on by a thread, and so instead she said, "What a coincidence." She had bigger fish to fry. Such as holding on to her sanity, something that was getting increasingly harder and harder to do.

"You in pain?" he asked, probably because he'd seen her face contort as she tried to refrain from crying.

"No." And, oh Lord, was that her lip quivering?

"You look like you're about to cry."

And he sounded so concerned, so caring—and all right, a little bit panicked—that she found herself taking a deep breath and saying, "You ever go through times when you feel like a fish being slowly digested in the belly of a giant whale, bile eating at your flesh, bacteria nibbling at your eyeballs? And then, just when you think it can't get any worse, you get regurgitated and you're floating in some water current, flailing about with giant sharks circling overhead?"

She looked over at him. He was blinking in a funny way, kind of like a dog the first time it saw a toilet flush.

"Uh…no."

"Well, that's the way I feel."

"Why?"

She took another step closer to tears. "Because in the space of a week I've been publicly humiliated, lost my job, been hit by a car. And now…*now* I'm about to embark on a career driving a bus for some famous race-car driver. I'm a *kindergarten* teacher, not a bus driver."

"Then teach instead."

"I can't," she said. "Not back home at least."

"Why not?"

"Because of the pictures," she said in total, absolute frustration—forgetting for a moment that he had no idea what the heck she was talking about.

Which was why he probably asked, "What pictures?"

Which made Sarah realize she didn't really *want* him to know about them. "Nothing," she said quickly.

"Oh, no," he said, a half smile alighting on his face. "You can't say something like that and take it back."

"I'm not trying to take it back. I just refuse to expand on it."

"What kind of pictures?" he asked again.

"Forget it," she said, trying to get out.

He locked the car doors with a pop. "What pictures?" he asked again, giving her a wicked grin.

Sarah was suddenly aware of the fact that she

was alone, with a near stranger, parked in front of a deserted home. "Let me out."

"Did you pose for *Playboy?*"

Her face suddenly felt like a barbecue. *"I did not."*

"Hustler?"

"I'm leaving." She tried the door again. He let her go this time. That made her feel a bit better, though the sticky North Carolina air did nothing to cool her heat-embarrassed cheeks.

"Wait," he said, getting out, too. "You can't leave me hanging like this."

"Yes, I can," she said, turning toward the house, though she suddenly realized she had no idea what to do. Wait for Mr. Cooper? Go back for her car?

Get hit by a bus next time?

"You *were* in *Playboy,* weren't you?" he asked, coming around the front of his car. "C'mon, tell me what issue."

She gasped in outrage. "Why you…sleazeball! I was *not* in *Playboy.*"

"Sleazeball?"

She crossed her arms in front of her. He chuckled a bit. *Oh, wow.*

Sarah almost melted into the fancy stone driveway. She'd never, not ever, been in the presence of a man who looked like Lance before. Gorgeous smile with just a hint of razor stubble lining his masculine jaw. Lips that curved up in a wicked way, a more pronounced patch of razor stubble right below his lower lip. And his eyes; they were a playful gray filled with laughter that seemed to poke fun at her.

"It wasn't *Playboy*," she said when she realized those eyes were staring at her in unabashed curiosity, too.

"Then what?" he asked.

"Is there a hose I can use to wash off my knees?" she said, turning away.

Lance stayed with her. She stopped, her gaze darting to his. He'd wiped the laughter from his face, but a film of humor still drifted in his eyes. "I'm sorry. I forgot for a moment that I'd just run you over with my car. C'mon. We have Band-Aids and stuff inside." He motioned for her to follow.

Sarah stood there for a second, watching him turn away. "I didn't pose naked," she found herself confessing.

He stopped. She met his gaze, feeling her chin lift in dignified pride. "I was wearing undergarments. And I took the pictures in college. Driving a bus wasn't paying the rent and this was a way to make some quick money."

"And you got fired over something that happened years ago?" he asked. "How could that be?"

She should have let the matter drop. But he seemed genuinely curious, and perplexed, and Lord knows, she'd been dying to talk about it to somebody who might understand. "The photos were published *this* year," she said. "And they were put in a maga-

zine that makes *Playboy* look like *Reader's Digest*."
She shuddered. "I can't even say the name. But the
worst, the absolute worst was that they took my underwear off and replaced it with someone else's—"
She couldn't finish, humiliation making it impossible to speak.

"Somebody else's..." he prompted.

"Somebody else's *you know*."

"No, I don't know."

"Body parts," she admitted.

"Body parts?" he asked.

"Yeah, body parts."

But he still looked confused.

"I was wearing somebody else's you-know-what,"
she confessed, pointing to the appropriate area.

He drew back, and for a second he looked incapa-
ble of speech. Then he started laughing, a big, booming laugh that filled the air and all but vibrated her
skull.

"You were wearing someone else's—" His
words got choked off by his laughter.

"It's not funny." Only, suddenly, it kind of was.
"I got fired for this!"

She heard him bite back a laugh before choking
out, "Why?"

"One of the parents found out. Other parents heard
about it, too. Someone brought the magazine in to
show the principal. There was a formal review…"

She left out the part about dating one of the school's officials. And that he'd turned his back on her during the whole affair. That little humiliation she managed to keep to herself.

"I packed my bags and headed for North Carolina. I'd heard teaching jobs were more prevalent here, but they're not, so I had to take the first job I could find."

"Driving a motor coach."

"It was better than nothing. Plus it came with living quarters. I was, ah, living with someone at the time, someone who frowned upon my illicit past."

"Your boyfriend," he surmised.

Well, and now that cat was out of the bag, too. Not that it mattered. After today she'd probably never see Lance again.

"He kicked you out," he said softly.

Sarah met his gaze, surprised at the sudden compassion she saw in his eyes. "Well, it *was* his apartment."

Silence filled the air, the kind of heavy quiet that seemed to amplify everything. Her breathing. His breathing. Her scent. His scent…

And then his lips began to twitch a bit. He moved in closer to her. And then there was noise, loud noise—her heart as it echoed in her ears like the slap of water against a rock.

Her cheeks heated all over again, especially at the brief glimpse of…something she caught in his eyes.

Then he flicked her chin up with his hand.

And Sarah knew the moment he touched her that she was in deep, *deep* trouble.

CHAPTER TWO

"C'MON IN," Lance said, his hand dropping back to his side, fingers tingling as if the steering wheel had been jerked out of his grasp during a wreck.

That was bizarre.

"Let's get you fixed up," he added.

She nodded wordlessly, Lance feeling something warm seep though his insides. She looked so forlorn. So completely downtrodden—like Bluto, the dog he'd found by the side of the road when he'd been a kid. In need of food and a good hug.

Hug?

Okay, maybe not that. After all, he didn't want any lawsuits on his hands. But he sure sympathized with the way she felt. He'd been there himself.

"Where are we going?" she asked as Lance turned back to his house.

"Inside," Lance repeated.

"Wait. Inside? We can't do that," she said, stopping on the path.

Oh, yeah. That's right. Damn it. He was supposed to be the pool boy. Unfortunately, she didn't look any

more capable of handling the news of who he was
now than she had a few minutes ago.

"I have keys," he said. "In, ah…in case of an emergency."

Lame. Really, really lame.

She bought it. Nodded. "Do you think he'll mind
if you let me in?"

"Nah. Lance Cooper is a great guy." Okay, so that
might have been a little over the top, but he couldn't
resist. In fact, he was beginning to find the whole
thing kind of amusing.

He opened his front door, turning to the left and
disabling the alarm. If she thought it was strange
that he had the alarm code memorized, she didn't
show it, though to be honest he had a feeling she
was too distracted to notice much.

Maybe not.

When he glanced back at her, her mouth was
open, her eyes darting left and right, then up and
down, then left and right again.

"Holy guacamole."

"Yeah," he said, glancing at the vaulted ceilings,
numerous skylights and tall paned windows. "It is
kind of big."

Though he hardly noticed it anymore. He'd had
a decorator work on the interior right after he'd
bought it, but most of her "homey touches" had
faded away, replaced by his own personal items: a
Gatorade bottle saved from his first victory at

Pocono. He doubted his prissy decorator would have approved of the yellow lug nuts inside the bottle: they clashed with the rose-colored Tiffany lamps. There were other souvenirs from his years on the track, too, most of them stashed atop shelves in his cherry-wood entertainment center, the big-screen TV reflecting back their distorted images. Helmets. A battered pair of asbestos shoes—they'd been the shoes he'd worn his first year Cup racing. And then there were the pictures.

Lots and lots of pictures.

Uh-oh.

"This way," he said, lightly grabbing her arm and steering her toward the back of the house.

"But I wanted to look at the pictures."

"I don't think Mr. Cooper would like that."

"Oh, yeah," she murmured.

Close. That had been really, really close.

She followed him along, looking left and into his private office which faced the front of the house. There were pictures in there, too.

"He's a bit of a slob," he said, wincing at the papers all over the place. "Anyway. We, ah, we better get this over with. I'd hate for the boss to return and get mad at me for letting you in here."

She nodded, her Shirley Temple hair bouncing along.

He led her to the kitchen. No pictures there. At least none that he remembered. She paused for a moment beneath the multifaceted chandelier that he'd always thought was a bit overkill, but that his decorator had insisted upon.

"Wow."

"You like it?"

"Well…" And then she surprised him with one of those I'm-going-to-be-honest-with-you-even-though-I-don't-know-if-I-should-be looks. "Not really," she admitted.

He laughed, nodding his head. "I don't really like it either."

Her expression cleared and she looked a bit more relaxed when she started to follow him again, though now that he watched her closely he saw that she limped.

Poor thing. She'd really had a tough time.

And he'd just lied to her.

Yeah, but it was for a good cause.

"Good golly," she said, his hand sliding off her arm when they reached the kitchen. "How much does driving race-cars *pay?*"

"Big bucks," he said. "If you're any good at it."

"Lance Cooper must be very, very good."

Oh, yeah, I'm good.

Or I used to be.

He shook his head, walking past the blue-tile counter to the stainless steel sink to his right.

"C'mon. Let's get you cleaned up."

She shuffled forward, her eyes darting all around.

The whole kitchen was decorated in a Mediterranean theme: maroon walls, dark cabinets and thick-leaved banana plants. A skylight oozed filtered light, copper pots and pans hung over the island, and glass-fronted cabinets were filled with the blue-and-white dishes that his decorator insisted on calling "crockery." Whatever.

"You could dance the Coco Cabana in here," she mumbled, her eyes on the island.

"Yeah, well, you won't be doing any dancing any time soon. Sit down," he said, wetting a paper towel, then guiding her to the wrought-iron kitchen table and chairs.

"Do you serve drinks when he has guests over?"

He paused in the act of opening up the cabinet where he kept suntan lotion, medicine and first-aid items.

"When who?"

"Your boss."

"What makes you think I'd be asked to do something like that?"

"Well, look at this place. All it needs is Hugh Hefner and few Playboy Bunnies to make it complete. So scratch that. He probably has the Bunnies serve the drinks."

"He's not like that."

"No? Could have fooled me. So if he doesn't have a huge ego, he must be lacking in other departments."

He almost choked. "What?"

She blushed, looking instantly contrite. "I'm sorry. That wasn't very nice. I've never even met the man and I'm certain he's perfectly nice."

"You think the house is pretentious?"

She gave him a look that she must have practiced on her kindergartners. "Nobody needs this much space."

"Maybe. Maybe not. Maybe he built such a big house because he wants kids."

"Is that what you think?" she asked, looking curious.

And suddenly, with her head tilted to the side, her curly hair falling over one shoulder, her hazel eyes wide and more green than brown, Lance found himself saying, "Yeah. He does."

"Then he better get busy 'cause he's got a bunch of rooms to fill."

"I'll tell him you said that."

Her eyes widened. "Don't you dare!"

She had really thick lashes, he noticed, with sweeping, dark-brown brows above them. Pretty eyes.

Gorgeous eyes, he quickly amended.

"What's the matter? Afraid he might think you're volunteering for the job?" he teased, kneeling down in front of her and giving her a smile.

"No." She half snorted, making that funny noise people made when they were trying not to laugh, sort of a combination snort/cough. "He'd only need to take one look at me to know I wasn't his type."

"And what makes you say that?" he asked, opening up a tin of Band-Aids. He stored a tube of antibiotic lotion inside.

"Look. I may not know anything about race-car drivers. Heck, I don't know anything about racing at all. But I know something about celebrities. Famous men, as a rule, don't date women like me."

"Yes, they do."

"No, they don't."

There was such a self-deprecating look of acceptance in her eyes that he found himself almost bristling. "Jeez, don't tell me you think you're ugly?"

"Not *really* ugly. But I'm not exactly a candidate for *America's Next Top Model*."

"So? What's wrong with that?"

She looked away. "Want to hand me the antibiotic lotion?" she asked. "I'll put it on myself."

Changing the subject. So she *didn't* like her looks. "No. I'll do it," he said.

"That isn't necessary."

"Yeah, it is. I ran you down. I'm taking care of you. Lift your skirt."

She blushed, mumbling. "Really. There's no need."

And the way that color spread from her neck up into her face… She blushed so bad he knew in an instant what the problem was. She was attracted to him.

He almost sat on the floor.

She thought he was good-looking. And she didn't even know who he was.

Cool.

"Lift up your skirt."

"No," she said, holding out a hand. "I've doctored more scraped knees than I can count. I can do my own."

"Just the same, I'm doing it for you. Lift up your skirt."

She looked ready to protest again.

"Do your kindergartners give you such a hard time?" he asked. "You know, when you want to doctor them up?"

Her eyes narrowed. He found that kind of cute, too. But then her expression turned to one of long-suffering resignation. She even let out a huff of exasperation.

Lance tried not to laugh.

She was adorable. There was no other way to describe her. Adorable and completely unaware that he found her makeup-free face and curly hair more attractive than a hundred made-up models.

She reached down, pulling up her pretty floral skirt. "There," she said.

He glanced at her knee. "Uh-oh."

"What?" she asked, leaning forward, her hair hanging next to his face. It smelled good. Kind of sugary.

"We're going to need to stitch it up."

"No, we're not," she said, leaning even closer. Lance didn't move.

"I'm just teasing."

She looked up then, their faces inches apart. Both of them went still. No. That wasn't right. She opened her mouth a bit, a plump, fully kissable mouth (funny he hadn't noticed *that* before), the word, *Oh* escaping on a sigh.

"We'll need to ki—clean it," he said, mentally wincing at his near slip.

She didn't appear to notice. "Yeah."

She had freckles. And the cutest little dent right at the tip of her nose. And a sexy mouth. And if he leaned forward just a bit...

"Lance!"

They jerked apart.

"Lance, where are you?" a masculine voice called. "I know you're in here. Saw your car out front."

He heard steps. Shit. It was Sal, his business manager.

"There you are. Oh. And there *you* are," Sal said to Sarah. "I thought you stood him up. What happened, Lance? She show up after you called me to complain?"

And Lance knew he was busted.

Sarah looked up at him, little flames all but flicking out from the center of her eyes. "*You're* Lance *Cooper?*" she asked in a low, tight voice.

"Guilty," he admitted with the smile of a ten-year-old who's just knocked his baseball through Mom's kitchen window.

CHAPTER THREE

SHE WANTED to hit him. No. She wanted to scream. No. Maybe what she wanted to do was run out the door. That seemed a much better solution to all her problems. Run out the door and keep on running.

"You're Lance Cooper," she said again. And it was a statement, a flat, unemotional statement, which was hard to accomplish given how furious she felt.

"That's what I said." And then his smile turned playful. She'd seen little boys do that, too. Catch them gluing paper to their desk and they'd look up at you with that same aren't-I-funny? grin.

As if by smiling at her like that she'd forgive him.

As if she should be all smiles, too.

As if.

She'd been dealing with far too many adolescent males lately to have much patience for the opposite sex.

"You, sir, are no gentleman."

It was a lame thing to say. Very Scarlett O'Hara, but she didn't care. She didn't swear and she didn't like to call people names. That said, if ever there was a time when she felt like cussing, this was it.

"Uh-oh. What'd he do now?" Sal Lowenstein, the man who'd interviewed her and who was Lance Cooper's business manger, asked.

"He told me he was the pool boy."

Which made the big-breasted man's eyes widen so fast, his head actually flicked back a bit. And then he laughed, his meaty jowls opening and exposing perfectly bleached teeth. Sarah's lips tightened. She crossed her arms in front of her, giving both Lance and his portly manager a look that would have turned her kindergarten class silent in an instant.

"Look, Mr. Lowenstein," she said. "Obviously, Mr. Cooper has a sense of humor I don't appreciate. Thus, I don't think I'm suited for this job. I'm sorry I was late, but now that I've met Mr. Cooper there's no sense in wasting our time. I don't want the job."

She had a car to fix. A job to find. Rent to pay.

You don't want the job?

"Whoa, whoa, whoa," Lance said, his movie-star smile morphing into a frown. "You can't leave."

"I beg to differ, Mr. Cooper. I can."

"Don't blow an ignition over this."

"Blow a *what?*"

"An ignition."

"I'll do whatever I want."

"Great. As long as it's with me."

"You're impossible," she said.

"I try," Lance said.

"And it's just one more reason why I shouldn't take the job. You're a flirt, Mr. Cooper, and right now I've had it up to here with lying, cheating flirts."

"Whoa, whoa, whoa," he said again. "Who said anything about cheating?" He turned to his manager. "Have you been blabbing?"

"Not me," Sal said, his wide arms spreading as he lifted his hands. The result was that he lost all semblance of a neck. Sarah thought he looked rather like an egg with a gum ball on top of it.

"I've got to go," she said, standing. When she wobbled a bit, Lance Cooper shot forward, trying to steady her with a hand. She leaned away so his fingers never connected.

"Don't touch me," she snapped.

His amusement faded. In fact, he looked so sympathetic, she found herself staying still despite what she told herself.

"Look," he said. "You're right. It was wrong of me to pretend I was a pool boy. But you looked so distraught after I hit you with my car that I didn't have the heart to tell you who I was."

"You hit her with your car?"

Lance glanced over his shoulder. "Yeah. When she was a half hour late, I quit waiting and went out— When I came back, I didn't see her in the driveway until I ran into her. She claims she's okay, but I'm not buying it."

"I *am* okay," she contradicted.

"That's what they all say and then they drop dead the next day from fluid building up around the brain."

"You think I have a brain injury?"

"I don't know, do you? Let me look in your ears and see if I can tell."

And all she could think to do was stare at him because he'd lost his mind. He'd completely lost his mind.

"Just kidding," he said.

She turned for the door.

He stopped her with a hand, a big, warm hand that made her suddenly flush with heat and embarrassment and, and—she didn't know what else.

"I'd like to take you to a doctor," he said gently.

"I'm not going to a doctor."

"I'll pay for it."

"No thanks. What I need is to get back to my car."

"Did it break down?" Mr. Lowenstein asked.

"Yeah," she said, testing her leg with the knee injury. Pain shot up her thigh. She tried not to wince, but she had a feeling Lance Cooper saw it anyway.

"Was it a VW with faded blue paint?" Sal asked.

Sarah froze, pain momentarily forgotten. "Yeah?" she asked warily. "Why?"

"It's being towed."

"That's impossible. It's been on the road for less than two hours."

"Yeah, well, someone must have reported it

because I saw them loading it up with my own two eyes."

"No," she said with a quick shake of her head.

"Did it have a yellow smiley-face sticker in the back window?"

Her shoulders slumped. "They're towing my car," she said, desolate.

"We'll get it back," Lance said.

"But I don't have the money to pay an impound."

"I do," Lance said.

"I don't believe this," she said breathlessly. "I just don't believe this." And horrors upon horrors, she could feel the tears begin to build again in her eyes. "This has got to be a cosmic joke. There's got to be some kind of conspiracy going on. Drive Sarah Tingle crazy. And, you know what, it's working. It's really, really working."

"Come here," Lance Cooper said.

"No," she warned. "Stay away from me."

But the man just ignored her, pulling her into his arms before she could stop him. She tried to pull away, muttering, "If you don't let me go, I'll sue you for sexual harassment."

"Go ahead," he said, his big hand cupping the back of her head and forcing it against his chest. "Go right on ahead," he said softly.

She gave in then, she just gave in and did the girliest thing she'd ever done in her life. She started sobbing in a total stranger's arms. A stranger who was supposed to be her new boss. A stranger whom she could never work for because even while she was bawling all over his polo shirt, she couldn't stop herself from noticing how muscular his chest was, how big his arms, how perfectly nice it felt to be held in a man's arms.

That wouldn't do. That just wouldn't do *at all*.

IT FELT NICE to hold her.

"Sal, can you hand me that box of tissue?"

"Lance," his manager started to say, obviously seeing big attorney fees in his future. "Maybe you should let her—"

"Shh," he said, both to Sal and the woman in his arms. "It'll be okay." He even rested his head atop her hair, liking the way the curls turned to silk beneath his cheeks. "Shh," he said again, slowly rocking her.

"I can't believe this," he heard her mumble. "I can't believe I'm crying in some stranger's arms."

"I'm not a stranger."

"You are to *me*. I've never even seen your Wheaties box."

"No big deal. It's a bad picture, anyway."

"*That* I find hard to believe."

"It's true," Sal piped up.

But she ignored him, mumbling, "It's just that from the moment those darn pictures appeared in that magazine, everything's gone wrong. I feel like

God's got a vendetta out for me. Like if I try to do one more thing, I'm going to be struck by lightning."

"I've had days like that."

She drew back, looked up at him. Lance's heart melted at the tear-streaked face that stared up at him. "Oh, yeah?" she asked. "What happened? All four tires fall off your race car or something?"

"No. Just two. We had a new tire changer and he didn't get all the lug nuts tight. Back tire fell off which tweaked the car enough that the front tire came off. My car looked like something you'd find in a ghetto."

She was staring up at him like she thought he was crazy.

"I'm serious. Looked like someone had stolen my rims. One of the boys back at the shop even spray-painted some graffiti on the side to make it look more authentic."

"Seriously?" she asked in a small voice.

"Seriously."

"But did you break a leg while trying to get out of the car? Because that's the kind of thing that would happen to me right now."

"No. But one of the other drivers got mad at me because my tire ended up in the middle of the race-track, which he hit. It tore apart his front end, caused him to go a few laps down, which ultimately caused him to miss the top ten in points, thus eliminating him from the Chase. He threw a wrench at me in the garage."

"Yeah?"

"Yeah."

"Here," Sal said, holding a box of tissues out to her.

"Thanks," she said, wiping at her eyes. "I'm sorry," she said to them both. "It's just been a bad day."

"Well, we're going to make it better," Lance promised. "Sal, get on the phone with the city. Find out who they use to tow cars. I'm going to get my cell phone to call Doc Brown. I want him to give you the once-over—ah, ah, ah," he warned her when she opened her mouth to protest. "For my sake, not yours. I'll worry about you all night if you don't get yourself checked out."

She didn't look any more enthusiastic about the idea, but at least she stopped protesting. "Now. C'mon. Let's get you settled in the family room."

"You mean the one with all the pictures of you in it?"

"Yeah," he said, giving her a smile. "That's the one."

"I should have known something was up when you all but dragged me away from the room."

"I didn't *drag* you."

"No. But it was clear you didn't want me loitering."

"I didn't," he said with a wide smile. "I was having too much fun pretending to be a pool boy."

Her eyes dimmed a bit.

"C'mon, you gotta admit. I'd make a good pool boy." He flexed one of his arms.

"Yeah…well, don't quit your day job, 'cause your acting skills leave a lot to be desired."

He clutched at his heart. "Ooo."

She smiled a bit. And that's all he'd wanted to see. A smile. Just one tiny little grin.

They got her settled onto his burgundy-colored couch, the thing practically swallowing her up. Lance helped prop her injured knee up on his glass coffee table, saying, "You realize you're hired, don't you?"

She caught his gaze, wariness in her eyes. "I'm not so certain that's a good idea."

"Oh yeah?" he asked. "And why's that?"

"Because…" She looked away, her lower lip being sucked into her mouth for a second, a blush lightly staining her cheeks.

He just loved the way she blushed.

"Because I just don't think it'd work out."

"So what're you going to do? Go home in a taxi, take a bus to your next job interview, use up the last of your savings while you try to find a new job?"

"I don't have any savings."

"Well, then, it's going to be awfully hard to get your car out of jail, isn't it?"

In went her lip again, her eyes moving to the floor once more.

He tipped her chin up. It was a completely personal thing to do, something he wouldn't normally do to a woman he'd just met, but with Sarah, it felt right. "Drive my bus. Just give it a try. If it doesn't work out, at least you'll have one paycheck to help see you through."

She met his gaze, and that thing happened to Lance again, that odd sort of mushy feeling he got in his stomach as he stared down at her.

"All right."

"Atta girl," he said, dropping his hand back to his side, rubbing his fingers together because it felt as if he'd been shocked by a loose spark plug wire.

"Okay," Sal said. "I'm, ah, I'm going to go call the city."

Lance held Sarah's gaze for a second longer before forcing himself to look away—and he really did have to force it. "Great," he said, telling himself he just felt sorry for her. He knew what it was like to go it alone. It wasn't easy. "I'll go call Doc Brown."

Thankfully, she didn't protest again, but when Lance turned to go, Sal grabbed his arm, waiting until they were out of the room before saying, "I should probably use the phone in your office."

"Why's that?"

"Because I don't want her to know I'm really calling a tow truck company to tow off her car."

"You're *what?*"

"Shh," Sal instantly said. "Not so loud. I don't want her suspicious."

"You mean to tell me her car isn't really gone?"

"Nah," he said, shaking his head and pressing his lips together so his jowls hung down like a bulldog. And that's exactly what Lance's business manager was. A bulldog, even if he was a bit overzealous in his protection. "I just told her that so she wouldn't take off on us."

"Why the hell'd you do that?"

"Because I didn't want her trotting out of here, mad as hell, and thinking later on that she might have a good lawsuit on her hands. This way, she's here. We can soothe her ruffled feathers, maybe even convince her to stick around for a while, see a doctor. We really should have her checked out."

"I know. That's why I'm calling Doc Brown now."

"I know, I know, and he'll tell us if he thinks her injuries are real or faked."

"You think she might be faking?" Lance asked in disbelief.

"It's possible."

"Doubtful," Lance corrected. "That woman doesn't have a dishonest bone in her body. It's why I like her. And why I want her to stick around. So you better have the tow truck company bring her car here. I want her happy."

Sal gave him a strange look. Actually, it was more of a concerned look. "You're not attracted to her, are you?"

"No," Lance denied. "Not my type."

But Sal's eyes narrowed. "You better watch yourself," his business manager warned.

"Don't worry. I will."

But Sal didn't look convinced. Not surprising because Lance wasn't convinced himself. He had a feeling Sarah Tingle might prove to be a huge distraction. And that wasn't good.

That wasn't good at all.

CHAPTER FOUR

IT AMAZED SARAH how quickly Lance and his manager arranged everything. Within an hour they had her car parked in the driveway, the doctor examining her leg, and a couple of guys from "the shop" examining her transmission.

Sarah didn't know whether to be impressed or intimidated. It seemed to her that only the very wealthy and the very influential could order mechanics to repair a car and have a doctor show up on their doorstep.

In North Carolina, apparently, race-car drivers ranked right up there with the Pope.

So she waited for the doctor to finish poking and prodding her (diagnosis: superficial wounds) then sat in Lance Cooper's fancy family room while she waited and waited for the mechanics to be equally brilliant in diagnosing her car.

It wasn't good news. It was terminal.

"What do you mean you can't fix it?" Sarah asked a little later, feeling as if every molecule of blood had suddenly dropped to her heels.

"There's a lot of miles on that motor, Miss Tingle. Over two hundred thousand by the looks of it," a blond headed guy said. "Sorry, but the block gave out. It's cracked. Given the number of miles on it, I'm surprised the engine lasted this long."

She'd bought the car used in college by saving money from working nights and weekends. She'd nursed the blue Bug through a leaky radiator, a bad transmission and a whole host of other problems. That it had finally died made her feel…resigned. She felt resigned. What else could go wrong in her life?

"So what do I do with it?" she asked. Three male faces stared down at her—only three because one of the male mechanics was still outside with her car, like it was a dying patient or something.

Would you like some oil, Mr. Bug?

"Well," said the mechanic, glancing at Lance, hero worship in his eyes. "We could put a new engine in it."

"That sounds expensive," she said.

"It won't be too bad if we run the parts through the shop," Lance soothed in his Carolina voice.

"I'll have to find out where to get them from, but that shouldn't be a problem," the mechanic said.

"We can pay for your car to be repaired and take it out of your salary," Mr. Lowenstein added. "Not all at once, but a little bit at a time. That way you'll have a car to drive when you're not busy driving for Lance."

And she would have to drive for Lance, she

realized. She'd driven across the country in a burst of misplaced optimism, had hoped to find one of the jobs that she'd been told were so prevalent in booming Charlotte, North Carolina. It'd taken her two weeks to realize that North Carolina school board politics prevented those on the outside from getting in, no matter what the woman on the phone had told her. When she'd seen the help wanted ad for a bus driver, she'd thought it might be for a private school, thought maybe she'd get to know a few people, maybe move up the waiting list for a teaching job. She'd been shocked to realize the "bus" she'd be driving had actually been converted into a coach and that she'd be driving it from race to race for a famous driver. Even still, for some reason, she'd pictured a local-type driver, not…not…

A drop-dead gorgeous hunk of a man.

"Oh, jeez," she said, dropping her head into her hands.

"It'll be okay," Lance said, sitting down next to her. "You'll have your car back in no time."

"Well, I don't know…." his mechanic started to say.

"In no time," Lance repeated. "I promise."

He completely contradicted everything she'd heard about professional athletes, Sarah admitted. He wasn't a jerk. He didn't appear to have an ego. And he'd treated her with nothing but respect ever since they'd first met—well, aside from the pool-boy incident. Of course, she wasn't his type and so it wasn't like he'd try and make a pass at her. Ever. And he'd run her down in his car and so he *had* to be nice to her.

Her eyes suddenly narrowed. "You don't have to worry I'm going to sue you."

He drew back, then smirked at his business manager. "Looks like she has you pegged, Sal."

"I'm not worried about a lawsuit," Sal denied.

But years of handling tiny little males stood Sarah in good stead. "Yes, you are," she corrected. "And I understand *why,* but you don't need to be."

"And *you* don't need to worry, either. We'll fix your car," Lance interjected. "Heck. That's the business we're in, so before you start protesting, just remember we fix cars every day. And if you like, we'll get you a rental so you can get around town. We get great deals through some of the rental car agencies. And if you don't feel up to driving my coach out to Daytona tomorrow, you can start next week."

"No, really—"

"No arguments," he interrupted. "This is how it's going to be done. Now. Let's go get your stuff out of your car. You're spending the night with me."

HE ALMOST LAUGHED at the look on her face.

"I don't mean in my bed," he added.

Which, of course, made her blush, and made her instantly say, "No, no. Of course not."

He almost contradicted her.

Of course not?

Could she really think he didn't find her attractive? Was she that beaten down?

What's more, there was no flirtatious comment back, no look of pure, sexual interest pouring from her eyes. He almost smiled just because it was so nice, so damn nice, to be looked at like a human instead of a walking dollar sign. No wonder Sal had hired her on the spot.

"I really think you should stay here. Doc Brown said it's all superficial, but I'd feel better if you had someone nearby. Or are you living with somebody?"

Again, no flirtatious glances, no look of invitation, no nothing. "No. Just a few dozen cockroaches."

"Well then, good. You can sleep in one of my guest rooms," he added, not giving her time to answer, just standing up and saying, "And when you feel up to it, I can show you the motor coach."

"A guest room isn't necessary. I'll be fine on my own. And I can look over the bus on my own. You don't need to go to any trouble."

"It's not trouble and there are some special features you'll need to be shown how to operate, but we can talk about that later. In the meantime, let's get you settled in your room."

He saw her release a breath, the kind that was directed at a hank of hair. "I really don't want to impose."

"Will she be imposing, Sal?"

His business manager rolled his eyes. "In a house this big? I don't think so."

"Stay," Lance said again, and when she still looked hesitant, he added, "If it makes you feel any better, I won't be here this evening. I have a *Raceday* interview in a couple hours. I won't be back 'til later. Sal's gonna keep an eye on you."

"I am?" Sal said, bushy brows arching.

"You are."

"I still don't know...." she murmured.

"Are you worried about Sal making a pass at you?"

"No," she said, looking torn between amusement and horror.

"Then stay."

"It's too much to ask."

"No, it's not. Look how easy it'll be. I think half your clothes are in the back of your car."

She gave him a "You noticed that?" look that was part humiliation, part resignation.

"Do you always travel around with half your clothes?" he teased, trying to set her at ease.

She looked away, giving him her pretty profile. "Actually," he heard her mumble. "Those are *all* my clothes."

"All?"

She nodded. "The place I'm staying at. It's not exactly the best and so I keep my clothes in the car in case I need to make a quick exit."

"You're kidding."

"I'm not."

"Then it's settled," he said quickly. "C'mon. I'll show you to your room. You can have your choice."

And this time he didn't give her the opportunity to protest. He just walked out of the room, resisting the urge to turn around and help her up. He'd let Sal do that. If he turned back to her he just knew she'd argue some more. Stubborn. He could tell that already.

To his surprise she didn't argue. So he showed her upstairs, Sal acting like the concerned citizen by helping her up the sweeping staircase when, in fact, he was probably more concerned about her falling and slapping him with a second lawsuit. He showed her to the flower puff room, so dubbed by him because it was a total chick room. The decorator had let her inner estrogen fly, using roses and white chintz (or so she'd called it—looked like cotton to him) to create a room Martha Stewart would be proud of. Sarah looked a bit wide-eyed, Lance leaving her behind with firm instructions to take some of the painkillers Doc had left her and get some rest.

WHEN HE GOT BACK from his interview a few hours later Sarah's car had been towed, a rental car had been delivered, and Sarah Tingle herself was sound asleep, Lance noticed. He stood in the doorway, observing her for a moment, her fully clothed form sprawled out on the "chintz" bedspread. Sarah Tingle slept a lot like Lance suspected she lived, no holds barred and everything wide open—in this case, her mouth.

She snored, lips parted, a strand of hair having been pulled into the black hole by the tractor beam of her breath.

He stood there for a second listening to the discordant sound, a chuckle escaping him.

"She's out," Sal said, coming up behind him.

"Obviously she needed rest."

They both stood there, another growl being let loose.

"She snores," Sal observed.

"Yeah. I don't think I've ever heard anyone snore quite like that."

"Amazing."

His business manager, tie loose around his dress shirt, jacket discarded, glanced at her and then back at him then back at Sarah Tingle again. "I still can't believe she had no idea who you were. I mean, when I interviewed her for the job she told me she didn't know anything about racing but I still thought she knew who you were."

"And I still can't believe you pretended her car had been towed."

"Got your best interests at heart, buddy."

"Well, do me a favor and camp out here tonight. I don't want her freaking out thinking I'm going to molest her or something."

"You think she'd think that?"

"I think she doesn't trust men."

"Yeah. Maybe," Sal agreed. "Wouldn't do to have her claim something happened that didn't happen."

"She wouldn't do that."

"You never know," Sal said with a shrug. "And I've already got an overnight bag in the back of my car for emergencies, so it's no big deal."

"You really do think of everything, don't you?"

"Why you pay me the big bucks," Sal said, turning away.

But Lance lingered in the door.

Sal came all but running back, which was a sight to see given his size. "I *told* you, no distractions."

"She's so cute."

"Wait a minute, wait a minute. You're going to allow someone to work for you whom you find *cute?*"

"And frisky."

"Frisky? What are we talking about here, a woman or a golden retriever?"

"I like her," Lance said, his eyes roving over the curls that lay strewn across the pillow, then back to her gaping mouth. He still couldn't believe the sounds coming out of her mouth.

"This could be bad," Sal said, echoing Lance's own fears. "This could be very bad."

"You think we should hire someone else?"

"I'm thinking that's exactly what we should do. I mean, I thought she was perfect for the job earlier, but now you're telling me you think she's cute."

But Lance was already shaking his head. "Nah. Can't do that. She needs the money."

"And you need to focus on *your* job."

"I will. Don't worry."

But it was plain to see Sal was worried.

"We should probably wake her," Lance said, sidestepping his own concerns. "Doc said she might have a concussion and to keep an eye on her."

"You're sick, you know that?" Sal asked. "You're really sick. You can't stay away from her."

"She needs her dinner."

"That's it," Sal said. "I give up."

"No, wait," Lance said, frustrated with himself, too. "You're right. I should let her sleep."

"Yes, you should. And you should stay away from her, too."

"I will," Lance said.

And he did stay away from her. Right up until the next morning.

CHAPTER FIVE

SARAH WAS HAVING a really great dream, one of those fantasies where everything is so good, you just know it's a dream. And so when you feel yourself waking up you try to keep yourself under, try to wiggle and shrug and worm away from the hand that. Wouldn't. Leave. Her. Alone.

"Go away," she moaned.

"Sarah," a voice said. "It's time to wake up."

No. It wasn't time. She wanted to sleep. She wanted to keep enjoying the dream that she was a famous swimsuit model with a race-car driver boyfriend and a house on the beach.

Lance Cooper.

The name clanged through her head like a cymbal in a marching band. Sarah sat up so abruptly her hair fell over her face. She shoved it back over the top of her head, spitting out strands of hair that had somehow made it into her mouth.

"Whoa there, Sparky. Settle down," the voice said.

Lance Cooper.

Her gaze shot to his, her hands lifting to her face as she let out a loud moan.

"It wasn't a dream."

"What wasn't a dream?" he asked.

"Never mind," she said, horrified that she'd obviously been dreaming about *him* and that was bad, bad, bad. Men were taboo. They were all jerks. She didn't trust them as far as she could throw them. She had no business, no *business,* dreaming about Lance Cooper.

"Those drugs Doc gave you give you bad dreams?"

"They gave me nightmares," she amended, dropping her hands back to the bed. "What time is it?"

"It's morning. You slept the whole night through without dinner. That's why I woke you. You should eat some breakfast."

Breakfast. Ugh. Her stomach turned at just the thought of eating. "I'm not very hungry."

"It's the drugs. They make you nauseous."

"You sound like an expert."

"I *am* an expert. In my line of work you get a lot of bumps and bruises."

Yeah. She supposed he did. "Look. Could I have a minute?"

"Sure," he said. "I had Sal take your stuff out of your car." He pointed.

A green garbage bag of clothes wilted in the corner of her room.

He followed her gaze, saying, "I don't think I've ever heard of anyone using a VW as a suitcase."

"Yeah, well, it's not like I've had the money to do a lot of traveling."

"No. I suppose not."

Sarah glanced up and when she looked into his eyes it wasn't a look of pity she saw; it was a look of understanding.

He understood.

She felt her whole body relax before she remembered that she shouldn't go looking for sympathy from her new boss, even if he was a hottie.

A *famous* hottie.

"Tell you what," he said. "I'll send some food up. You can eat it in bed. When you're done, if you're feeling better, you can come downstairs and I'll show you the motor coach."

"That's right. I'm supposed to head out today."

"Only if you feel like it."

"I'll feel like it."

"We'll see."

She watched him walk away after giving her a chipper smile, then hid her head in her hands.

How had it happened?

How had she ended up here, in this fancy house, working for a sexy race-car driver when three months ago she'd been happy, living with a man she'd thought might be "the one," teaching little ones their ABCs? No more putting up with drunks late at night while she drove a county bus to pay her way through college. No more living from paycheck to paycheck.

She'd moved in with Ron and things had been looking up.

And then creepy Peter, her ex-boyfriend, had decided to get even. Okay, so he had a good reason for being kind of peeved at her. She'd left him a few weeks before graduation. But to be fair, he'd been freaking her out with his growing possessiveness. So she'd broken it off. And, yeah, she'd gotten involved with Ron pretty quickly after that. But he was a teacher just like her and they'd had a lot in common. Peter had wigged out. Just went off the deep end. She knew he'd known about the pictures she'd taken, but she never, *ever* thought he'd dig them up and sell them to some porn magazine just to get even. He even had to forge her signature on the model's release. And then to send the magazine to the principal and a few of the parents when the pictures got published. It made her sick just thinking about it. And then Ron had dumped her. That hurt the worst and very obviously proved her point: Men couldn't be trusted.

"Here we are," a female voice said, Sarah looking up to see a Hispanic woman enter the room, a tray of food dangling off a Great Barrier Reef of breasts presently contained by a tight red tank top. "I'm Rosa, the housekeeper."

Rrrooddsa.

That's how she said her name. Not Rosa like Sarah, a bona fide Anglo Saxon would say it, but R-r-r-o-d-d-d-sa.

Rrodsa leaned down, setting the tray on the nightstand, apparently unaware that her low-waisted jeans didn't fit her quite right and so when she bent, they slid down like she was a plumber bending over a pipe. Sarah about to warn her that her "something" was in danger of falling out. Fortunately, Rosa straightened just before the critical moment.

"You going to be driving the big banana boat from Mister Lance?" she asked, hands on her hips, her brown eyes narrowing as she glared down at her. She had hair like a wand of cotton candy, only black, and a mole that was too dark to be real. It sat near the corner of her mouth like a fly.

Sarah had to replay the sentence in her mind. "Beg your pardon?" she asked when she realized she'd been so distracted by the pants, she'd missed what the big woman had said.

"You know," Rosa said. "Drive the big bus." She mimicked the holding of a steering wheel with her hands.

"Oh," Sarah said. "Yes, I am."

"That's what he told me. He also told me he hit you with his car. You not going to sue him, are you?"

Sarah drew back. "No. Of course not."

"Good," she said, eyes narrowing like a bird of prey. "Mister Lance, he a good man. If I no married to my Jose, I snatch him up myself." She snapped her fingers for good measure.

"Er. Okay," Sarah said, not sure what to make of

the woman. She was like the Mama Corleone of housekeepers, staring down at her with such suspicion, Sarah wouldn't be surprised if a horse head showed up in her bed the next morning.

"Here," she said, reaching down to pick up Sarah's bottle of pills. "Mister Lance told me you gotta take your medicine."

"No, no. Really. I'm fine—"

"You take medicine. Then eat food. That's what he said to do. You do it."

Sarah held out her hand. Rosa poured a single pill into her palm, then stood there until Sarah picked up a glass of water and gulped it down. The thought of chasing the pill with what looked to be chorizo and eggs should have turned her stomach, but funny, the moment she smelled food she was instantly hungry.

"Good," Rosa said after she'd taken a bite. "You eat. I be back to check on you."

And that was her first encounter with Rosa Perez.

THE CHORIZO AND EGGS, as it turned out, settled into her stomach like a missing relative at a family reunion. Sarah felt better. Or maybe it was the medication, but the fact remained that after she'd consumed a few bites, got up and washed her face, checked on her knee (her leg was still attached), then changed into a pair of loose-fitting jeans and a bright pink blouse, she felt reasonably human.

Enough so that she didn't mind going down to confront Lance Cooper.

She found him in his family room, sitting in the same spot she'd been sitting in last night, and for a moment she just stood there watching him. Sunlight poured in from both sides of the room. His blond hair was slightly mussed as if he'd run his hands through it. Gray eyes peered intently at the television screen opposite him. Sarah noted that even though he was a man, he had the most sensual pair of lips she'd ever seen.

Just then he looked up, those lips curing into a smile. "Hey," he said. "You feeling better?"

Be still my heart.

"Much," she said, looking away. What should she do? Sit down next to him? Stand? She settled on putting her hands in her jeans pockets.

"Good."

"Umm, I was thinking maybe now would be a good time to show me your bus."

"You sure you're up for it?"

"Sure I am."

"Okay then. Follow me."

She had to look away when he stood because if she didn't, she had a feeling she might just check out his rear end, which was not something an employee should do with her boss.

"You keep your bus in your kitchen?" she said as they headed toward the massive room, a cool breeze brushing her cheeks in a way that made her want to close her eyes and tip her head back.

"No. You get to the shop through here."

"You have a shop?"

"Well, yeah."

He opened a door and reached inside. A row of fluorescent lights flicked on with a tink-tink-tink, one after the other, exposing a garage that was easily the size of a department store.

Okay, maybe not that big.

But it was as big as a Wal-Mart service center, and she should know because she had a lot of experience with those.

"Holy guacamole," she breathed because at the far end, in its own private bay, was the most beautiful bus she'd ever seen.

"Like it?" he asked, stepping down and into the garage.

"I get to drive that?" she asked, unable to keep the glee from her voice.

"You do," he said, her pleasure obviously amusing him.

"It's like a rolling Trump Tower."

"It's my home away from home."

She stepped past him, the grin on her face so big it actually hurt her cheeks. "For some reason I thought you had a diesel pusher."

"Really? I thought Sal put in the ad that we needed someone who knew how to drive a bus."

"Well, he did, it's just that when he said motor coach I thought he meant an RV, but this looks like something a celebrity would drive."

He almost told her he *was* a celebrity, except he had a feeling she wouldn't believe him. "Actually, the company we got it from sells their conversions to a lot of rock stars."

"Wow," she said, feeling smaller and smaller the closer she got. And she had to walk fully fifty yards to reach the darn thing. His "shop" was practically the same size as his house, with shiny cement floors reflecting fluorescent glowing neon patterns that caught her attention for a moment. "It's gorgeous," she said, though she was really referring to the bright spots of light that pooled on the gray cement.

"Thanks."

She looked up at the motor coach again, having to blink a few times to get her eyes to focus. "That's a very racy race pattern on the side," she said, referring to the black graphics that whipped back from the front of the bus like streams of paper, or the tentacles from a Predator's head. "I'm surprised it doesn't have checkered flags on the side."

"I'm a Raiders fan."

She looked over at him, feeling light-headed all of sudden.

He must have seen her wobble a bit. "You okay?" he asked.

"I'm fine," she said. "I feel just fine." And she really

did. In fact, she felt better than fine. "Good. Really, really good." She smiled, a huge, wide smile that puffed up her cheeks until she could practically see them. She tried doing exactly that for a while, crossing her eyes until realizing that made her *very* dizzy.

"C'mon," he said.

She followed him, having to correct her directions a few times before making it to the door. Odd.

"Whoa," she heard Lance say. "Easy there, Sparky."

She felt hands steady her. Big hands. Warm hands. She'd like it if they held her for the rest of the day.

"That medicine makes me woozy."

"That medicine makes you *something*," she heard him murmur, amusement leaking out from the words.

"How do you get in this thing?" she asked, patting the door like it was a thug she'd just apprehended. "Is there a handle?"

"There's a keypad," he said, letting go of her shoulders, though she thought he might have hesitated a bit, as if he didn't want to let her go. "Here," he said, pushing on a hidden panel, the thing flipping around à la Star Trek to reveal a numeric keypad.

"Neat-o," she said.

"Yeah, neat-o," he echoed.

"You're laughing at me," she accused, having seen his lips twitch.

"Nah," he said, a metallic beep-beep-beep ringing out as he pressed some numbers.

"Why are you laughing at me?" she asked, feeling suddenly miffed.

"I'm not laughing. It's your smile. It's infectious."

She felt her shoulders droop a bit. "Oh," she said in a small voice. Then gasped as with a whoosh and a hiss, the bus door opened, and to be honest, she was surprised a peal of little choirboys didn't ring out as the interior was revealed.

"Hole. Lee. Shit."

"I thought you didn't swear."

"This is definitely a situation that calls for swearing. How much did this thing cost?"

"You don't want to know."

She turned back to him, getting woozy again, but that was okay because he steadied her again. "How much?" she insisted, partly horrified that she asked such an audacious question.

"A million two."

"A million two!"

She saw his lips twitch again just before he said. "A million two."

"I'm driving a million—" She stepped back, wobbling a bit before she caught herself. "Nope," she said, waving her hands. "Nope, nope, nope. I can't drive something that costs that much. No way."

"Whoa-ho-ho," he said, placing a hand against her back. "Calm down, Sparky. It's no big deal."

"No big deal?" she said. "You try driving a rolling bank vault."

"It's not like that. It's just a motor coach. Besides,

if you wreck it, the insurance company will replace it."

"Yeah, right. And hike up your rates."

"Sarah," he said, stepping closer to her. "It's just a motor coach. That's all. Don't think about how much it's worth."

"Easy for you to say," she muttered.

It looked like he had to bite back a smile again. "C'mon," he said. "Let me show you inside."

"No."

And then he did something completely unbosslike. He framed her face with his hands, leaned down close to her and said, "There's nothing to worry about. It's just a bus. That's all. If you drive it off the Brooklyn Bridge I wouldn't care. Seriously."

If she thought she was dizzy before, it was nothing compared to the way she felt with his face so close to her own, his soft gray eyes filled with warmth and understanding. It took a second or two for her to remember to breathe.

She could really like this man.

The thought just popped into her head, there, despite the fact that she warned herself not to think such ridiculous thoughts.

"Okay?" he asked.

She couldn't move, didn't want to move.

"Okay," she heard herself say.

She thought he'd let her go, even braced herself for it. But he kept his hands right where they were, his thumb drifting along her cheek—back and forth, back and forth, his fingers stroking her scalp. She almost closed her eyes, but something inside the depths of his own eyes held her, made her feel all warm and gooey.

Wow.

"Silly Sarah," he said softly.

"Silly Sarah," she murmured back.

And then she heard him take a deep breath, the pressure of his hands slowly easing. "C'mon," he said, his hands dropping back to his sides. "Let me show you inside."

CHAPTER SIX

HE'D WANTED to kiss her.

He couldn't believe how much he'd wanted to bend down and touch his lips to hers. But he didn't. *He couldn't,* he quickly amended. To do that would invite trouble and he didn't need trouble right now. As Sal said, he needed to focus, not lust after his new bus driver.

"This is unbelievable," she said after climbing into the coach, her hand on the back of the passenger seat as she stared around her, slack-jawed.

Bracing herself, he quickly amended, because if ever there was a more important reason why he shouldn't kiss her, it was because she'd obviously been overmedicated.

What the hell had Doc Brown given her?

"Wait," he said, eyeing her with concern. "You haven't seen nothin' yet. Sit down," he ordered, swiveling around the passenger seat because he didn't want her falling down. Lord knows, she was so loopy she might freak out.

"Comfy chair," she said.

"Yeah," he agreed, flicking a switch.

The coach rumbled. Sarah gasped. He shot her a reassuring look as air from the hydraulic system emitted a sharp hiss. And then, with a low-hummed vibration, the sliders began to push out.

She gasped.

He grinned. He couldn't help it, watching as both walls began to push outward, doubling the size of the coach with a simple flick of the finger.

"Wait," he said again, heading to the galley which was in the middle of the bus. From a cabinet designed specifically for them, he pulled out three black bar stools which he deposited beneath an S-shaped countertop—black—that he'd had specially designed to look like a waving race flag.

"What do you think now?" he asked.

Her mouth hung open. He saw her gaze drop to the checkerboard laminate floor which matched his bar, only the squares were bigger, and if he didn't miss his guess, it did something to her eyes because she got that bug-eyed look of optical confusion. She blinked a few times, shook her head again, and when she opened her eyes, it must have passed because she met his gaze again.

"It looks like someone from OPEC lives here."

"OPEC?"

"Yeah, you know, one of those Arab princes with eighty wives and more money than God."

"Are you saying my motor coach looks gaudy?"

"Well," she said, waving an arm, the motion causing her to momentarily lose her balance. She clutched the back of the chair again. "You must admit, the fiber optic lights are a bit much. I mean, do they really need to snake around the bottom of the floor like that? They do something to my eyes."

He just bet they did, he thought, suddenly feeling…miffed. He liked the inside of his coach. Loved to show it off to all his friends. And, hell, it wasn't half as gaudy as some of the rigs at the racetrack.

"What else bugs you?"

She looked around, her head swinging back wildly for a moment and he knew he'd get the absolute truth out of her. She was well and truly stoned. His pique faded as quickly as it'd come. Hell, this might be kind of fun.

"Well, the black leather couches are a bit bachelor pad-ish. I'm surprised you don't have zebra-striped throw pillows."

"Oh, yeah?" The couches had actually come with those pillows, but they'd clashed with his custom checkerboard bar and floor.

"And what's up with the bar?" she asked. "Does a race-car driver really need a bar?"

"It's not a bar bar, it's just a place to eat. You know, sit down on a bar stool and eat your breakfast like you did this morning."

But she'd spun away from him, her low, "Weee,"

as she turned her chair bringing an instant smile to his face.

Wasted. No doubt.

"But this," she said, leaning forward and stroking the dash. "This is nice. Nicer than the county bus I used to drive, that's for sure." She stroked the leather dash, leaning forward and inhaling the scent. "Smells like new cow—"

"New cow?"

"And look," she said, ignoring his question and sitting up too sharply so she had to clutch at the dash. "Something I finally recognize." She turned back to him with a wide smile. "Windshield wipers."

But Lance was suddenly struck dumb, didn't even really notice when she switched seats.

Damn, what a smile.

"Will they work?" she asked over her shoulder.

Would what work?

She fiddled with something. The wipers, one sliding along the right side square of glass, the other sliding along the left, both emitted loud crii- iiicks in protest. The dry glass caught their edges before they swished back to their original spot, upright, alongside the dividing pane in the middle of the bus.

She laughed, her head bobbing side to side as she began to sing, "The wipers on the bus go swish, swish, swish. Swish, swish, swish. Swish, swish, swish."

And he couldn't help it. He started to laugh.

She peered up at him. "Maybe I could take it for a spin and do wheels next."

"Maybe not," he said.

"Ah, come on. It'd be fun."

"And I think you've been hanging out with kindergartners too long. Plus, you're not driving anywhere. Not today."

And all at once she looked sad.

"But you can drive it soon," he quickly amended, because jeez, he couldn't believe how much he wanted that smile to return.

"It's not that," she said quietly, turning off the wipers which had been swishing in the background. "It's that I'll never watch my kids get on a bus again."

Surprise held him quiet a moment. "Your kids? You have kids?"

She sat sideways on the driver's chair, her arms resting on the back of the seat, her chin resting on her arms. "My class," she clarified.

And why did that fill him with relief? It wasn't because he'd been afraid for a moment that she'd been married, was it?

Was it?

"I used to bake them cookies every Friday. It was a game," she said, her head tipping sideways, Lance thinking she looked adorable with her curly hair falling over her arms. "We used to make a game out of it. They had to learn to spell the animal's name before they could eat the cookie. You should have seen the trouble they had with the hippopotamus cookies."

"You really liked teaching, didn't you?"

"I didn't like it," she said. "I *loved* it."

"Why don't you do it again?"

"I'm going to," she said. "Just as soon as I find someone who'll hire me with a big gaping hole on my employment record."

"A hole?"

"Yeah," she said. "I can't exactly put down my last job on my résumé. They'll want a reference and I'm not going to get that. Not after what I did."

"C'mon. It's not as if you endangered a child's life."

"Yeah, but that wasn't the only reason I got fired."

"It wasn't?"

"No. I also got fired for ripping the toupee off the principal's head."

"*You what?*"

"Only he wasn't just the principal to me. He was my boyfriend."

"You dated a man with a toupee?"

She sat up. "I didn't know it was a toupee," she said, her eyes wide and, yup, glassy. "I mean, I *suspected* it might be, but that's not exactly something you ask a guy on a first date. Nor a second. And then I realized he was really nice and I didn't care that he wore a piece of fur on his head. Shows you what I know," she mumbled. "Never trust a man who wears fur, especially when it's not his own."

She looked up at him with such complete seriousness he began to laugh yet again. When she started to stand, he rushed toward her. "I'll try to remember that," he said softly.

She looked up. And there it was again: that surge of energy reminiscent of when he put the pedal to the metal. It was the same sense of exhilaration. The same wild sense of anticipation. The same need for…something.

"You do that," she said softly.

Screw it, he found himself thinking. Screw this. He wanted to kiss her and by God he would.

"Sarah," he said softly, blowing her name across her face, his lips getting closer, ever closer, the adrenaline building in him like it did when he neared a white flag.

"You're going to kiss me, aren't you?" she asked.

"Yes," he said, so close now he could feel the heat radiating off her face, count the number of freckles on her nose (ten), see that she had a tiny scar just above her eyebrow.

"I don't think that's a good idea."

He was just a breath away when he said, "Actually, I think it's an excellent idea."

CHAPTER SEVEN

SARAH FELT the gentle touch of his breath and closed her eyes. And when he pressed those lips against her own, she almost moaned.

She wanted this, she wanted him to kiss her so passionately that she'd forget for a moment where she was, and who he was, and what had happened in the past.

Forget.

Yes.

His lips were cool, but his breath— that was hot, as was the way he made her body feel. The pressure increased, razor stubble sliding against her chin as he turned his head, changing the angle in such a way that it encouraged…her…to…

Yes, she inwardly sighed as she opened her mouth, his blazing hot tongue stroking against her own and, oh, how it excited her, made her burn and sizzle with anticipation. She arched into him.

He pulled back.

Pulled back?

"This is a bad idea," he said quickly, his hands firmly setting her away from him. "A *really* bad idea."

"What are you doing?" she asked. "Why'd you stop?"

"Because you're stoned and I'm in no position to be flirting with you."

"Stoned? I'm not stoned."

"Yes, you are," he contradicted. "I don't know what Doc gave you, but whatever it is, it's pretty potent stuff."

"*I* am *not* stoned."

"As a gravel pit," he said.

"Hah," she said with a flick of her head, turning away from him in outrage.

Only when she turned, she almost fell, and that's when the weird buzzing she'd been experiencing suddenly became more pronounced. But even more telling, the floor suddenly seemed to undulate, the black checkerboards seeming to wave like a living flag.

"I'm stoned," she admitted in shock, looking up at him, her body quickening at the sight of his masculine, handsome face.

Damn, but he was hot. And she was, too. Burning, actually, burning for *him*.

"Let me help you down," he said.

"No, thank you," she said primly. "I can walk."

"No, you can't," he quickly corrected.

And, darn it all, the moment she took a step her

head did something weird. It sort of sagged, her neck muscles so weak she felt like she might fall. "Oh, man," she said, trying to clutch at something. Him. Her hands found him.

When she opened her eyes, she couldn't help the accusation that came pouring out of her. "What did you give me?"

"*Me?* I didn't give you anything."

"Then Doc Brown must be a crackpot." And even her voice sounded funny, she noticed, like it came from far, far above her head.

"They always tell you not to handle heavy machinery when on painkillers."

Then she noticed the way it felt to be so close to him. Or rather, her body noticed because it instantly flared to life. "How about sexy race-car drivers?"

He froze.

She did, too—and then clapped a hand over her mouth. "Please tell me I didn't just say that aloud," she mumbled. "That was in my head, right?"

"Yup, in your head," he said, little laugh lines sprouting out from the side of his eyes, and from the side of his mouth, too, because he was smiling at her. That gorgeous, naughty-boy smile that made her pulse pound.

Or maybe that was the medication.

"I think I should probably lie down."

"With or without the sexy race-car driver?"

Her face suddenly lit up like the high beams on a car. "I need to get out of here."

"Yeah," he said softly. "As much as I hate to admit it, that's probably a good idea. We should probably *both* get out of here."

HE HELPED HER back inside, running into Rosa in the kitchen who, thankfully, helped her back to her room.

Lance sat down on a kitchen chair, head in hands, knowing he'd narrowly escaped doing something really, really stupid.

He'd almost slept with his newest employee.

But, no, he wouldn't have slept with her. He'd only wanted to kiss her. He'd been curious what it might be like. If she kissed like a gentle little schoolteacher, or a ferocious kitten. A half hour ago he'd have laid bets she'd be meek and mild. Not anymore.

Eeyowza.

"She be settled in the bed," Rosa said, sashaying into the kitchen in that wide-hipped way of hers, brown eyes staring at him in disapproval. "What you been doing in that bus o' yours?"

"Nothing," he said. "Just showing her a few things."

"Yeah. I bet," she said, narrowing her eyes.

Rosa wasn't just his housekeeper, cook and help around the house. Rosa was Mother Theresa. Rosa was the Virgin Mary. Rosa kept him in line. She booted the women out that he'd brought home on the occasional basis—the ones who thought that because he'd slept with them, he wanted them to stick around. But he never wanted more than a night.

Until now.

And, see, that was crazy. Just plain *nuts*. How could he be having thoughts like that about someone he'd just met?

"You look like a man who eat one too many prunes."

"I *what?*"

"You heard me. You like this new employee of yours?"

"Rosa, I don't like her. I'm just concerned about her. I'm wondering if maybe I should call Doc Brown and tell him about her reaction to the drugs."

"Yeah, right," Rosa said, black eyes narrowed.

Lance got up from his chair. "How many milligrams did he give her, anyway?" he asked, ignoring the way Rosa's eyes followed him about like one of those paintings—the kind with holes where the eyes should be, a real pair of eyes tracking his every move. He grabbed Sarah's medication that was sitting alongside the sink.

"That's no what I gave her," Rosa said.

Lance spun around. "What?"

"It's no what I gave her. You said to give her the pills that were in the cabinet above the counter," she said, pointing to a bottle near the sink.

"No, I didn't. I said her pills were *not* the ones

in the cabinet above the counter. That they were by the sink."

"Yeah. In the cabinet, above the counter, by the sink."

"No," Lance corrected, suddenly horrified. "Not in the cabinet, but by the sink."

"Uh-oh," Rosa said.

"What the heck did you give her?"

"I don't know. Who knows what's up there, you always banging and crashing into things. I can no keep track of your medicine and now hers." She erupted into Spanish, a sure sign that she was upset.

Lance went to his cabinet, grabbing the only bottle of prescription medication that was stashed amongst cold remedies and cough medicine.

"Percocet," he said. "Seven hundred milligrams. Jesu—"

Okay, okay. No need to panic. Obviously, she hadn't had an adverse side effect, well, aside from double vision and a loss of balance. But, still, he'd better call Doc Brown just to be sure.

"Couldn't you tell it had my name on the outside?" he asked, swinging back to Rosa.

"You know I no read English very good."

"But surely you recognized the name Lance Cooper on the bottle."

"I look for the name of your doctor and that good enough for me."

And when she assumed a man's combative stance,

her arms crossed in front of her and her toe tapping
the ground, he turned away and called Doc Brown.

An hour later he'd been reassured that no harm
would result. He'd sent Rosa up to check on her; the
housekeeper reported that she was snoring away.

And despite himself, he found himself smiling,
and then frowning, and then smiling again and then
shaking his head in exasperation because this was
just the sort of thing he didn't need right now. Distraction. Of the feminine kind.

Sal would kill him.

HE'D KISSED HER.

Sarah opened her eyes hours later with that exact
thought on her mind.

He'd kissed her and she'd opened her mouth and
wanted more.

Stupid, stupid, stupid.

And fie on him. She should be outraged that he'd
taken advantage of her when she was...

Stoned.

Okay, no doubt about it. She'd been high as a kite
and done something really, really stupid.

"It 'cause I give you the wrong medication,"
Rosa confessed a half hour later, after Sarah tiptoed
down the stairs with her heart pounding. She didn't
want to bump into Lance.

"The wrong medication?"

Rosa nodded, her black hair turned nearly blue

by the light that ebbed in from the kitchen window. "He tell me to get the medicine from the cabinet above the sink. I get you that medication. Only your medication is by the sink, not above it."

"Oh my gosh," Sarah gasped. "So what'd I take?"

"Percolate, or something like that."

"Percocet?"

"Yeah. That it," the big woman said, pointing a finger. "Percocet. Mr. Lance, he call the doctor this mornin', but Doc tell him not to worry. You be fine in a couple hours."

"You gave me the wrong medication," Sarah repeated.

"I did, but you no sue me, 'kay? And you no sue Mr. Lance. It was accident. No harm done."

No harm done.

She'd just about thrown herself on top of "Mr. Lance." No harm done, indeed, Sarah thought, watching as Rosa started scrubbing the counter, a hint of bacon and eggs lingering in the air. Rosa must have cooked that for Lance after she'd passed out.

"Where is Mr. Lance?" Sarah said, unable to stop the wince from crinkling up her face as she waited for her answer.

"He go out. Big meeting with the mucho grande sponsor. Not be home 'til dinner. He say not to drive the big bus today."

She wouldn't have to face him. Oh, thank God she wouldn't have to face him. Not yet at least.

"I'm fine," Sarah said. "That medicine just knocked me for a loop, but I can drive now."

"I no think that's a good idea." But something in the woman's eyes made Sarah think she actually thought that was an *excellent* idea. "Mr. Lance, he might get mad."

"Well, Mr. Lance can just get mad then. If I don't leave today, I won't make it to Daytona in time."

"I still think you should wait for him."

"But then he'll insist I stay here another night."

"Yeah, but then he no get mad at me."

"Hmm, well, if you really think it's a bad idea—"

"No, no," Rosa said quickly, confirming what Sarah already suspected—she didn't want her around. "You leave if you think you have to. I pack you a lunch."

THREE HOURS LATER she was on her way, Rosa having come up with the idea of enlisting Sal as an accomplice. An hour after the housekeeper's call, Lance's business manager had arranged for someone to come over to Lance's house and show her how to operate the million-dollar bus.

One million dollars.

One *million* dollars.

The words kept replaying through her head in the voice of *Austin Powers'* Dr. Evil.

Stop it, she told herself. She would not think about how much the darn thing was worth.

And so she didn't, putting it from her mind and pretending she was once again driving for Alameda County Transit, but even that was hard to do given that fact that county buses didn't have a GPS display taking up a portion of the dashboard. They didn't have lead crystal odometer displays and twenty-thousand-dollar stereo systems hanging above a person's head. They didn't have plush leather seats and they sure as certain didn't have an automatic dial-up system that phoned OnStar when you didn't wear your seat belt. The first time Sarah had heard the discombobulated voice say, "Hello, OnStar," she'd just about jumped out of her driver's seat. And when the woman had told her they had a seat belt alert, she'd felt like Big Brother was watching her.

Gradually, very slowly, she began to relax.

A man whistled when she parked the bus later that night. The guy was an eighty-year-old Johnny Carson look-alike whom Sarah had thought at first might be a pervert (she'd heard RV parks were famous for them) but for the fact that when he whistled, he had his eyes on Lance's bus, not her.

"Sure is a beauty," he drawled in a voice as southern as Lance's, and in a tone usually reserved for speaking of the Pope, patron saints and other sacred things. "Bet you she cost a fortune."

"You don't want to know," Sarah mumbled.

"You a Lance Cooper fan?" the guy asked, spotting a white number twenty-six sticker on a side window.

"Um, yeah," Sarah said, and in her mind she could hear Lance's sexy voice drawl sarcastically, "Oh, yeah?"

Argh. Even now she couldn't get him from her mind.

"Really? I am, too," he said, motioning to his diesel pusher.

Sarah's eyes widened because this man, this eighty-year-old retiree from Florida (she assumed), had all kinds of stickers on his RV's windows. Race car stickers. From some type of air filter to his favorite type of oil. But what shocked her, what made her mouth drop open, were the dozens of different car number stickers on the side—all in various shapes and sizes, and all Lance's car number.

"Sure wish he'd fire his crew chief or something," the man said. "If he did that, he'd start winning again."

"Uh, yeah," Sarah said, having to blink when she looked back at the man again.

"You going down for the race?"

"E-yeah," Sarah drawled.

"Terrific. What spot are you parking in?"

"Uh." What to say? She had a feeling if she told the guy she was supposed to park in the driver/crew area, he'd freak out. "In a special spot?" she said lamely.

"I have a special spot, too," the man said, completely misunderstanding her. "Been parking there for ten years. Where's your spot?"

"Um, look, I, ah, I've got to go inside. I left something on the stove." Which was as dumb an excuse as she'd ever heard because she'd only just pulled in. But the man nodded, seeming to be content to take her at her word—her being a Lance Cooper fan and all.

"Sure, sure," he said, lifting a hand. "I'll talk with you later."

Sarah lifted a hand, too, diving into Lance's bus with a pounding heart.

Why? Why had seeing that man's RV made her suddenly feel nauseous?

Because you've been telling yourself that Lance Cooper isn't really a celebrity. Because you'd deluded yourself that racing couldn't be that popular. Because until you'd seen those stickers you'd believed exactly that.

But it wasn't until the next day that she realized just how famous Lance Cooper really was. She'd popped into an Internet café, her fingers flying as she Googled her new boss's name.

There were 900,000 hits.

Well, okay, obviously there were a lot of Lance Coopers in the world. She narrowed her search down a bit, typing in: Lance Cooper, race car driver.

This time 441,200 hits.

She felt her eyes widen. Lance Cooper, race-car driver was mentioned nearly half a million times on the Web?

Just for comparison's sake she typed in her own name, kindergarten teacher and then hit the return key.

Results 1 of 1 for "Sarah Tingle" "kindergarten teacher":

Naughty (and Naked!) Teachers!

She gasped, quickly hitting the return key, glancing over her shoulder to make sure nobody had seen that. Why, that low-down, no-good, dirty—

She almost picked up the phone and called her ex right then, but, she quickly reminded herself, what good would that do? The man purposely tried to get her goat. She'd checked her e-mail earlier and found half a dozen messages from him, each with a header like, I'm Sorry, and, Forgive Me. As if. Only a pervert like Peter would send her photos to Naughty (and Naked!) Teachers. But she wouldn't call him, and she wouldn't answer his e-mail, either. The sicko was just fishing to see how upset she was. He'd just sit there and gloat the moment after she hung up with him.

Still, her hands shook as she went back to her original search, all the while chanting, "What's in the past is past. What's in the past is past," to make herself feel better. As luck would have it she soon became distracted because she found Lance Cooper's Web site.

It was a shock to see his smiling and—yes, she could admit it—sexy face staring back at her own. It made her blush, a ridiculous reaction given he wasn't even within four hundred miles of her. But she blushed nonetheless, and then quickly clicked on the *Bio* button. To be honest, it felt a bit like poking around someone's underwear drawer, as if she was doing something bad by snooping on him, but her overwhelming curiosity made her do it anyway. Sarah averted her eyes from the tiny, less intimidating picture that cropped up to the left of the bio. It gave his stats, including his age (twenty-nine, she noticed, five years older than herself), his height (six feet—ai yi yi) and his marital status (single), but not much more than that.

Further surfing revealed a picture of his car. It was white. In the middle of the hood was a large orange star. Bright, there's-no-way-you-can-miss-me fluorescent orange, the words Star Oil in black cursive beneath that. She wondered for a moment who Star Oil was, only to discover a few clicks later that they imported oil, reselling it to refineries.

It was a few clicks after that that she finally discovered a bio worth reading. In it were all the pertinent facts of Lance's racing career. Of how he won a midget championship at age eight (whatever a "midget" was), and how he joined USAC at age seventeen (whatever USAC was, although she assumed it wasn't the opposite of MY-SAC), dropping out of high school to do so. But his lack of education must have paid off in this instance because he went on to win the USAC championship two years later. He'd raced "open wheels" next, and then in the NASCAR

Busch series, and so then she assumed Busch was a *type* of race car, and not, as one might think, a car decorated with shrubbery. Finally, when he was twenty-four, he'd entered the NASCAR NEXTEL Cup series with Blain Sanders as his team owner. That threw her for a moment because she'd assumed the driver owned the car, and yet that wasn't the case, apparently. He'd been with Sanders Racing his entire career, although by the sound of another article, it hadn't been the best season so far. Heck. It hadn't been good for a couple of years.

Further snooping revealed other facts, such as Lance's lack of family—he and his father appeared to be estranged. That Lance Cooper was revered by many, and yet, oddly enough, hated by an equal number of fans. The reason for that, she found out later, was because Lance had scored too many wins (obviously before his losing streak), thus irritating the fans of the other drivers who didn't win. What an odd sport.

Her cell phone rang.

She just about jumped out of her chair. The cell phone actually belonged to Lance Cooper, Inc., which meant the caller was either Lance's business manager Sal, or—

"Are you wearing underwear?"

Lance Cooper himself, she realized, blushing yet again.

"You know I could sue you for sexual harassment," she found herself saying, feeling more emboldened because he was miles away from her, while she was staring at his picture.

She quickly closed the screen, almost as if he might know she was snooping on him in some Star Trek, mind-melded way.

"I know," he said. "But you won't. If you were the suing type, you'd have already filed a lawsuit against me for felony hit and run."

"You didn't run."

"That's true," and she could hear the smile in his voice. "How about kiss and run?"

The skin on her lips tingled just before her cheeks heated up. "I'd rather not talk about that," she mumbled in a low voice, looking around her again as if someone might have heard him.

There was a pause. "Yeah. We probably shouldn't."

But she wanted to. Curse it all, she wanted to ask him all sorts of questions about that kiss. Had he enjoyed it? Did he like the way she kissed?

Was he going to kiss her again?

"How are you feeling?" he asked, suddenly all seriousness.

Stop thinking about his kiss. "Well, aside from a few scrapes and bruises, I appear to be fine."

"Taking the medication?"

She snorted. "No. I shudder to think what would happen if I did that. I might decide to head toward Hawaii, damn the Pacific Ocean."

"That wouldn't be a problem as long as you took your scuba gear."

"Actually, I bet your bus has pontoons somewhere."

He chuckled and she waited for him to say something else, getting that uncomfortable feeling one got when someone whom you kissed calls you and you're not quite sure how to react, or what to say.

"Well," she finally heard him drawl. "I was just making sure you were all right."

And that was the thing about Lance Cooper. He really cared. There was no artifice. None of the aloof pretentiousness that she might have expected from a man who'd been mentioned on the Web nearly half a million times. There was, of course, a hint of flirtatious innuendo in his voice, but she suspected that had more to do with simply being Lance's way than any real interest in her. Earlier, she'd imagined the look in his eyes as his head had lowered toward hers. It'd been the medication, that's all.

She just wished she knew why she felt so disappointed.

"Well, thanks for checking in," she said. "I'll see you in Daytona."

But would she? She had instructions to get the bus to Daytona by Wednesday. She'd have one night at the track and then she'd check into a hotel room. There'd be no need to go back to the track after that, or so she'd been told, because Lance only used his bus from Thursday to Sunday—the rest of the time he was at home or off doing media appearances. She'd only return when it was time to take Lance's motor coach to its next destination, Chicago.

But he said, "Yeah. I'll see you there."

And that was that. She said goodbye, coming back to earth and remembering she sat in a coffee shop where she'd been spying on Lance Cooper. And it seemed strange to be there, strange because when she'd answered the phone she'd forgotten her surroundings. She'd just about forgotten everything, including where she was. She even had to think hard to remember what city she was in.

A new customer walked into the dimly lit coffee-house, the man wearing a black T-shirt with bright markings on the front. A race fan T-shirt, she realized, the things suddenly sticking out like extra heads on a dog. This one was for a driver whose name she didn't recognize, but she would bet Lance knew him. Gosh. Lance was probably friends with the man pictured on the back of the shirt.

How surreal.

It was like working for a rock star, right on down to the bus.

And so why in the heck are you secretly thrilled that he's called? a voice asked.

Why in the heck did you have the urge to look around the coffee shop and tell people you were speaking to Lance Cooper. The Lance Cooper?

The man was famous. Much more famous than she would have ever surmised. Ergo, she had no business having a crush on him. Celebrities did not date kindergarten teachers. Besides, she had no business dating anyone—celebrity or no.

But that's exactly what she wanted, she admitted in dismay. She wanted to date him.

You're not seriously thinking you could rein in Lance Cooper?

No, she quickly reassured herself. She wasn't that silly. Besides, she probably had it all wrong. Lance Cooper might be a famous race-car driver, but she doubted anyone would know who he was outside of that venue.

That thought lasted right up until the moment she maneuvered the big bus out of the parking lot, lasted until then because as she was passing a gas station she caught sight of a vending machine—one with Lance Cooper's full-length picture on the front, his grinning face seeming to say, "That's what *you* think."

Oh, jeez.

CHAPTER EIGHT

HE FLEW to Daytona early.

It was a stupid thing to do, Lance realized. Why hire someone to drive your motor coach if you were going to fly down early so that the motor coach hadn't even arrived yet when you got there?

But that's exactly what he did, having told his pilot to meet him at the airport Wednesday evening in an attempt to beat Sarah Tingle to the racetrack. Ridiculous. What about his routine?

Thursday: Leave for the track, arriving in time to settle into his motor coach for the night.

Friday afternoon: Practice and then qualify.

Saturday was happy hour—usually. This weekend it was Friday, the whole schedule moved up a day because they were racing Saturday night.

And while he was at the track he didn't leave his motor coach, aside from media appearances. He never had women to his motor coach. He never even went out with the boys. He focused.

Until now.

"You're here early, Mr. Cooper," the infield guard said when he pulled up in a rented Lincoln Navigator.

"Media appearance," Lance lied, smiling at the man through the car's lowered window.

"Good luck on Saturday," he said, waving him through.

"Thanks," Lance said, rolling up the window and resisting the urge to bang his head against the steering wheel as he drove through the narrow tunnel painted to look like a giant checkered flag.

He was doomed.

Doomed, doomed, doomed. He'd broken his routine and now there was no telling what might happen.

Fortunately, someone else was at the track early, too. Todd Peters, the driver of the number forty-eight car. Lance spotted his blue-and-black motor coach the moment he entered the private parking area.

His friend gave him a curious stare when he opened up the door, saying, "Lance Cooper. What the heck are you doing here so early?" Todd had thick black brows that matched his equally black hair, and so when he lowered his bushy brows like he did now, he looked a lot like Mr. Potato Head. They even called him Spud, although they called him that because of his spud-shaped body.

"Sal had me scheduled for some radio show, but it got cancelled at the last moment," Lance lied. "Now I'm stuck with nothing to do."

"Stop the press," Todd said, smiling. "You agreed to come to the track early?"

Lance almost groaned. "I did."

"You breaking your routine now?" he asked. "You that desperate?"

"Can I come in?"

"No," the stocky driver said instantly. "Not after spinning me into that wall last week."

"Me?" Lance asked, pointing to himself. "You got loose all on your own, Spudly."

"Yeah?" Todd said, stepping back from the door. "I can still blame it on you."

And so he would, Lance thought, familiar with the tactic. "You here all alone?" he asked as he took the first step up, knowing Todd wasn't really mad. And, indeed, his friend stepped back to let him pass.

"For now," Todd said with a fox-in-the-henhouse smile. "Don't plan on being lonely for long."

Lance rolled his eyes. "By the way, what are *you* doing here early?"

"Aw, I gotta go do some lunch thing for Super Tools. Supposed to be there at noon, along with a few other drivers, reporters and TV cameras."

"Man, I hate those things."

"Yeah, but you can't get out of them, not and keep your sponsor, even if Super Tool is just an associate. I'm still required to go," Todd said with a shake of his head, "Hey, look. There's your bus now."

Lance paused, turning back from the top step to

peer in the direction Todd pointed. Sure enough, there it was, the familiar black-and-silver paint scheme shiny even beneath Daytona's partly cloudy skies.

"Who's that driving?" Todd asked, squinting those eyes to the point that his thick brows became one.

"That's Sarah."

"What happened to Frank?"

Lance looked away, refusing to admit he felt any sort of reaction. "You're not going to believe what happened to Frank," he said, forcing himself to stand there and not rush over like an excited puppy.

"Try me."

Lance bit back a smile, watching as Sarah stopped the bus near "his" spot.

"He ran off to drive for Mötley Crüe."

"He what?"

She hadn't seen them watching her, and Lance bit back a smile as he watched a look of intense concentration cross her face as she put the bus in reverse, the backup warning chime beep-beep-beeping. He had a perfect view of her, white teeth raking her bottom lip, eyes narrowed as she flicked her gaze between the two side mirrors, red ponytail swishing like an angry horse.

Lance finally looked back at Todd. "He took off on us to drive for the Crüe."

"Frank? The man who's been driving your motor coach for the last four years? Frank who was in his forties?"

"He grew up listening to them, apparently, and when he heard about their need for a driver, he bailed."

"Unbelievable," Todd said. "You've been thrown over for aging rock stars."

Lance chuckled. "I suppose that's one way of looking at it, but it left me in a bind. Fortunately, Sal found Sarah."

"Sarah looks cute," Todd said, squinting his eyes again, unibrow back in place.

"Sarah's off-limits," Lance said.

Todd's brows took off, gaze flicking back to him. "Like that, is it?"

"No," Lance denied. "She's just off-limits. I don't want to lose another driver."

The beeping stopped. Lance looked away from Todd, which was just as well because he could tell that his sometimes fishing partner, most-of-the-time best friend (when they weren't out on the track), didn't believe him.

"Yeah, right," Todd said as Lance stepped down from his bus.

Yeah, right, his own conscience echoed. Because there was one thing Lance couldn't deny: as he approached his motor coach he felt just like he did before a race.

And that wasn't good. That wasn't good at all.

SARAH WANTED to rest her head on the steering wheel.

She'd made it.

She'd driven Lance Cooper's rolling Taj Mahal all the way to Daytona without once sideswiping a car, cutting a corner too close, or driving off the road.

"Thank you, Lord," she silently whispered. "Thank you, thank you, thank you." Now all she had to do was level the bus out, set up the generator, pop out the three sliders and she'd be all set and frankly, she was looking forward to relaxing in a hotel room. Lance and company weren't due to arrive until tomorrow, which meant she wasn't due to check into her hotel until tomorrow, which meant she could spend one more night in The Palace. More importantly, it meant that she wouldn't be bumping into Lance Cooper anytime soon. As silly as it sounded, she was really worried she might run into him—

"Hey, Sarah."

The door, the hiss of the hydraulic lock, and her scream all erupted at the same time.

"Did I scare you?"

She spun around, wondering why the heck people always asked that when it was plain as the noses on their faces that they had, indeed, frightened someone? "No," she said sarcastically. "I always yelp when sitting in drivers' seats."

"Oh," he said. "And here I thought you just sang 'Wheels on the Bus.'"

She narrowed her eyes. "What the blazes are you doing here?" Her heart was pounding against her chest so hard, it sounded like bongos in her ears.

"I came early."

"But," she swallowed, then swallowed again because she was not, absolutely not ready to face Lance Cooper.

"But what?" he prompted, that boyish smile of his back in place.

"But I'm supposed to sleep here tonight."

"You can sleep with me."

"I can't do that."

"I didn't mean that the way it sounded," Lance quickly corrected, making his way up the narrow steps so that he stood over her. "I meant you could sleep on the couch like you've done the last couple of days…"

On the couch? While he slept nearby?

No, Sarah. No, no, no. "I'm sorry, Mr. Cooper, but I wouldn't feel comfortable sleeping in the same bus as you."

"Mr. Cooper is it now?" he asked.

Race-car driver, she reminded herself. *Hugely famous. Fantastically gorgeous.* And, even more importantly: *man not to be trusted.*

"I really think it best if we keep things on a more professional level."

She waited for him to disagree, waited for him to smile at her and tell her that was the last thing he wanted to do was keep it professional. But instead he looked—well, he looked almost relieved. "Yeah, you're probably right," he said, running a hand through his hair. "I just thought…"

"Just thought what?" she prompted, and for some reason her heart had started to thump against her chest like she faced a dentist's drill and not just a handsome man.

"I just thought, I don't know, that maybe we could do lunch."

We could do lunch? she almost said aloud.

"But you're right. This was a bad idea—"

Someone knocked on the fiberglass door.

"That's probably Todd," Lance said. "Come over for an introduction." And then, she could have sworn she heard under his breath, "Sneak."

But it wasn't Todd. It was the skinniest, leggiest blonde Sarah had ever seen.

"Lance," she said in a rush, stepping into the bus without being invited, a yellow polo shirt with the words *Super Tools* on her tiny little body. The color should have made her look like a kidney patient; instead, it made her skin glow. Not fair.

"I'm so glad you're here early—oh," she said, turning to Sarah, giving her the once-over, deciding she didn't know her, and then turning back to Lance with a perky little bounce of her heels (though actually, they were tennis shoes). "Dan Harris had to pull out of our lunch and I would be really, really, really, *really* grateful if you could take his spot. Would you please, pretty please, please, please, please?" she said, tipping her head sideways and looking up at Lance with a pleading expression on her face.

"I don't know…"

"You can bring your friend," she said, glancing back at Sarah.

"I'm not his friend. I'm his new driver," Sarah said.

"Oh, well, you can still come," she said.

"That's okay," Sarah started to say.

But the blonde had already turned back to Lance saying, "*Please.* You'd really be helping Super Tools out."

The mention of his sponsor seemed to clinch it for Lance because he nodded his head.

"Good," the blonde said with another bounce. "I'll have a driver pick you up in a half hour. It's at the Renaissance Hotel and the event starts in less than an hour so you'll have to hurry." She turned back to Sarah. "Can you make sure he's ready?" she asked as if Sarah was his caretaker or something.

"Um, sure, but there's really no need for me to go."

"Oh, it's not a problem. The more bodies there, the better. Makes it look good to the press when the place is packed."

Sarah thought about protesting one more time but figured if she did that she'd come off sounding ungrateful or something. But when the woman left, Sarah said to Lance, "I'll stay here."

"Nah. You should come," he said, crossing his arms across his chest, his biceps bulging as if he lifted weights for a living instead of driving race cars. Jeesh, no wonder he'd been voted sexiest driver two years in a row. "You're new to this sport, so you might find it interesting to see the fans in action. Plus, you'll meet a few of the other drivers."

She almost told him she'd already interacted with a few of his fans. Every time she'd stopped to refuel, someone had come over and asked, "You a Lance Cooper fan?" That little twenty-six car sticker had been like a neon Open sign. Perfect strangers came up and chatted with her like they'd known her forever. Even her lame-sounding "I'm new to racing" hadn't deterred their friendliness. They'd just gone on to list all of Lance's outstanding capabilities, then congratulated her on picking such a good man as her driver.

Her driver. Yeah, right.

"Look, Sarah. I, ah…I wanted to apologize for kissing you the other day. It was a stupid thing to do. You're just coming off a bad relationship and I need to focus on my job."

And for some truly ridiculous reason the blood drained from her face. "Yeah. Sure. Absolutely."

He looked relieved and then maybe sad, but definitely more relieved than anything.

"I need to go get dressed."

"And I need to start up the generator."

"Do you need help?"

"To flip a switch?" she asked brightly, too brightly if he knew her better. "Don't be silly. Plus, it'll give you some privacy."

"Yeah, thanks," he said. And then he smiled at her, holding out his hand and asking, "Friends?"

No, she wanted to scream. No, no, no—you are *not* my friend.

"Friends," she echoed.

Because no matter what she'd told herself the whole way down to Daytona the truth of the matter was that she'd kind of liked his kiss. She'd even thought he might have liked it, too.

Obviously, she'd been wrong.

CHAPTER NINE

SO SHE WENT to the autographing, although to be honest, mostly to prove that she could interact with Lance and not make a fool of herself.

As they climbed into the waiting car, Sarah told herself to relax. The hotel was close by, or so the driver told her. She could sit next to Lance and act as if nothing had happened between them. He sure did a good job of it.

But the fact of the matter was, she couldn't just dismiss it as he apparently did. Every time she came near the man her pulse rate elevated like she had hypertension. A chronic blush tinted her cheeks. Within two minutes of climbing into the rental car, Sarah realized that despite all the times her heart had been stomped on in the past, she seemed to have developed a crush—a bona fide, heart-pounding, palm-sweating crush—on her new boss.

What.

An.

Idiot.

A little voice inside her head told her she should

quit, but she was fresh out of courage and quitting meant sinking even further into debt, not to mention owing Lance for the repair of her car. No, she was kind of stuck trying to stick it out. As long as she nipped her crush right in the bud she was safe. And if ever she needed further proof that she didn't stand a chance at catching Lance's interest, all she had to do was glance around the spacious ballroom and look at the women who'd come with the very obvious intention of becoming the Saran Wrap to Lance's Tupperware.

She'd entered Babeland.

Seriously, there were so many pretty women in the room, it looked like a cattle call for The Rolling Stones' next video. Oh, not every woman was decked out to the nines, some even had husbands and boyfriends with them, but the majority of the women had come with the very obvious intent of scoring themselves a driver—if only for a night. Sarah watched as each woman turned toward the door, breasts thrusting up, hair swishing over one shoulder, mental "welcome" signs all but hung around their shoulders.

She, apparently, was immediately dismissed as a nonthreat. More than one woman looked at her and glanced away without a single sign of visually wishing for her death.

Too plain. Not flashy. Must be a friend.

Sigh. Story of her life.

"Lance," Miss Super Tools said, coming forward

in her too-tight pants that made her waist look so narrow, Sarah wondered if a McDonald's French fry had ever passed her lips. "I'm so glad you could make it. There's drinks over there for you and your driver," she said, glancing in Sarah's direction before pointing toward a corner of the room. "We're having an autograph session in an hour over there." And now she pointed to another side of the room. "Todd is here. And so is Brock Ashton—they'll both be signing with you. Feel free to mingle. I'm sure the fans are dying to talk to you."

Lance nodded, glancing in her direction. Sarah smiled brightly as she said, "Go ahead. I'll be okay," all the while wondering what the heck she was doing here. Why had she come? Had she really needed to prove to herself that she could act disinterested in Lance?

You came because you wanted to see what his life was like. Because you were curious about how fans would treat him.

But to her surprise, he didn't abandon her. What he did was say, "No way," the words all but whispered in her ear, which caused shivers to slide down her back and her cheeks to color. "I'm not leaving your side. Not with so many barracudas in the room." And then he looked momentarily pained, as if he regretted his words, Lance adding, "We might be friends, but they don't know that."

Friends. Yeah. Right.

"C'mon," he said. Sarah's blood rushed to her thighs at the way he smiled at her, a smile that was obviously meant for their audience. "Let's go get a drink." And then—*then*—he placed a hand at the small of her back.

And suddenly, Sarah became The Competition. If the lights had suddenly been dimmed, if eyes had suddenly turned into laser beams, she would have had a million little red dots all over her torso.

"What do you want?" he asked when they stopped before a portable bar, the man behind the chest-high counter staring at Lance in awe.

You.

"Just some orange juice, please."

Lance's eyes widened. "No Cosmopolitan? No martini? No foo-foo drink?"

"Actually, I'm a beer and pretzel sort of girl— when I drink, which isn't very often."

He held her gaze, his face softening into a look that could only be called approval. "My kind of girl," he said, patting her back and turning to the bartender.

Sarah just stood there, frozen, her whole body flushing with pleasure.

It's just an act, remember Sarah. Think "professional."

Yet after her drink was served—a double shot of OJ, over ice—he stayed by her side, introducing her to the other drivers there, all of whom she gleaned drove Fords because heaven forbid you should mix a

Chevy driver with a Ford driver (or so she surmised). Fans came up to them and asked questions, Lance always answering with a smile and a funny quip. She found herself smiling, too, and falling deeper and deeper into crush mode as the afternoon wore on. And then, when it came time for him to do his signing he gave her waist a goodbye squeeze. She blushed, feeling pleasure even though she told herself to not, not, *not* take the gesture personally.

When he turned and left (and the haze of hero worship wore off) Sarah looked around.

And felt like a fish head tossed into a tank of sharks. A blonde eyed her up and down, the look she gave her saying, "He's mine next, honey."

Sarah just smiled, flicked her chin up, and retreated to the balcony like the coward she was.

Not a coward, she swiftly corrected, taking a deep breath of salt-scented air, *realistic*—or at least she was trying to be.

She closed her eyes, tilting her head back. Over the hum of conversation in the ballroom she could hear the roar of the ocean. When she tipped her head back she noticed the fluffy clouds of the morning had turned into serious thunderheads, the sand on the beach turning gray beneath the shadow of a cloud. Yes, she would be realistic, because no matter how much she wished she were a different person, she wasn't about to risk getting involved with Lance. Not even for only a night, which she quickly reasoned she could probably entice him into having with her. He might have agreed with her "let's keep things professional" but she'd caught a look in his eyes once or twice this afternoon, one that made her think that maybe he wasn't quite as disinterested in her as she'd thought. He'd hugged her waist, too. A man didn't give a woman a hug like that unless he liked her. Maybe more than liked her.

And then she heard it.

"He's washed up, anyway," said a woman whose voice drifted to her from inside the ballroom.

"Yeah," said another woman. "What's the big deal?"

"But I'd still like to know what he sees in her," said the first. "I mean, she must be good in bed or something because she sure isn't much to look at."

If humiliation had been flames, Sarah would have combusted on the spot. They were talking about *her*. Obviously.

"Maybe that's the best he can do now that his career is on the skids," said the second woman.

"Shame, too," said the first. "He used to be such a good driver."

"Well, after the way he tanked last year, I'm surprised Blain Sanders let him come back *this* year."

"Rumor has it he and Sanders are good friends. He probably let him come back out of pity."

"He's probably with that *woman* out of pity," said the second voice. They both laughed.

Sarah turned, blindly staring out at the ocean. Her hands clutched the rail as her hair whipped around her in the wake of a sudden breeze.

How dare they? she thought. How dare they criticize Lance? How dare they criticize *her*? They didn't know her. And they sure as certain didn't know Lance. So what if he'd been having an off year? Okay, an off couple of years. From what she'd read on the Internet, that wasn't unheard of in the racing industry. More than one reporter had predicted he'd pull it together again. Who's to say he wouldn't do it this year? Or next?

She stewed at the injustice of it all. People could be so cruel. So mean and petty. She'd dealt with it all the time in her job, not so much with the children—no, she saw it in the parents. The well-off, well-dressed moms would roll their eyes at the moms that drove beat-up cars instead of a new SUV. They'd form cliques just as they had in high school, some of the moms "in" and others "out," and Sarah witnessed the hurt those "out" moms would try to hide when they weren't invited to play Bunko or whatever else the "in" crowd was doing that week. It wasn't fair. It was childish and she couldn't stand people like that.

Thrusting herself up, she almost turned back to the ballroom, but something stopped her. What did she expect to do? Find those two women and then blast them with a look? She didn't even know who they were. Besides, it wasn't in her to be rude. But it still angered her to no end that they'd been so cruel when talking about Lance. The criticism to herself she could take. After all, she'd known for years her looks weren't much more than average. But criticizing Lance was another story. He might not be an "in" driver, but he was a nice man. That should count for *something,* certainly for more than his driving skills.

"Hey," said a familiar, masculine voice.

Sarah jumped. But when he came up alongside her, she tried to give him a wide smile. It wobbled.

"Don't let 'em get to you."

"What?"

"Those women. Don't let what they said get to you."

"You heard that?" she asked, aghast.

"I came in through the other door," he said, pointing to a door at the far end of the balcony. "And it was kind of hard not to hear."

"Oh, jeez," she said.

His face softened, his eyes holding hers so tightly, it was like he held her face between his hands. "Don't let it upset you. It's what race fans do. Their favorite sport, besides racing, is bashing other drivers. Men and women do it, only women seem to think it's okay to attack a driver's wife or girlfriend, too. It's not right, but it happens."

"I'm not your girlfriend."

"No," he said instantly, making her think the glimmer of interest she might have seen in his eyes had been all in her imagination. "But they think you are."

She couldn't argue that point, didn't want to argue the point. "It's not their comments about me that upset me," she admitted. "Really, Lance, what they said about me is nothing worse than what I've heard before. What bothers me is that they attacked you."

"Don't let it," he said again. "It comes with the territory. Yeah, sure, sometimes it stings, but that's the nature of the beast."

It more than stung. For a second there she'd caught a glimpse of it, the anger and humiliation he felt at being a public figure of scorn. He might try to hide it, but she'd seen it.

"Lance, you're a great driver. Don't let people bring you down."

He snorted. "This from someone who's never watched a race in her life."

"I'll watch you."

"Will you?" he said, peeking at her in a boyish way that made her heart melt.

"Well," she sighed with long-suffering resignation, "If I have to."

He chuckled a bit. "Good."

She turned, knowing if she didn't look back out over the ocean he might see something in her eyes she didn't want him to see.

"You're not an object of pity, Sarah," he said softly. "You're witty and you make people laugh, not to mention sing a stirring rendition of 'Wheels on the Bus.' So no matter what those so-called ladies might have said, you're twenty times prettier than they are and any man would be lucky to have you as a girl-friend."

Just not Lance.

Sarah gulped and swallowed back something that felt suspiciously like tears. She tried to distract him by saying, "Are you sure you didn't wreck your car last weekend?"

He looked puzzled. "No. Why?"

"Because I think you must have double vision or something if you consider *me* prettier than some of the women in there."

She wasn't fishing for compliments. Really, she wasn't.

Yes, you are.

He leaned toward her, something that made her breath catch and her heart give a giant leap.

"Sarah," he said, "You have a beauty that has nothing to do with your physical appearance and ev-erything to do with the soul inside of you. Nobody in the room can hold a candle to you."

And there it went. It was happening again. A massive swell of bona fide crush filled her heart and made it difficult to breathe.

"Thanks," she said softly.

He seemed to recall himself. When he drew back Sarah wanted to weep. "Let's blow this taco stand," he said quickly.

Too quickly.

"Ah, yeah, sure."

CHAPTER TEN

HE TOOK HER BACK to a hotel after commandeering a room from one of his team members. But when he'd left her there, all Lance could do was clutch the steering wheel and think: *what the heck am I getting into? You can't afford to be distracted, buddy. Not now.*

Maybe in a few months, when he'd gotten his driving back on track again, but not now.

When you get your driving back? a little voice asked. *What if you don't?*

That was part of the problem. His need for complete and total concentration was at its maximum right now and he couldn't be distracted, not even a little bit. Not to mention, a relationship with a woman like Sarah was doomed from the outset. She didn't "get" racing, and while that was something that attracted him now, he also knew it would lead to problems down the road.

Damn, it had been adorable the way she'd tried to make him feel better.

Stop it, Lance. No more thoughts about Sarah. Time to focus.

HE COULDN'T FOCUS.

Crap. He was a frickin' nervous wreck.

And to top it off, the whole world knew it. All right, maybe not the whole world, but those watching ESPN had seen him climb into the number twenty-six car, his team owner, Blain Sanders, helping him in. They watched him wipe the sweat from his brow, and then nervously fasten his helmet with hands that very obviously shook.

And it was just a practice.

To wit: it was the first practice of the weekend, which meant if the car performed badly, they had time to fix it. Unless he wrecked, and then he'd have to go to a backup car.

You're not going to wreck.

Why? he kept asking himself. Why were these sudden thoughts of doom and gloom consuming him? It drove him nuts, he admitted, waiting for the okay to start his engine so he could back his car out of the garage and head on out to the track. In front of him Allen, their crew chief, spoke to a television broadcaster, a white star in the center of the hood reflecting their image back thanks to the fluorescent lights above their heads. Blain had left the garage and gone back to the hauler parked out behind them. Lance glanced left and right. All the other drivers were in their cars, crew members buzzing around and making last-minute adjustments. In front of him a wall of Plexiglas allowed fans to peer into the garage, their gazes transfixed on the action.

He's washed up, anyway.

The woman's words echoed in his ears, the same words Sarah had heard, too, along with the not-so-flattering things those women had said about herself. He'd been right at the entrance to the balcony when they'd spewed their poison. Lance was furious for Sarah's sake and, it would appear, subconsciously affected by the words, too. There was no other explanation as to why he suddenly felt as if he were about to run his first race.

Washed up.

Stop it, he ordered the voice. It's nothing worse than you've heard before. Crap, half the reporters who followed racing had said much worse. Washed up. A has-been. Lost his edge.

It was the look on Sarah's face that made him furious. That's what had him so nervous, not because he was afraid of practicing his car, but because he knew his concentration wasn't what it was supposed to be and that had him worried. Never before had a woman intruded on his time in a race car. Never.

"Start 'em up," came his crew chief's voice, Lance looking up only to realize Allen wasn't giving an interview anymore. He stood alongside his car, his crew chief for the past three years tapping on the roof. Lance flicked the starter switch. The roar of the motor instantly filled his ears, even through his mask, ear pieces and helmet. Usually the sound of the engine worked as a filter, a white noise that helped him to focus. Not today.

She hadn't come to watch him practice. He'd told her to stop by when he'd dropped her off at her hotel. He'd mentioned it in a casual way and she'd nodded and smiled a bit—

"Lance?" Allen asked.

Lance jerked, brought back to reality by the sound of his crew chief's voice.

"Any day now," Allen added.

And when Lance glanced left and right, his movement restricted by the safety restraints attached to his Day-Glo orange helmet, he noticed all the other drivers had already pulled out of the garage.

Son of a—

He jerked the car into reverse, backing it out with barely a look at the crew member who directed him. Jeez. Talk about spacing out.

"Okay, buddy," Allen said. "We've put new springs, new shocks and a different track bar on the rear than what we had in for the 500."

In other words, they'd started from scratch. Again.

"She shouldn't be as loose as she was in the spring, so just take it out and let me know how it feels."

It felt like crap, Lance admitted a few laps later, the grandstands a blurry gray as he passed by at a hundred and eighty miles per hour. His lap times were crap, too.

"She's too loose, Allen," he said, as he pulled in, nearly hitting his crew chief's orange-clad legs when he pulled into the garage. "Doesn't matter what line I take, the rear end is swinging around like a ballroom dancer."

"Ten-four," Allen said, consulting his clipboard. Other crew members stood around waiting to be told what to do. He pressed the talk button on his headset. "Blain, you got any ideas?"

His car owner came on the line. "Try some tire pressure adjustments."

"All right, let's take it down a half a pound in the front and a pound out of the rear. Frank, take a round of wedge out, too. Let's see if that makes it any better."

And that's what he did for the next hour. He'd drive around for a few laps, see if the changes helped (they didn't), then come back in, his crew chief's blue eyes looking more and more puzzled each time he rolled into the garage. In the end they took out numerous rounds of wedge (and put them back in), took out a few rubbers (and added a few, too) and fiddled with the tire pressure, all to no avail. The car was crap and everyone knew it. The white shirts they wore above their orange pants were looking as pale as their faces. Even Blain climbed down from the hauler, trying to offer advice. Didn't help.

Not good. And with the vice president of Star Oil showing up to root him on...

"Too bad we can't just pull out the backup car," Blain said after Lance had taken off his helmet and pulled his earplugs out. "It couldn't be any worse."

"Very funny. Though with the way my luck is going," Lance said, setting his helmet down on the aluminum platform to his right, and then inhaling a fresh blast of cool air. Damn, but that felt good. "It probably could."

"Starting at the back just might be better. Too bad it's not legal."

Car owner and crew chief said nothing, Lance meeting their gazes. He had a sinking feeling in his stomach again, the feeling he'd had more and more of late.

"I don't know what the matter is, but every time I take her into the corner she's so loose it feels like I'm on skates."

"Loose is good," his crew chief said as Lance wormed his way out of the car, his firesuit catching on the hooks for the window netting. And Lance didn't need to be told what his crew chief's un-spoken words were: *You should still be able to drive it.*

"There's loose and there's loose," Lance said, leaning up against his car, his firesuit and the humid day making him feel like a caterpillar wrapped up in a cocoon.

"We've tried everything we can," Allen said. "I don't know what else to do."

"Too bad," Lance said, feeling edgy. "Because when this car is loose, it's really loose and when it's tight, it's really tight. There's no in-between."

Allen and Blain exchanged looks. Lance shook his head and walked away.

"Lance, wait," his car owner said.

"I can't," Lance said, walking toward the hauler. He wanted out of his firesuit; the high collar all but choked him. "Courtney set up an interview for me."

"The interview's not for another half hour," Blain said, stopping him right in the middle of the road between the garages and the haulers.

Lance should have known their PR gal had filled Blain in on his media appearances. She always did.

"Look, I don't know what's eating you today, but you gotta relax."

Lance forced himself to meet the gaze of the man who he'd idolized for just about as long as he could remember. Blain Sanders was an icon in the racing industry, a man who'd pulled himself up from the ranks of tire changer to car owner in the fourteen years he'd been in the business. Not only was he a brilliant engine builder, he was a good man, and Blain and his wife Cece were two of the nicest people Lance had the privilege to know. Any other team owner would have tossed him out on his ear after two years of poor performances.

And it killed him that he wasn't driving up to par.

"You're not yourself," Blain said. "Even Cece noticed it, and she's watching from home."

Terrific. Just as he'd thought. That ESPN camera

crew had trained their lens on him just a little too close.

"Look," Blain said. "I know you're struggling. Everyone in the garage knows it. But you've never had a problem driving crap cars in the past."

He had in the last year.

"You're one of those rare drivers that can make a bad car look good and a good car look excellent. But something's got you messed up here," Blain said, tapping his black hair, now liberally salted with gray hair, compliments of his first child—or so he liked to tell people. "Figure out what it is so you can start driving like the Lance I remember."

Which was as close to an ass-chewing as Lance had ever gotten from his owner. That was the thing about racing for Blain and Cece Sanders. They were special people in the industry, which made his crap driving all the worse.

"I'll do my best, boss."

"Good," Blain said, patting him on the back. "'Cause I miss the wisecracking Lance of old."

"Oh, I can still make wisecracks."

"I don't doubt it."

"I just hate for you to grow self-conscious about your thinning hair."

"Very funny," said the man whose hair was every bit as thick as it'd been the day Lance had first met him.

"I thought it was," Lance said.

Blain shook his head, patting him on the back again. "Go."

And Lance went.

HE SMELLED COOKIES.

It was the first thing he noticed when he went up the aisle between his motor coach and the next, the driver parking area so crowded with buses and fancy RVs that it looked like a dealership. The blue-and-white Prevost next to him belonged to Sam Kennedy, NASCAR NEXTEL Cup racing's current brightest star and a man who had the good fortune to be married to a wife that cooked. Man, those cookies smelled good. Made his stomach growl.

It was only when he opened the door that he realized the smell was coming from *his* motor coach, and that the person cooking them was Sarah Tingle.

His knees went weak.

That's exactly what seemed to happen when she straightened up from pulling a batch of cookies out of the oven, a wide smile on her face. Granted, that smile seemed a bit forced—as if she wasn't sure he'd be happy to see her—but when she held out the aluminum tray and said, "Want one?" he forgot all about weak knees and strode forward to grab an... animal cookie?

She'd baked him animal cookies?

He almost laughed, almost leaned down and

kissed her. It was amazing how close he came, considering all the times he'd told himself in the past few hours to forget about her. The cookie he plopped into his mouth melted on his tongue. Sugar and butter flavored his mouth, causing him to purr. "Mmmm," he said.

Her smile turned genuine. He could see her tension fade, although she didn't look him in the eye for a second or two. Instead she busied herself with taking the cookies off the tray.

"The secret is waiting for the tray to cool down in between batches. A tray that's too hot will burn the bottom and so I wash my tray off before I put another batch in."

He watched as she did exactly that, grabbing another cookie from the cooling plate while her back was turned to the sink.

"I saw that," she said.

He laughed. And, man, he almost felt like crying, so good did it feel. His tension just seemed to melt away, the smell of fresh-baked cookies so familiar and from such an achingly good time in his life that he wanted to pull her into his arms and kiss her in gratitude.

What you should do is marry her.

He jerked as if the thought had dive-bombed his head.

But he couldn't deny how good it felt to stand there watching her bake cookies. It made him want to do something to ensure that feeling happened again…and again, not because he was falling in love with her or anything, but because he needed the calm she provided after the chaos of driving a car.

"Sarah Tingle, you're a woman after my own heart."

She peeked up at him. It was one of the things he loved about her. There were no boldly sexual looks of invitation on her face, just a sweet innocence that made him want to cuddle her.

Innocent?

Remember, Lance, she'd been wearing someone else's privates a few weeks ago.

Okay, well, maybe not that innocent, but certainly less worldly than the women who'd been a part of his recent past.

"You looked nervous on TV."

Ahh, so she'd been watching. "I was."

Her expression turned serious for a moment. "It's just a race, Lance."

He took the tray of cooling cookies with him as he sat down at his bar. "Only someone who doesn't understand racing could say that."

She looked stricken.

"No, no. Don't look like that. I know you don't get racing and so let me explain," he said, placing a half-eaten cookie back on the plate. She gave him a kindergarten teacher frown. "Sorry," he said, moving the cookie back to his hand.

"We don't spread our germs by putting half-eaten food on other people's plates."

He almost laughed. "Okay, Miss Teacher. And like I was saying, you have no idea how important this is—at least to me."

"No?" she asked.

"No."

"Then tell me."

"I don't think I can," he said with a frown. "I don't think I can explain how it makes me feel to go 190 MPH down the front straightaway. What it's like to know that you're right on the verge of spinning out of control, but that if you hold on to it, you'll come out in front, maybe. What it's like to feel that adrenaline rush during the last few laps when you know you might just win, or not, but finish good enough that you might get a shot to race for the championship. There's nothing like this, nothing like this in the world."

"Yes, but what if something happens? What if you're not able to drive again? What will you do then?"

He shrugged.

She shook her head. "Look," she said. "If I asked the average fan who won the championship in 1968, assuming there was a championship back then—"

"There was. David Pearson won it, one of the few to snag two in a row."

"Okay, you know who won, but do you think the average race fan would know?"

"I don't know." He shrugged a bit. "Probably. Maybe."

"And that's my point. Probably. Maybe. You're not curing cancer here."

"Ouch."

"I'm sorry," she said, running her fingers through her hair in an agitated way. "I'm really sorry. You just looked so nervous on TV, Lance, and there's no need to be. It's just a race. You're not saving the world. You're not helping to promote world peace. You're just driving a car in a circle and I have a feeling you used to have fun doing it, but it sure doesn't look like it anymore."

"So you baked me cookies," he said with a half smile, not sure if he should be offended at how inconsequential she made his job sound, or touched that she tried to help.

"I used to do it for my class," she said. "Back when I was a student teacher, my third graders would get upset on test days, too. So I'd bake them cookies. Just by taking the test you'd get one cookie. If you got all the answers right you got *five*."

"How many would I have had to have gotten right for eating four?"

"You would have had to have gotten a B on your test."

"Then I guess I better do good during the next practice session because that was very definitely an F performance."

"You will."

"I will if you're there with me."

It surprised him how much he wanted that. She was so completely unimpressed by what he did that he wished he could capture some of that. Maybe if he went back to just having fun, his driving would improve.

"I can watch from here."

He shook his head. "Nope. I want you there in the garage, holding up a bag of cookies every time I come in."

She laughed, and the realization that he'd put a smile on her face—well, it made him feel almost as good when he roared down the straightaway.

Actually, it felt better.

"You're not serious," she asked.

"Yes, I am."

Her look turned somber. "I can't do that. I don't know the first thing about being in the garage."

"What's there to know? Stay out of everyone's way and when you hear a car coming toward you, make sure you're not in front of it. Drivers have been known to run people down—by accident, of course."

Which made her lips twitch again. "Lance, I can't."

He bent down and kissed her on the cheek, the cookie scent of her hair filling his nostrils. Suddenly Lance felt so filled with pent-up longing that it was all he could do not to pull her to him. But he didn't.

He just straightened, unable to resist cupping one side of her face with his right hand.

Stupid, Lance. Stupid move. She might read more into it than she should.

But he didn't care. Her skin was as soft as it looked. No, softer.

"Please, Sarah, come be in the garage with me." Because, damn it, he needed her.

"Jeez," he thought he heard her murmur, the word so softly muttered that it was barely audible over the sound of A/C humming in the background. He felt his whole body still, wondering if maybe she'd felt the same thing he did whenever they made eye contact—as if some sort of charged energy stretched between them. If she did, she hid it well. Then again, she didn't exactly hold men in high esteem.

"Please," he said again.

She looked away from him, her brown eyes flecked with tiny streaks of mint green that sprouted from their centers. Pretty eyes, he found himself thinking yet again.

"All right," she said at last. "When do I need to be there?"

"In an hour."

"Okay," she said, nodding, then moving away from him. Lance was smart enough to let her slip away. If he touched her again, if he bent his head and kissed her like he wanted—well, there was no telling what else might happen. And while he was selfish enough to insist on her company in the garage, in hopes that she might be able to help him get his head on straight, he knew that anything more than that would be a serious distraction.

Serious.

CHAPTER ELEVEN

IT BOGGLED SARAH'S MIND that after suffering a horrible humiliation at the hands of her wacked-out ex-boyfriend, she was actually considering—yes, truly considering—jumping into bed with Lance Cooper.

There. She'd said it...or thought it. Whatever. She could admit that when he'd walked into his motor coach, his eyes having gone all warm and gooey at the sight of her baking him cookies, she'd just about told him the cookies weren't the only things available for consumption.

She moaned aloud as she took the latest batch of cookies out of the tiny oven, depositing them on the counter, all the while wondering if she should do as he asked and show up in the garage. For some reason she couldn't help but think that showing up at the garage meant something. She didn't know what, exactly, she just thought that making him cookies had straddled the line of the boss/employee relationship and so going into the garage in order to rah-rah Lance, well, it just seemed too personal.

But she wanted to.

In the end she decided she really had no choice. She'd given her word and so she needed to show up. If she didn't she worried he might get mad at her, which might distract him, which might affect how he practiced.

The heat just about slapped her back when she stepped out of the motor coach, and the humidity, too. If she'd thought North Carolina humidity was bad, it was nothing compared to Florida. It was one of those days where so much moisture filled the air, it turned the atmosphere a hazy gray.

It wasn't hard to find the garage. All she had to do was pause, listen for the sound of revving engines and follow her ears. She glanced at the grandstand; three layers of seats rose up, red and blue chairs on the bottom two, seats painted in a checkerboard pattern signaling the uppermost grandstand. There weren't a lot of people up there, something that surprised her. The brief glimpses she'd caught of racetracks on TV showed grandstands packed to capacity. But maybe this type of racing didn't have a high attendance, she thought, her eyes catching on the word DAYTONA that stretched across the white retaining wall near the center of the track.

"Credential?" a wizened old security guard wearing a blue hat with Daytona Security emblazoned on the front asked her. Sarah stopped in surprise, eyeing the chain-link fence at the same time the realization hit her that access to the garage appeared to be restricted.

Credential? Oh, yeah. That was that postcard-sized thing that she'd been told to carry around with her. She reached in the back pocket of her jeans, having to unfold and smooth down the paper so the darn thing could be read. The security guard looked at her like she was nuts, and by the time he'd finished looking at it Sarah felt the familiar sting of embarrassment. What? Was she not supposed to fold it or something? She had her answer less than two seconds later when someone walked out of the garage, a clear plastic holder bobbing around with each step he took. Inside was the credential.

"Guess I need to buy one of those holder thingies," she said to the guard, who just frowned. Okay, so maybe he wasn't used to people being friendly.

In fact, the whole atmosphere seemed a bit tense, Sarah noticed as she stayed to the right of a thick yellow line that she assumed had been painted there as a way of keeping unwary tourists like herself out of harm's way. Multiple garage doors with race cars inside were the focus of some mighty serious stares as men in brightly colored outfits dashed between the garage and the big rigs to her right. Someone started an engine; Sarah just about shot out of her tennis shoes. Jeez, those things were loud.

"Excuse me," she asked a man in a bright-blue

outfit, the name of an auto parts store emblazoned across his chest. "Do you know where Lance Cooper's garage is?"

The man didn't smile, didn't flinch, didn't do anything other than point in the direction of the car stalls. "Name's on top."

Name's on—?

"Ah," she said, seeing that, indeed, someone had had the foresight to put the driver's name and car number above the garage door. "Thanks," she said, only to realize a second later that there appeared to be no rhyme or reason as to the order they were placed, which meant she had to walk all the way to the other side of the garage before finally spying LANCE COOPER in big, bold letters.

Okay, so now what? She stopped directly opposite the garage, near a stack of tires on a red dolly. Did she go into the stall? Lance had said to meet him there. But those men inside the garage looked awfully scary, and she didn't see Lance.

She looked around for help again, only to spy the logo of Lance's sponsor on some tinted glass doors, doors that appeared to belong to the truck that carried Lance's race car around. Above the doors was a metal flap that hung off the back of the big rig like a castle drawbridge, only elevated so that it afforded some shade. Someone had placed lawn chairs along one side, orange coolers with white lids snuggled beneath the truck's rear bumper.

How…bizarre, she found herself thinking. It appeared to be some type of mobile office. But where did they put the race cars?

Just then one of the doors opened, a man Sarah recognized from TV and the World Wide Web stepping outside, his white shirt with a bright orange star on the left shirt pocket. What was his name? Billy? Bo? Burt?

"Hi," she said, catching his attention as he started to walk by. "Do you know where I can find Lance Cooper?"

Blain, she suddenly remembered. Blain Sanders, the owner of Lance's race team.

"He's inside," he said, eyes narrowing. "If you want an autograph, you'll need to wait until after practice."

"Autograph?" she said, brows lowering. "Oh, no. I'm Sarah, his new driver and he asked me to—"

"Sarah," Blain Sanders interrupted, his expression undergoing a dramatic change. The guarded look was instantly replaced by warmth. "Lance told me all about you."

"It's not true," she said, smiling up at him. Dark-haired and green-eyed, he was a man that made you want to smile back. "Whatever he told you, it isn't true."

"You mean he didn't try and turn you into a hood ornament?"

"That he did do," Sarah said, feeling somehow better now that she'd found a friendly face. "Unfortunately, I ended up looking more like bug guts. I did a belly flop atop his window."

Blain Sanders winced. "That had to hurt."

"It did," she said, nodding.

"Well, Lance is inside. We've got to go out in about twenty minutes so you're just in time."

"Should I wait here?"

"No, no," Blain said. "Go on."

"Thanks," Sarah said, suddenly nervous again. Actually, she'd been nervous since the moment she'd passed through the chain-link fence. For some reason she'd thought this was a lot less—she frowned, trying to find words for what she'd thought—she'd thought it'd be a lot more casual than this. But this was no casual operation. This was a big deal. Most of the crew members ran around with expressions on their face akin to Irritable Bowel Syndrome sufferers, something that told her there was a lot at stake. And if that hadn't tipped her off, the fact that TV crews darted around attempting to catch all of the drama on film would have. She was almost glad to get inside.

"I'm looking for Lance," she said to a crew member who stood just inside the door, fluorescent light glinting off the lenses in his glasses.

"That way," he said, pointing toward the front of the big truck, the finger he used to guide her covered in grease.

Sarah thanked him, realizing the big rig wasn't so much of a mobile office as it was a garage, one that smelled of burnt grease and chemical cleaners. Dark gray cabinets stretched down either side of an aisle with a rubber mat covering the floor.

"Pretty cool, huh?" said a familiar voice.

It happened again. Her body shot what felt like a hundred volts of energy to various parts of her body.

"It's bizarre." She said the first thing that came to mind, although what she was actually referring to was her reaction to him, not the big rig.

"What's bizarre?"

Think, Sarah, think.

"Umm, that race cars appear to travel in as much luxury as their drivers."

He smiled, his tan skin making his perfectly symmetrical white teeth stand out. Obviously, he'd had braces as a child.

"I guess they do," he said. And then his eyes warmed as he crossed his arms in front of him, his firesuit turning his skin a nutmeg brown that turned his eyes even more blue. "Thanks for coming."

"You're welcome," she said.

"Do you want me to show you around? I don't have to climb inside for another fifteen minutes."

"Ah, sure," she said, thinking the last thing she should do is spend more time in his company. But she was like those bugs that dove into a pool of water only to end up drowning themselves—she couldn't seem to keep away from him. And what was it with the bug analogies lately, anyway?

"Come on," he said.

It was a short tour, as necessitated by Lance's impending duties, but during that time she was introduced to his crew in the garage, then brought back to his big rig where she learned that microwaves and refrigerators were standard options on a "hauler" and that computers had become a necessary part of stock car racing. Of course, it ended with a glance at his watch, Lance's face growing tense as he said, "It's time."

And she felt her own heart thud in response.

"C'mon. Let's get you a headset," he said, brushing by her as he headed to the front of the transporter. Inside one of the cabinets about a half-dozen headphones hung on a metal rod, the things looking like plastic earmuffs.

"Put this on," he instructed.

"Why?"

"Because you'll be able to hear me."

"You want me to listen to you?"

"Of course," he said, the smile he gave her a pretty pathetic one given what she knew he was capable of. "Maybe you can tell me some jokes while I'm out there."

She shook her head. "I have a feeling the knock-knock jokes I'm familiar with won't be as amusing to you as they were my kindergartners."

"Try me," he said, then handed her a headset. "Put this on. The black strap goes across the back of your head. Leave the mike retracted unless you want to talk. You have to press the button on the side in order to speak."

"Okay," she said, sliding the thing over her curls, which became an immediate problem. Obviously the people at Racing Radios didn't realize that women wore their equipment, too, women who had long hair and curls that liked to tangle. Lance started to help her, and when he lifted his hands, she saw that his fingers trembled.

She wasn't sure why she did what she did next, but one moment she was standing there, waiting for him to help her and the next she was clasping his fingers, the radio forgotten.

"Wait," she said.

"What?" he asked, his fingers cold and clammy.

"You're nervous."

"No, I'm not," he said.

"Yes, you are," she contradicted, almost laughing at the way he'd said, "No, I'm not." He'd sounded exactly like one of her students when she'd caught him trying to pull the feathers off one of the class's baby chicks.

"Are you talking about the way my hands shake?" he asked. "That happens every time I'm about to climb into a car. Adrenaline."

"Yeah, right," she said, placing a hand on her waist. "You're nervous, Lance Cooper."

"I'm not nervous—"

"You're about to strap yourself into a car that goes 190 miles per hour. It's only natural that you'd be a little nervous."

"Professional drivers do *not* get nervous. They get edgy."

"Edgy," she said with a slight grin. "Is that what you call it?"

He crossed his arms in front of him and didn't say anything.

"Well, what you call edgy, I call nervous. And before you start up again, I'll tell you right now that the look on your face is the exact same look as my third graders used to get before a test. They might have been eight years old. They might not have understood what real stress is, but their dilated pupils looked the same as yours."

"And your point is?"

"I'm going to tell you the same thing I used to tell my students."

"What? That it's just a test? That it's no big deal in the scheme of things?"

"No," she said with a shake of her head. "I'm going to tell you a story."

She saw his brows lift, saw the brief glimpse of surprise on his face before his eyes narrowed. "What kind of story?"

"Once upon a time there lived a man who predicted that airplanes would never fly, radios would never broadcast, and who proclaimed that the good people of Earth had discovered everything there was to know about physics. Obviously, this was a pretty stupid man." She waited for him to ask because she knew he would.

"All right. Who was it?"

"Thomas Kelvin, the man who revolutionized thermodynamics. The same man who outlined major principles about heat and its conductivity and whose Kelvin scale scientists use to this day."

He smiled a bit, though it was really more of a smirk, one that seemed to say, "And your point is?"

"Even some of the world's most brilliant people blow it sometimes, Lance. Nobody's perfect. Nobody's going to always get it right. The most you can hope for in life is to get it right *some* of the time."

CHAPTER TWELVE

THE MOST YOU CAN HOPE FOR is to get it right some of the time.

The words repeated in Lance's head, his crew chief's voice nothing but a warble of noise as he drove his car off pit road, pressing the accelerator to begin his warm-up lap.

And she was right, he thought, as the grandstands began to flow by faster and faster. Nobody could ever be perfect all of the time. Hell, history was dotted with the tales of brilliant men who'd said and done some really stupid things. Fermi had won a Nobel Prize for the discovery of new radioactive elements that had turned out to be not so new after all. Einstein had told the world that the universe was stationary, even though his own equations had pointed to the fact that it was expanding.

Lance threw his car into turn two, the back end sliding out from under him. Loose. The rear tires wouldn't grip the track. His hands gripped the steering wheel, his foot lifting a fraction as he fought for control. But no sooner had he lifted his foot than he was pressing it down again, allowing the car to drift higher in the hopes that he'd find better traction in the higher groove.

Like magic, the car straightened out.

And Lance felt elation fill him. That's it. That's the way to drive.

The most you can do is to get it right some of the time.

Other cars came up alongside of him. Lance recognized the blue paint scheme of the number seventeen car, Todd ducking down to take the inside line right as they moved toward turn three. Once again he felt the back end begin to break loose. He eased off the gas, feathering the brake to tighten things up a bit and trusting the high banking turn to transfer weight to the inside rear tire. The car bobbled. His hands tightened. But he held on to it and Todd's car faded back. He'd beaten through the turn.

The front stretch came into view, the white line nothing more than a brief blur of white as he zoomed toward turn two.

"Inside low," came his spotter's voice.

"There you are," Lance said as he drove it into turn two again. "I wondered where you'd gotten to."

Brad Jeffries, his spotter on every day but race day when he was busy changing tires, said, "Shoot, Lance. We didn't expect you to get all racey on the first lap."

"She feels good," he said, sailing through turns

two and three with nary a bobble. He'd started to get a feel for her now.

"What's she feel like, driver?" Allen, his crew chief asked.

"A bit loose going into the turns, but if I keep her high and feather the brake a bit I can keep her straight."

"You want a track bar adjustment?"

Lance thought about it, heading for turn four and shocked to see that Todd was now behind him, and a good three car lengths behind him at that. *Hot damn.* The seventeen had been one of the fastest cars during the last practice. Of course, they might have made some adjustments that set them back, but Lance wasn't so sure. Back in the old days he'd actually won the 500, and the car he drove now felt fast. Really fast.

"One-eight-eight-point-six-seven-oh," Allen said, and Lance could hear the exaltation in his voice. "Damn, Lance. That's a full tenth faster than the pole winner last year."

"She feels like a hot banana," Lance said.

"She *is* a hot banana," his crew chief echoed.

"I'd like to see how she does in traffic," he said, slowing down a bit so Todd could catch him.

"Inside," came his spotter's voice.

And this time when they came nose to nose, Lance let him pass, hearing the change in air pressure as Todd's car pulled up alongside of him.

"Clear low," his spotter said.

Lance ducked his car behind the seventeen, and immediately he felt the difference. The looseness got better. Much better. Rear spoiler, he thought. They should adjust that. Might fix the looseness when they ran in clean air.

Excitement made him smile. "Hot damn," he said, shooting past Todd a few seconds later.

"I take it that first lap wasn't a fluke," Allen said.

"Nope," Lance confirmed, and then, before he could stop himself he said, "Sarah, you listening in?" He was immediately stricken with the need to share this with her somehow. No, that wasn't it; he wanted her to know that she'd helped. He wasn't exactly sure how or why what she'd said had sunk in. Half a dozen people had told him much the same thing as she had.

The image of eager young faces rose in his mind's eye.

He smiled. That was it. It wasn't so much what she'd said to him as it was the realization that once upon a time he'd been an anxious schoolkid— anxious because all he'd wanted to do was race cars. And look, here he was, doing that. He'd forgotten that for a moment. Lance took a deep breath, remembering to just enjoy the moment and to quit stressing the small stuff—just as Sarah had advised.

"Umm, yes," came a feminine voice. "Testing one, two, three."

He laughed into the mike. "Sarah, I can hear you."

"Um, you can?" she asked. "Ah, good. I had a little problem figuring out how to make the thing work."

His smile crept higher, the lining inside his helmet forcing his cheeks to crease uncomfortably. Lance didn't care. "Well I'm glad someone helped you figure it out 'cause I just wanted to say thanks."

There was a momentary silence, then the sound of the mike opening up and the metallic sound of cars roaring by from her end. "For what?" she asked.

"For everything."

"Oh," she said. "Oh," she said again. "I guess the talk worked."

"Talk?" Lance repeated. "It wasn't the talk. It was the cookies."

"Ooo," she huffed in exasperation. "It wasn't the cookies, and you know it."

"Well, whatever it was, it worked."

Another silence, then her small voice saying, "Good. I'm glad."

Lance opened the mike again. "And, ah, Allen. You better say hello to our newest secret weapon."

"Oh, yeah?" Allen repeated.

"Eyup," Lance said. "Sarah is now our official cookie baker."

"I'M WHAT?" Sarah said from her end, compressing the button on the side of the earphones. She had to have misheard him, although the headset was so tight against her head she was almost certain when she removed the things her ears would pop from the change in atmospheric pressure. "Did he say an official cookie baker?" she asked.

"He did," Allen said with a wry smile, ducking down next to her and screaming the words at her left ear—not that it was easy to hear him with the half domes covering her ears. They stood atop the hauler, Sarah having taken her life into her own hands by crawling up a narrow aluminum ladder, then half scooting, half crawling along the metal lift that led to a second ladder, this one shorter and leading to a sort of balcony that sat in top of the back end of the big rig.

"He's kidding, right?" Sarah yelled back.

"Knowing Lance, probably not," Allen called back, lifting his headphone away from his right ear a bit so he could hear what she said next.

"What do you mean?" Sarah asked.

Allen shrugged. "Lance can be superstitious at times. If he thinks something works, he's apt to do it again and again until it stops working."

"And he really thinks baking him cookies helped?" Sarah asked, having lifted her own earphone off with an ear-sucking pop.

"Who knows?" Allen said, shrugging. "All I know is something you did or said helped him out and so now he's not about to let you go."

Not let her go. Was he kidding?

"I'm bringing her in," she heard Lance say in her right ear, Sarah releasing the headphone so that it sucked itself back onto her head. It was such an odd feeling to hear Lance's southern drawl in her ears, as if he stood right next to her, when really he was out there, his white-and-orange car a blurred streak on the track.

"What do you want to change?" she heard Allen ask.

"Tire pressure," Lance answered. "And whatever you can give me on the rear spoiler."

She saw Allen nod, make some notations on the metal clipboard he'd rested on the balcony railing. "Roger," he said. "Will do."

"Clear low," came another voice—the spotter, she'd been told.

Allen shot down the ladder that led from the balcony to the lower deck with such speed and agility Sarah was left in awe. She heard the roar of an engine and a moment or two later saw Lance's car round the corner. It hurtled toward them, a few people darting out of the way as he pulled into the garage. Like a swarm of ants on an orange rind, his crew went to work, someone running forward and sticking what looked to be probes into the tire. Sarah turned away, having no clue what was going on and wondering if she should stay atop the transporter or not. She felt like a monkey on a poodle thanks to the way people stared up at her from down in the garage—fans, she surmised, because they looked as shell-shocked by the action as she felt.

In the end she decided to get down. The stupid

headphones made the skin around her ears itch and Lance wouldn't be out on the track again for a few minutes. But the main reason she decided to get down was because she really couldn't see a whole lot from up top, and so she slid her headphones off her ears (scratching around her ears like a dog), and headed toward the ladder. Getting down, however, was much scarier than getting up, she soon realized. It involved a death grip on some sort of chain and blind faith that the ladder's steps were where they were supposed to be. Thank God she was wearing tennies and not heels. By the time her feet hit solid ground, she almost kissed it in gratitude, the aluminum ladder having shaken and vibrated the whole way down.

"Steady there," said a feminine voice when she stepped away from the thing and almost collided with a body.

"Sorry," Sarah said, turning and meeting the eyes of a green-eyed woman who just about made her jaw drop, she was so darn pretty.

"It's hard to see behind you when you're concentrating on the ladder," she quipped with a smile.

"Yeah, it is," Sarah said, about to turn away.

"How'd Lance do?" the woman asked in a southern drawl that sounded entirely too smooth to be anything but upper-class. The clothes were a dead giveaway, too. Her jeans alone must have cost a couple hundred dollars with their custom beading and tailored fit.

"Good," Sarah said, not sure how much she should say. Who was this woman? She looked familiar, her red hair such a startling color that Sarah was certain she'd remember it. Was she a model? An actress?

"He was better than good if his lap times were to be believed."

"I'm sorry," Sarah said, "but I'm not sure I should be discussing this with you. I'm new to the sport and I'm still trying to figure out who everyone is."

"I know who *you* are. You're Lance's new driver."

Sarah felt her mouth flop open, but only for a second. "How do you know that?"

"Because I saw you pull the thing in the other day. Nice bit of driving. Obviously, you're used to handling buses."

"Thanks," Sarah said, now truly perplexed by the woman's identity, although she suspected she was the wife of a famous driver. That would explain why she looked so familiar. Sarah had probably seen a picture of her when she'd been snooping around.

"I'm Rebecca Newman, by the way."

Newman, Newman, Newman. Why did that name sound so fam—

And then it hit her. She knew exactly who the woman was, and why she looked so familiar. She'd been the wife of a famous race-car driver, and when he'd died, it had made national news. She'd read about it the other day when she'd researched Lance. Because of the husband's death, Lance had been brought in to drive his car.

"Hi. I'm Sarah Tingle," Sarah said, holding out her hand.

The woman took it, her hand warm and soft in a way that only fingers tended regularly by a manicurist could be.

"Nice to meet you," the woman said. "And I have to be honest, I've never seen one of Lance's bus drivers in the garage before."

"No?" she asked. "I mean, that's interesting. I don't think I'd be here, either, except I baked Lance cookies earlier and he was so grateful he insisted I come watch him practice."

"You baked him cookies?" the woman asked, red brows lifted.

Sarah's skin warmed like the hood of a race car. "I did."

"That was nice of you."

"He looked nervous on TV," Sarah admitted. "I felt sorry for him."

"So you baked him cookies."

"I didn't give him a lap dance, too, if that's what you're thinking."

The woman laughed, her pretty face tipping back, a look of surprised delight entering her eyes. "I wasn't thinking that at all."

Sarah liked her. There was no logical reason why

she felt instantly comfortable with Rebecca Newman (as evidenced by her lap dance comment), she just did. Maybe it was the kindness she saw in the green eyes. Maybe it was because she figured anyone who'd been through as much as this woman had, had to be nice. Maybe it was just that she saw friendliness in her face and Sarah felt the sudden need for a friend. Whatever it was, Sarah felt comfortable enough to say, "What *were* you thinking, then?"

"I was thinking if you baked him cookies and he drove as well as he did, you're in deep doo-doo now."

"Why?"

Rebecca crossed her arms in front of her, the smile on her face one that was as amused as it was pitying. Why did she pity her?

"Because one thing about race-car drivers— they're all superstitious. If you baked him cookies and he drove well, he's going to want those cookies every day now. Well, every day he has to drive."

It was no more than Allen had implied, but hearing Rebecca say it concerned her. "Why the heck is that?"

Another car came roaring into the garage, Rebecca and Sarah watching it pass.

"Because all professional athletes are superstitious, some more than others," Rebecca admitted after the engine shut off. "And Lance is at the top of the superstitious meter. The whole garage knows about his purple underwear."

"Purple *underwear?*"

"Only on race day," Rebecca said, her words all but a giggle. "And only at Daytona," she added. "Seems he was wearing them when he won here a few years back and so he wears them every time now, although they don't seem to be working as well. Todd Peters says that's because he ripped them last year when he wrecked and so now they don't work anymore."

Sarah felt speechless for a moment, but then she felt laughter well up inside of her. "Well, if he asks me to make cookies for him every week, I'll be sure to do it before I come to the track."

"Oh, yeah?" Rebecca asked. "Why's that?"

Sarah looked into her eyes and she knew Rebecca knew the truth. She even saw the woman's eyes flicker. "Like that, is it?"

How had she guessed. "Like what?" Sarah asked, pretending innocence.

"Don't give me that, Sarah Tingle. I might have just met you, but I'm not blind. Besides, Lance is one of the nicest drivers in the series. To be honest, I'm surprised someone hasn't snatched him up yet. Then again, racing's pretty much consumed his life. But, still."

"I haven't snatched him up."

"No, but he *wants* you to snatch him up."

"No, he doesn't."

Rebecca rolled her eyes. "Of course he does. He wouldn't invite you into the garage, give you a radio, and send you up on his hauler if he didn't want to impress you. Drivers may be men, but in some ways they're still little boys. They always, *always* like to impress the girls with the toys on their playground."

"No," Sarah said. "Seriously. He's just being nice to me."

But her words were drowned out when Lance started his car with a crack and a vroom that made Sarah jump.

"You going back up top and watch him again?" Rebecca nearly yelled, a knowing look in her eyes.

"No," Sarah said, watching as Lance backed out a few seconds later, and when he did, Sarah watched to see if he waved goodbye to her.

She *wanted* him to wave goodbye to her.

What. An idiot.

So when the garage had gone quiet again—or as quiet as a NASCAR garage could turn, what with whirring mechanisms and rumbling generators— she said, "I was actually going to leave."

Had she just heard Lance say her name on the headset which still rested on her shoulder?

She lifted one of the blue earpieces, but it was just Allen talking about a spoiler adjustment.

Rebecca cocked a brow at her, the look in her eyes asking, "Why are you so anxious to hear what they're saying if you're not interested in Lance?"

And that was the whole problem because she

thought she'd done a pretty good job of disguising her attraction. Allen's words—*he's not about to let you go*—had filled her with an instant panic that had made her want to flee, because if Lance insisted she accompany him to the track on practice and race days, she wasn't certain she'd be able to stop herself from doing something stupid.

"To be honest, I'm kind of bored by all this," Sarah lied. "And I thought I heard my name on the radio. That's all."

"Well, if you were going to leave, why don't you join me for some tea?"

"Tea?" Sarah repeated, surprised. "I thought only Brits drank tea."

"The British and people who don't like the taste of coffee and need a little caffeine. C'mon. We can get to know each other over a steaming cuppa," she said, mimicking an English accent.

"Oh, no. I couldn't do that…"

"Nonsense." Rebecca checked her watch. "Practice will be over soon. The car I own is total crap—"

At which Sarah's eyes widened because a) Rebecca Newman didn't look like the type to say the word *crap,* and b) she had no idea she'd owned the car.

"And to be honest," Rebecca finished, "I'm in need of female companionship. If you hadn't noticed, there's a lot of men around this sport."

There were, but Sarah had noticed quite a few women, too, although none appeared to be working with Rebecca.

"Come on," Rebecca said. "Cece's not here—Blain's wife," she added at Sarah's obvious confusion, "And so you're it."

CHAPTER THIRTEEN

AND THE FUNNY THING WAS, Sarah was flattered that Rebecca Newman had decided to adopt her. She left with the woman, telling one of Lance's crew members that if Lance asked for her, to tell him she'd gone back to the motor coach.

When they got to Rebecca's own million-dollar motor coach, one that was every bit as luxurious as Lance's—only in a feminine way—she didn't protest when Rebecca turned on the TV. The engine sounds coming from the speakers didn't match the sound of the cars out on the racetrack, thanks to a five-second time delay, but it was still kind of neat to know that what was being televised was happening outside. And Lance did even better this time around, even the announcer sounding excited. In the end Lance had a lap that was a full second faster than the previous year's qualifier.

"Looks like your cookies really worked," Rebecca said, the smell of cinnamon tea filling the air. She had a whole bunch of different kinds of tea, Sarah noticed, making idle chitchat as she boiled water in a shiny black microwave, then pulled down cups from an off-white cabinet with crystal door handles.

"It wasn't the cookies."

"That's what you think, but the truth is something happened today that must have worked. I haven't seen him hold on to a car that loose in almost two years."

"Don't tell me that," Sarah mumbled, putting her head in her hands.

"You like him, don't you?" Rebecca asked, setting a delicate floral cup and saucer down in front of her.

It was on the tip of Sarah's tongue to deny it again, but after being so sweet, not to mention making her tea, Sarah realized she couldn't. She despised fibbing, and if the truth were known, she desperately needed another woman's advice. And since she didn't have a sister, or even a close friend, Rebecca Newman was it.

How sad was that?

"I'm such an idiot," she admitted, pouring sugar into her tea and then moaning as sugary-sweet cinnamon flavor burst onto her tongue. "Oh my gosh, that's to die for."

"It is, isn't it? I buy it from a tea shop in Charlotte. You should try the lemon." She placed her spoon down on the edge of the saucer with a delicate clink, and Sarah thought Rebecca Newman had to be the most elegant woman she'd ever met. She had good taste, too, because her motor coach was stunning. The interior was decorated in pale greens, the color exactly matching Rebecca's eyes. If someone had told her she'd be sitting down in a million-dollar coach, confessing her deepest, darkest secrets to a woman she'd only just met, she'd have called them crazy. But there you had it. That's exactly what she found herself doing.

"He's the nicest guy I've ever met."

"He is," Rebecca agreed, taking a sip of her own tea, French manicured fingers holding the cup gently.

"But he drives race cars for a living and, come on, I'm hardly the type to hold his interest for long."

"You think not?" the woman asked.

"I *know* not."

Rebecca set her cup down. "Let me show you something," she said, getting up from the table to go to a drawer in the kitchen. "Where is it?" Sarah heard her mumble. "I just saw it the other—ah. Here it is." She turned back to Sarah. "Look at this." She placed a photo on the table between them.

Sarah looked. A woman with tied back hair and a funny half smile on her face stared back at her with all the wide-eyed innocence of a virgin about to be pushed into the maw of a volcano—well, maybe not *right* before she was about to be pushed. "Is that your sister?" she asked, suddenly seeing the resemblance.

"No," Rebecca said. "That's me."

Sarah sat up straighter, cocking her head to get a

better look. "Wow. You've..." Changed, she almost said, except she didn't want to sound insulting. "You look different," she finished at last.

"I look like a housewife," Rebecca said. "Not that there's anything wrong with that, I just wanted you to see that I didn't always dress like this and get my hair done and my nails painted on a regular basis."

"You didn't?"

"Nope. But then my husband became very, *very* famous, and believe me, it only takes a few times hearing yourself described as a dowdy housewife before you decide to change."

"Someone called you a dowdy housewife?"

"That and more. And the higher my husband's star climbed, the worse it was for me."

Their gazes caught, Sarah saying, "Well, as much as I wish it were otherwise, I don't think a haircut and some new clothes are going to help me with *my* looks."

"You sell yourself too short."

"And I wouldn't change," Sarah added. "Not for any man."

"No?"

And Sarah suddenly remembered the way she'd felt when she'd overheard those two women talking about her.

"Well, maybe."

Rebecca smiled, the light that ebbed in from a window to their right turning her red hair a burnished blond. "That's what I thought. But I didn't show you that picture because I thought you should change."

That was good, because Sarah was just beginning to wonder if she should be insulted at the direction this conversation was taking.

"I showed you that photo because I wanted you to see what the woman who married Randy Newman looked like. When we met, he was already a rising star. He'd won the Busch championship and everyone predicted he'd win a Cup championship, too. But he didn't choose to date some leggy blonde, or glamorous starlet, he chose to date me. I think, at heart, a lot of drivers feel that way. What they want is a woman who will love them for them, not what they do for a living. You told me you didn't know anything about racing and so I bet Lance is liking you a whole lot more than the fans that constantly throw themselves at him. Toss in the fact that you're cute and you're a dead duck."

Oh, great. "But he hasn't done anything to make me think that he wants to, you know…that he wants to *date* me."

Rebecca just looked at her. Sarah had to shift her gaze.

"Nothing?" Rebecca asked after a lengthy pause.

"Nothing," Sarah lied.

It was apparent Rebecca didn't believe her. And when she leaned back and said, "The man I saw talking to you in the garage was not a man who thinks of you like a sister."

"You saw us talking?"

"Mmm-hmm. And let me tell you something else. I have never, ever heard of Lance inviting a woman to watch a practice. Never."

"Oh," Sarah said, the word spilling out of her mouth before she could think better of it. "This is not making me feel better."

"Why not? You should feel flattered," Rebecca said, leaning forward again and taking a sip of tea. Sarah did the same. It really was good tea, and it felt good on her suddenly queasy stomach.

"Look," Sarah said. "It's not that I don't think Lance would be a great boyfriend because, obviously, I do. It's just that I'm not sure I could deal with the whole racing thing. I'd worry that when push came to shove Lance wouldn't be able to commit to someone like me."

"Why not?"

"Because I just don't have *it*."

Rebecca smiled. "No, but you seem nice, and that's twenty times more important. And as you can see, Randy didn't marry me for *my* looks." She smiled, but the grin turned melancholy. And then sadness entered her eyes, so much of it that Sarah felt her heart clench in sympathy.

"I'm so sorry, Rebecca."

Rebecca smiled, saying in a low voice, "Call me Becca. And don't be sorry. Randy's death was tough, but I'm over the worst of it now. It still hurts from time to time, but not as bad."

And Rebecca wanted *her* to date a driver.

Some of what she felt must have shown in her eyes because Rebecca gave her a half smile. "With all the new safety devices the drivers have on board their chances of getting hurt are actually pretty slim. I suspect it'll only get better in the coming years."

But Sarah was frowning and shaking her head. "The danger of his sport doesn't worry me." And it was true because the more she talked to Becca, the more Sarah realized the whole professional driver thing had her scared. The publicity. The fans. The traveling. "I just don't think I'm cut out—"

A knock startled them both. Sarah looked at Becca with wide eyes.

"That'd be Lance," Becca said.

"What would *he* be doing here?"

"Word gets around and I'm sure someone told him you and I trotted off together." Becca got up and walked to the door as she spoke, Sarah cringing when she opened the door and said, "Hey, Lance. What brings you here?"

Becca turned back to her, giving her a smug grin, Sarah trying to tell the woman without words that she didn't want Lance to know if she was here. She mimicked cutting her throat, which, in Sarah's opinion, was the universal sign of don't-you-dare-tell-him-I'm-sitting-here.

But when Lance said, "I'm looking for Sarah,"

Becca didn't act surprised, and she didn't pretend not to know who "Sarah" was.

What she said was, "Sarah? Sure. She's here," stepping back from the door to let Lance in.

So much for their burgeoning friendship.

Some of Sarah's pique faded when she saw the look on Lance's face. He all but charged up the steps, an expression on his face of unmistakable concern. She swallowed hard.

"Thank God," he said. "I thought something had happened. Jeesh. You shouldn't have left like that. I blew my last few laps, I was so worried about you."

"I—you what?"

"I was worried about you."

"Well, I think I'll give you two some time to chat. I have to go back to the garage anyway where I can listen to my charming driver complain about the inferior equipment we give him and how his crew chief is a complete waste of a salary."

"Becca," Sarah said, half sitting up.

But she was gone.

"I didn't know you knew Becca Newman," Lance said, still standing over her.

"I don't," she said. "She just sort of…adopted me."

"She's like that," he said, his eyes darting to the chair Becca had vacated before pulling it out and sitting across from her. It felt better to have a table between them, kind of like a lion tamer probably felt when he had a chair in his hand.

"She's nice," Sarah said.

"Yeah, but she's been struggling with that team of hers."

This was good. Nice, impersonal conversation. This she could handle. "I didn't know she even owned a race team. Of course, I didn't even know who *you* were before I came to work for you."

"Randy, her husband, owned a truck team when he died. She sort of expanded the operation, more to keep her busy, I think. This is her first year Cup racing and I think she regrets it. The driver they promoted isn't up to snuff, which means she'll probably have to find someone else to drive. That's never an easy thing to do."

"What isn't?"

"She's going to have to demote her driver. Send him back to racing go-karts. He probably knows it's coming, which is why he's complaining about everything, but the garage knows the truth. Mike doesn't have the goods."

"Is that his name, Mike?"

Lance nodded, fiddling with the spoon that he'd picked up from Becca's abandoned cup of tea.

"You left."

She looked up sharply, surprised by the abrupt change of conversation.

"I couldn't see anything up top there."

"You could have moved to the lounge."

"I couldn't have done that. That's your office, or your crew's office. I don't belong there."

"Yes, you do."

She felt herself color again. Felt the need to look away. Felt suddenly, ridiculously shy in his presence. Jeesh, she hated the way he could do that.

"Lance, look. You've been really nice to me—"

"Will you have dinner with me tonight?"

Sarah felt her eyes widen in shock. She didn't know what to say at first because, sure, he'd been acting all concerned and what not, but this was the first time that he'd actually asked her out on a date.

"Lance, I don't think that's a good idea."

"Why not?"

And so it came to this. "I'm not ready," she said.

"Nobody's ever ready for a relationship," he said, the same light that had turned Becca's hair blond making his own hair snowy white. Gray eyes stared, so clear and serious Sarah felt the urge to look away as he peered across at her.

"Is that what we would have?" she asked. "A relationship? Or would I be a quick fling, Lance?"

"I don't know," he said, setting the spoon down and enfolding her small hands in his big one. He was warm, the air-conditioning in Becca's motor coach perhaps a little too cool. Or maybe it was just that whenever he touched her it felt like his fingers charged her own with a heat she couldn't explain.

"I don't know," he said again. "I just know there's something about you that I like and I think maybe you feel the same way. But I don't know where it'll lead. We might discover one of us loves broccoli and the other hates it and that'll be that."

He smiled and Sarah felt the dread all over again. "I can't," she said with a shake of her head. "I just can't, Lance. I have the worst luck with men and I worry you'd be mistake number two-hundred-and-twenty-two."

"You've dated two-hundred-and-twenty-one men?"

"No," she said miserably. "That's just what it feels like."

"So tell me about them."

"Nah. You don't need to hear all my horror stories."

"Why not? I'd like to know what I'm up against."

"But if you hear about all the losers in my life, you'll only use it as ammo against me for reasons I should date you."

"Try me."

"No. It'll make me feel dumb."

"You're not dumb. You're a kindergarten teacher, which is as noble a profession as being a doctor, in my opinion. You couldn't look dumb to me if you tried."

"You might be surprised."

"Tell me," he ordered.

She debated with herself, but for all the arguments there were against telling him about her former boyfriends, there were just as many arguments for it.

Frankly if she told him the truth, maybe he'd realize how serious she was about not getting involved again.

"Well, let's see," she said, looking away from him because she couldn't, just couldn't, look him in the eyes. "There was my very first boyfriend, a guy who threatened to kill himself when I told him I was breaking up with him. I didn't believe him, but when I was riding my bike home later that week, he pulled his own bike up alongside of me and threatened to dash out into oncoming traffic if I didn't go out with him."

"What'd you do?"

"Told him to aim for a semi. He'd die faster."

Lance chuckled, though that wasn't the reaction she'd been aiming for.

"The next memorable loser was the campus hunk, a man that spent more time checking his reflection in his rearview mirror than he did looking out the front windshield. Boy, was I ever pleased with myself for snagging his attention. We would study together, but then he passed calculus, at which point he dumped me."

Lance grimaced.

"Then there was Peter, I dated him my last year of college. He was funny and sweet. And then one day I used his computer and discovered his Temporary Internet File was filled with porn sites—and I'm not talking adult porn sites, either. He was the one who released the photos of me, and the idiot still sends me e-mails to this day, but I refuse to open them."

"You're better off without him."

"Then there was Ron, the toupee-wearing Judas." And the wound, apparently, was still fresh from that one because her stomach twisted. "The man that refused to believe that I didn't take my clothes off for those photos. He was on the school board, the same board that voted to have my contract terminated by unanimous decision."

"What a putz."

"Yeah," she agreed. "But, see, that's just it. He didn't seem like a putz when I first met him. I even thought that maybe, just maybe, he just might be…" *The One.* But she couldn't finish the sentence. It still hurt when she thought about it. Still stung when she recalled the condescension on his face. The way he'd acted so sanctimonious while she'd tried and tried and tried to tell him that she was *not* the woman in the magazine. Well, she was, but not really.

"It still hurts, huh?"

When Sarah met his gaze, she felt an unmistakable burning in her eyes.

"It does, doesn't it?" Lance asked again gently, concern and caring in his eyes.

And all Sarah could do was nod.

CHAPTER FOURTEEN

SHE WAS GOING to cry.

Lance could see it in the way she looked immediately away from him. She was going to cry and he was helpless to make her stop.

Maybe not *completely* helpless.

He got up from his chair. Her gaze shot to his again, her eyes widening when she saw him cross around toward her.

"Lance," she said, her tone low and almost a warning.

But he ignored her, just went to her and drew her up, telling her with his eyes that he was going to kiss her and if she truly thought this was going to be a bad idea, if she truly didn't want him to do it, he gave her time to protest.

But she didn't. What she did was close her eyes right before his lips connected with hers. To be honest, he didn't want to kiss her out of any sort of physical desire. He wanted to kiss her because he felt an overwhelming need to comfort her.

That lasted until the moment their lips met.

Zap.

That's what it felt like. Whether it was a static charge from their two bodies touching, or some kind of physical reaction, he didn't know, all he knew was that the moment his lips touched hers all good intentions went out the door because he couldn't believe how instantaneously hot he became for her. Nothing, *but nothing,* prepared him for kissing Sarah Tingle.

He felt her body tense, too, wondered for a moment if she might pull away. But she didn't. Instead her body seemed to collapse against his own, her hands going up and around his neck with seemingly no hesitation.

This was how kissing someone should be.

The thought popped into his head and he increased the pressure of his lips. This was how it should be between a man and a woman. There should be a connection, an instantaneous recognition that the person they kissed was perfect for them.

He drew back, staring down at her upturned face, feeling not so much wonder and awe, but confusion mixed in with a sudden surge of desire. What was happening between them?

Her eyes slowly opened, her pupils so dilated they looked almost black. He saw a look of confusion in those eyes, too, and a hint of fear. No, not fear, concern and, yes, he was almost positive, the same amount of sexual interest he himself felt.

"I'd hold on to you even if I saw a picture of you wearing three breasts."

Which made her eyes widen a bit, made a laugh pop out of her and her eyes soften. "I bet you'd like a three-breasted woman."

"I bet you I would, too," he said gently, lowering his head again. And this time when they kissed it wasn't gentle, it wasn't passive, it was a kiss that instantly proved the two of them were like high-octane fuel, their flesh sparking off each other in such a way that Lance felt the purely caveman urge to pick her up and carry her to bed. Except he wasn't in his own motor coach and so all he could do was kiss her, snuggling his hips up against her, showing her what she did to him and how much he wanted more. She didn't draw away. No. She pressed herself tighter against him.

Her mouth slipped open then, the vanilla taste of her causing him to groan again and one of his hands slid up her side at the same time he removed his lips from hers, the smooth skin at the side of her neck tasting as deliciously sweet as the rest of her.

His hand dropped to her waist only to slip beneath her shirt, his fingers sliding over her ribs.

"Lance," she said softly.

But he couldn't tell if she said his name in protest or desire. Desire, he decided when she didn't pull away. He found her lips and this time she opened for him instantly. Their tongues met, slid against each other's, entwined. The world seemed to slip away until all that was left were the two of them touching each other and stroking each other and—

"Stop," she said, pulling back and then stepping away.

"Sarah—"

"No, Lance. Don't. Don't try and confuse me."

"I'm not trying to confuse you," he said. "I'm trying to show you how I feel."

"But that's just it," she said, and he could hear her take a deep breath, see her fight for control. "It's just feelings. Physical feelings. They don't mean anything."

"How do you know that?"

"I don't, but I'm guessing I'm right. I mean, c'mon, Lance, we both know I'm hardly the type to hold your interest for long."

"You don't know that for sure."

"No, but I bet I'd never have to worry about you surfing the Internet for pictures of naked girls. I bet women send you pictures of their naked selves all the time."

He grimaced and then shrugged. "There's nothing I can do about that."

"Exactly. And there's nothing I can do about the fact that I don't want to get involved with you. I *like* you, Lance, but that doesn't mean I want to date you."

He could see how serious she was by the look in

her eyes. What he didn't expect was the disappointment he felt.

"I'm sorry," she said as she slipped out, Lance staying behind for half a second before following her.

"Sarah, wait!"

But by the time he stepped out of Becca's motor coach, she was rounding the front end. He chased after her for a few steps before realizing she didn't want to be caught.

"Damn it," he said.

"Problems?" someone asked.

Lance turned, thinking the voice had belonged to Becca. But it didn't. It was Courtney, his PR rep. She must have followed him from the garage because she had the look of someone who'd been waiting for him for a while, her ever-present clipboard in hand, brown eyes shielded by a pair of sunglasses, long blond hair pulled back in a ponytail.

"It's nothing," he said, waving his hand dismissively. But his eyes found Sarah again, watching as she made it to the end of the asphalt road, where buses were parked on either side. She paused there for a moment, a golf cart filled with crew members nearly running her over.

Where was she going?

But then she turned right, disappearing from sight.

"Is she your girlfriend?"

Lance started, having forgotten Courtney's presence. "Girlfriend?" Was she? Did he want her to be? "No," he said. "She's just a friend."

"Are you certain?" Courtney asked, looking at him from above the rim of her sunglasses, blond brows lifted. "You seem awfully distracted for someone who just got in an argument with a friend."

"We weren't arguing."

"No?"

"It's nothing, Courtney. Don't worry about it."

"Have you told her about the Bimbos Calendar Girl contest you're judging?"

"No. Why would I do that?"

"Just curious."

"Courtney. It's nothing. She's just a friend. Stop worrying."

But Courtney looked dubious, not surprising since she'd been a PR person for more years than Lance had been on the circuit. She'd seen it all, and right now she thought she was watching a driver get in over his head with a woman when his *head* should be focused on racing.

"What did you need?"

Courtney's eyes disappeared behind the sunglasses again. "I wanted to go over your media appearances on race day."

"Fine. Let's do it."

But as Courtney guided him through his schedule, Lance found himself looking around for Sarah, and wondering where she'd gotten to, and thinking that he probably should tell her about the

Bimbos contest because if she wasn't his girlfriend, what did it matter?

But therein lay the crux of the problem.

Because it would matter to her. She wouldn't approve. He was certain of it. And so he didn't want her finding out about—

"Lance?"

When he looked up, Courtney was staring at him over the rims of her glasses again.

"Sorry. Lost my train of thought."

She stared at him for a long moment, Lance growing more and more uncomfortable, especially when all she said was, "Uh-oh."

CHAPTER FIFTEEN

RACE DAY.

Sarah had planned to watch it on her hotel TV, but a call from Sal, Lance's business manager, had changed all that.

"He wants you at the track."

"What? Why?"

She'd slunk away and off to her hotel room after their last encounter, telling herself that she'd made the right decision in choosing not to get involved with him. The fact that Lance hadn't argued was proof of that. He hadn't called her, either.

And now he was having Sal issue her orders.

"He didn't give me a reason why," Sal said. "He just wants you here."

"But—"

"No buts, Sarah. There's a lot at stake and so if Lance wants you in the garage, you better go."

"Okay, fine."

But she was *not* happy about it. It meant leaving her hotel room and walking to the infield, something that didn't look easy what with the thousands of race fans making their way to the track. Obviously, race day would be better attended than she'd thought.

And so she'd walked, blending in with the stream of people out on the sidewalks. But where they wore colorful shirts splashed with various car numbers and sponsor's logos, she wore plain jeans and a white cotton top—and her precious credential stashed in a shiny plastic holder.

"At least this race is at night," she heard one woman say to her husband/boyfriend/guy pal.

"Yeah, but it's still hot."

And it was, Sarah admitted. It was late in the afternoon. The race wasn't due to start for an hour and a half, but the clouds of the previous days had melted away, literally melted away, giving way to high humidity and blazing hot asphalt.

And still, people poured into the track.

Her cell phone rang. "Are you on your way?" a voice asked.

Lance.

"No," she lied. "I'm still in my hotel room."

"What?"

She smirked into the phone, not that he could see. "Kidding, kidding. But it would serve you right if I decided not to come. I'm not a walking rabbit's foot, Lance, and I don't like to be ordered around."

"But I need you." And he sounded so desperate, so afraid that Sarah stopped walking.

Someone bumped into her. She mumbled an

"Excuse me" and said to Lance, "You're going to be fine."

"I feel better when you're here."

"That's just because you think I'm bringing you good luck."

"No. It's because I'm a better driver when you're around."

"You are a good driver, Lance. You've just forgotten that fact."

"See, that's what I'm talking about. You give me confidence."

"You could find that confidence all on your own."

He was silent for a moment, almost as if he were trying to absorb her words. But then he said, "Please, Sarah. Please come and watch."

She struggled with herself, struggled and finally gave up because no matter what might or might not lie between them, she couldn't turn her back on someone in need. "I'll be there as soon as I can."

He exhaled something that sounded like relief. "Thank you."

"You're welcome."

Another silence. "Careful on your way in. A few people in the garage have had run-ins with security here."

"I've got my credential."

"Just be careful."

SHE THOUGHT it would be simple: walk up to the infield entrance, show her pass and away she'd go.

And it probably would have been that easy—if she'd remembered her driver's license.

A man wearing a yellow shirt with SECURITY emblazoned across the chest in black letters glared at her when she explained that she left her photo ID back at the hotel. No amount of cajoling, I know Lance Cooper (yes, really I do), I work for a driver, I'm part of a crew did one bit of good. The security guard, an Incredible Hulk of a human—except he wasn't green, and his hair was blond—took great pleasure in telling her to get lost.

There were a few small trees to the right of the infield entrance, cars and RVs that were still streaming into the inner sanctum emitting noxious fumes. Sarah plopped down on a curb and dialed.

"I forgot my ID," she said before he could say a word.

"Uh-oh."

"I'll have to go back to the hotel and get it, which means I might miss the start of the race. It's packed out here."

"You can't be late."

"I'm sorry, Lance, but there's nothing I can do."

"Let me talk to security," he said sternly.

"You think they're going to believe you're really Lance Cooper?" she asked, putting her finger in her ear when a particularly loud vehicle rolled by.

"It's worth a try."

"Lance, please, you can call me before the start of the race if that'll make you feel better—"

"Put him on."

"This is a bad idea," she said *sotto voce*. "This guy's in a really bad mood. I can tell." And then a moment or two later she said, "Excuse me, Mr. Guard," to the man who was busy checking credentials of a young couple decked out from head to toe in racing apparel.

"What?" the guy asked, his expression full of impatience.

"Um, someone wants to talk to you."

"What? Who?" he cried impatiently, his craggy face and droopy eyes tightening with displeasure.

She held up her cell phone.

"Lady, I don't have time for this—"

"It's Lance Cooper."

To her surprise, that made him smile, and believe it or not, it didn't make him look one iota friendlier.

"Yeah, sure it is. And I'm channeling Dale Earnhardt right now."

"He doesn't believe me," Sarah whispered into the phone.

"Put him on," Lance said tersely.

"Here," Sarah said.

She had no idea what Lance said, but she could hear the security guard perfectly because what *he* said was, "I don't have time for this shit," just before he crushed the phone in his big hands with so much force, the battery on the back came off. He slipped the thing in his pocket before handing her the mangled carcass.

"Get out of here."

"But I need my battery—"

"Now," he all but roared.

People stared at her. Sarah felt like a mongrel about to be kicked out of the house. But she didn't teach kindergarten for nothing. "You really shouldn't use that tone of voice with me," she admonished. "We're all friends here and friends treat other friends with courtesy and respect."

"That does it." He grabbed her by the arm and led her to a curb, growling. "Sit here!"

"Why?" she asked, pulling her arm away. It stung where he'd clasped it.

"You can stay there until the police arrive."

"Police?" she said, torn between horror and outrage. "But I didn't do anything wrong."

The guy gave her a look that would wilt poison ivy.

She stared up at him for a moment in disbelief, thinking, *this can't be happening.* This really, truly couldn't be happening. She wasn't about to be carted off to jail for assaulting a security officer with her cell phone, was she?

It would appear so, and if Sarah thought people were staring before, it was nothing compared to the way they looked at her while forced to sit next to a bright blue Porta Potti, the security guard standing over her as if she were a suspected ax murderer and not a kindergarten teacher. There were literally hundreds of people passing by. She smiled at a few of them as if to say, "No problem. I'm okay."

Only she wasn't okay. It was humiliating. It made wearing someone else's private parts feel like a Hallmark card. She was going to go to jail. She knew this as soon as she heard the security guard speak into his radio and say, "I've got someone here who needs an attitude adjustment."

"Look. I really think you're making a mistake," she tried again.

Uh oh. The frown he shot her clearly said, "Lady, one more word out of you and I'll be tempted to find some duct tape."

She felt a burst of fear then, followed by an urge to cry, except she refused to let the guard have the satisfaction of seeing her break down. Besides, it wasn't as if she didn't know anyone in town. She'd call Lance just as soon as she was allowed to make a phone call.

Lance. This was going to upset him. And maybe throw off his race.

A tear pooled in the corner of her left eye. No. She would not. She. Would. Not. Cry.

She turned away, facing the Porta Potti like a truant child. The thing gave off an iridescent glow that turned her skin the color of a Smurf's, and its smell wafted toward her as the sun beat down on her. Terrific. Now she was blue. By tomorrow she'd be red.

Beep.

She heard the sound, but not really.

Beep. Beep. Beep.

It was one of those annoying sounds you ignore until it gets on your nerves to the point that you finally look around. She turned toward the infield tunnel.

"Lance!" she cried, darting up.

"Hey!" The security guard said, trying to force her back down.

Lance leaning on the horn of a careening golf cart, tore out of the checkerboard exit hole like a Sunday morning linebacker, the ball cap and sunglasses he wore doing nothing to conceal his face.

"What the hell?" he yelled. "Don't touch her like that!" he ordered as he tore around the security shack in the middle of the two lanes of traffic. Jumping out of the golf cart—stopping a minicamper in its path—he went right up to the guard, saying, "What the heck do you think you're doing?"

Sarah felt her eyes well with tears, though they weren't tears of humiliation or anger. They were tears of joy.

He'd come for her.

"He's taking me down to the station," she said, her voice sounding wobbly even to her own ears.

"What?" Lance asked, his eyes darting between hers and the security guard's. "Why?"

"For handing him my cell phone," Sarah offered as an explanation.

"Wait a second," the guard said, "It was more than just that."

"More than that?" Lance repeated as his eyes

narrowed. He did *not* look happy. "She's a kindergarten teacher. Somehow I doubt it was more than that."

"Hey," she heard one of the pedestrians passing by say, a quick turn of her head revealing that it was a man. A race fan man. "That's Lance Cooper," he said, Sarah feeling her eyes widen that he'd been recognized. Lance was in his pre-race garb—white polo shirt with the team logo on the pocket and jeans. Yet, still, the fans knew him.

That was evident when someone else said, "It *is* Lance Cooper."

There was a rush of people, which made the security guard give a shout of warning. Nobody listened. It was like feeding time at the ranch, scraps of paper pulled from who-knows-where and waved in Lance's face, people crying out, "Mr. Cooper, will you sign this?" and, "Mr. Cooper, can you sign that?"

Lance held up his hands, saying, "I'm not doing a damn thing until somebody apologizes to Sarah," which made the crowd go quiet, then turn as one to the security guard who, Sarah noticed with a certain measure of glee, looked like a man who'd been forced into underwear four sizes too small.

"Is that his girlfriend?" she heard someone say.

"Say you're sorry," Lance ordered. *"Now."*

To her surprise, the man did exactly that, looking like nothing more than a petulant schoolboy. "You could have told me you were his girlfriend," he said.

"I'm not his girlfriend," she muttered.

"You okay?" Lance asked, a gaggle of people having trailed in his wake.

"I'm fine," she said.

She thought he might touch her then, could plainly see the urge to do so in his eyes. But his hand fell back to his side.

"Now, who wants an autograph?" he asked, turning away from her.

HE WAS ALMOST LATE for a media appearance, but that was okay. Sarah was with him and so all was right in the world. His secret weapon was back by his side.

"I feel like I'm in the way," Sarah said after he'd finished doing a radio interview.

"You're not," he said, heading back to the hauler, Sarah trailing behind him, Lance stopping occasionally to sign an autograph.

"The crews look like they've contracted typhoid," he heard her say when they started off again.

"There's a lot at stake," he confessed, thinking he'd never been this chatty on race day. Usually he did the driver's meetings, spoke to whatever reporter wanted him (which lately, hadn't been all that many), then hid out until it was time for driver introductions. But not today. Today he felt the need to show her around.

"There was a man back there with a car on his head. An actual plastic car. I wanted to ask him what would happen if he sat on his hat? Would that qualify as a rear ender?"

Lance smiled, nodding to a man who used to work on his crew but who'd moved to another team, as people in this industry often did. Same bat time, same bat channel, so the saying goes.

"You might be surprised at some of the things fans wear."

"Or *don't* wear," Sarah said. "I couldn't believe all the people on top of their RVs in the infield. The last time I saw so many half-naked women was when I was ten."

He looked down at her questioningly.

"I had a lot of Barbie dolls."

Amazingly enough, he laughed.

"And what's with the viewing windows in the garage?" she asked.

They stopped near the back of his hauler, Lance moving close to the double doors so that fans would leave him alone. He'd changed into his firesuit for interviews and so he was easily recognizable to fans. Thus some of the more persistent NASCAR enthusiasts hovered, hoping to catch his eye. And this was nothing. Back when he was in the lead to win the championship, people were four feet thick. How things changed. From superhero to Lex Loser in two seasons flat.

"That's part of the Fan Zone," he said. "People really love seeing what goes on in the garage."

"Someone should put up a sign reminding them that tapping on the glass scares the fish."

"Yeah. Last year one of the teams taped up a sign that said the number ninety-six team had lug nuts they were giving away. Nobody on the ninety-six could figure out why so many fans were banging on the window."

It was her turn to smile, the afternoon sunlight turning her hair redder than usual.

Don't get distracted, Lance. Not now. Not with the race about to start.

"That wasn't very nice," she said.

"No, but it was funny as hell."

"I bet it was."

Lance glanced at his watch, instantly sobering. All at once her face drained of color, too, her freckles standing out beneath her dusky skin. "It's time to go, isn't it?"

"It is."

He saw her take a deep breath, saw her straighten her shoulders. "It's just a race," she said.

Only it sounded like she said the words to convince herself as well as him. "That it is."

"All you're going to do is drive round and round in circles."

"I know."

She nodded. "Well, then you'd better get to it."

He told himself to turn and leave right then.

Instead he found himself saying, "You could walk me out to my car."

Her black lashes flicked up in surprise. "No thanks. I'm tense enough as it is. I can't imagine what it's like out there." She motioned toward where the cars were lined up for the start of the race. "I couldn't do it."

"Then I guess you'll have to give me a kiss goodbye."

Damn. Why the hell had he said that? He needed to keep things impersonal between them. Avoid distraction.

But he couldn't deny that he ached to hold her, to let her soothe him, to tell him everything would be all right.

That was why, when she tipped up and kissed him on his cheek and said, "Good luck, Lance," he had to stop himself from pulling her to him. They held each other's gaze until a woman called out his name, interrupting them.

"Lance," the woman said again—Courtney, his PR person. "You better get a move on."

His gaze moved back to Sarah. "Guess I'm being paged."

"Guess so," she said.

"I'll see you after," he said.

"I'll see you after," she echoed.

And Lance had never, not ever, had such a hard time leaving someone's side in his life.

CHAPTER SIXTEEN

"FIVE MINUTES, Lance," Allen said, his voice low and tinny through the left earpiece.

Lance absorbed the words. Hearing, but not really hearing, his eyes staring straight ahead as he waited for someone—the governor or something—to call out the infamous, "Gentlemen, start your engines."

All you're doing is driving a car round and round.

The words popped into his head. Lance told himself she was right. That's all he was doing. Driving.

The sun had started to sink into the horizon, Lance making note of it because it meant the track would soon cool off. Would he be faster or slower? And how bad would the glare be coming out of turn three?

Was Sarah watching?

Don't think about her, Lance. Not now.

But he was thinking about her. What's more, the image of her face filled him with an odd sort of calm. Yesterday, just before qualifying, he'd felt it, too. It was such a welcome relief that he took a deep breath out of reflex, the sound of his own breathing echoing in his ears.

Relax, he told himself.

His mind tuned out everything but the sound of his own breathing until the moment when Allen said, "Start her up."

The words were like dynamite to his system. He flicked the ignition switch, holding his breath as he always did for that millisecond between fingering the switch and the actual firing of the engine.

Vroom-hoom.

The whole interior of the car vibrated with the force of the engine's power.

"Rolling," Terry, his race day spotter said a few seconds later.

Lance gripped the steering wheel, the tension he felt on race day the same and yet…different. No dread. No stomach flutters or butterflies. He usually had a whole herd of winged caterpillars banging around his stomach when he pulled off pit road.

Not today.

The most you can do is to get it right some of the time.

She was right. And if he didn't get it right today, it wouldn't be the end of the world. Blain and Cece weren't about to toss him out on his ears like some team owners might do. He'd have a job at least until the end of the year. Then maybe he'd go back to driving Busch cars.

He'd be racing.

He loved racing, something he'd forgotten for a while.

"We're getting the two to go call," Allen said. "Copy that, Lance? Two to go."

"Copy," Lance said, pressing the mike button on the steering wheel, weaving the car back and forth as he warmed the tires.

They picked up speed. People always thought drivers couldn't see the individual faces of fans, but that wasn't true. You could see them, especially at these slower speeds. You could see them and you could hear the excitement and the joy and the elation they felt. Many of those fans had saved money for months, maybe years. They'd used precious vacation hours and the dollars in their savings account to come watch them race.

Watch *him* race.

He owed it to them to give them a good show. *Damn it,* he would.

And so when a minute or two later his spotter called, "Green, green, green," Lance mashed the pedal from his position in the middle of the pack, not so much that the back end would break loose, but enough that the chassis torqued around him, the hood lifting and then dipping down as it hugged the track. Jimmie was in front of him, Lance knowing immediately that he had a better car.

"Clear low."

That was all Lance needed to hear. He ducked down, knowing that everyone else who was faster than Jimmie would follow. They did. A check of his mirror and he spotted the forty-one car, although in the past few months he'd been tailing the guy, not leading him.

"Clear high."

"Driver, how's it feel?" Allen asked.

"Still a bit loose."

"Track's cooling off. Maybe we could play with the wedge when we pit."

"No," Lance said. "Let's wait. I think we're fast enough to move up."

But it was tough. He thought clean air might tighten things up a bit, but moving out of the groove ended up being a mistake. He shot right back to twentieth.

"Damn," he said. "I shot back faster than a greased banana."

"No big deal, driver," Allen said. "It's still early."

A wreck on lap twenty-five didn't help matters. Lance had to stand on the brakes to avoid being scooped up by the ten car.

"Low, low, low," Terry said.

"Whew. Close."

"Yellow flag," Terry said, stating the obvious.

"Might have to change my underwear," Lance quipped.

"Okay, driver, what do you want to do?" Allen

asked. By now Allen had heard all his one-liners. Still, it'd be nice if every once in a while he'd laugh. That was everyone's problem. They were all too tense.

"Well, ideally I'd like to take off the restrictor plate, but since I can't do that, let's play with the tire pressure," Lance said. "But only a bit. I still think she's going to pick up some when the sun goes down."

"All right. Remember your RPMs. We're after the opening in the wall. Copy that? The opening midway down the wall."

"Roger that," Lance said, and when he came back around, followed cars onto pit road, a fiery red sky reflecting in their back windows.

"Okay, boys, nice and easy," Allen said. "Everyone remember their job and this'll be a piece of cake."

"Thirty-five-hundred RPMs," Terry said as his car approached the point of no return—a thick white line and the entrance to pit road.

Lance checked his tach. Should be good.

And even though he told himself not to tense up, even though he reminded himself it was just a race, he still felt his stomach tighten—not so much because he wanted to win, but because he worried about hitting one of his crew, or someone else's crew. Every time he ducked into a pit stall he looked around, but you could only turn your head so far.

"Three, two, one," Allen said.

There it was, the twenty-six sign dipping up and down like an excited little boy.

"I'd like a Big Mac, no cheese," Lance said as he stabbed the brake. "And fries," he added. "No, scratch that. Just give me a Meal Deal #3."

Allen didn't reply, probably because he was too busy making sure his crew performed up to par, his crew chief's "Go, go, go!" coming so fast Lance knew Allen would be proud of the boys.

"Good job, guys," Lance said. Their stop had moved him up four spots, back to fifteenth. "That was a helluva stop. Except you forgot my fries."

"Would you quit talking about food?" Terry said. "You're making me hungry."

Finally, someone had answered him. "Terry, you're always hungry."

"Hey, I'm not the one that can polish off a two pound porterhouse for a light lunch," Terry shot back.

"Yeah, but at least what I eat doesn't become a Goodyear around my middle."

Silence, then, "That was cold," but it wasn't Terry, it was Blain. "And totally not true," Blain said, but there was a hint of laughter in his voice. "Terry, he's just jealous." Truth was, Terry was rail-thin and everyone knew it.

"My waist size isn't the only thing he's jealous of," Terry said.

"Ooo," Lance said. "Now *that* was low," and he hoped his crew could hear the smile in his voice. "And also totally untrue."

Terry chuckled and Lance relaxed, realizing that he hadn't felt in this good a mood for months. Maybe even years. Damn.

When he mashed the accclerator after the "Green, green, green," and his car shot ahead, he didn't think the day could be any better. The track came to him and once he caught its rhythm he picked off cars one by one. There were the usual wrecks, but unless something broke, or majorly messed up, he might just have a shot.

Hot damn.

He tightened his hands around the steering wheel, seeing the word DAYTONA slide by him at one-hundred-and-eighty miles per hour. The sky had turned purple-black, bright lights flickering on the roof post and dash.

And then he felt it.

Just the tiniest of vibrations. Not much of one, but if he lifted his right hand from the steering wheel and rested his palm against the carbon fiber ring he could feel it.

Damn.

The word rang out in his head, as loud as if he'd screamed it.

"Got a vibration," he reported.

"Tell me you're joking," Allen said.

"Wish I was. But unless this here car suddenly turned into a washing machine, I'm shaking all over the place."

"Shit," someone said, Lance wasn't sure who. Blain or maybe Terry.

"Bring her in," Allen said.

It felt like Lance had eaten a dozen monster tacos. Son of a—for the first time in over a year, he'd been leading a race and now…

"Yellow, yellow, yellow," Terry cried out excitedly, his voice so loud and so full of relief there could be no mistaking how he felt. "We've got ourselves a caution."

"Lance, can you stay out until the pits open up?"

"Don't know," Lance said. "The vibration's getting worse. Must have cut a tire. Guess I don't have any choice but to try though."

"Roger," Allen said.

They were the longest two laps of Lance's life. Every second that ticked by felt more like an hour, every bump and vibration that shook his car making Lance's stomach twist.

But they made it.

They made it after changing a bad tire and by God, his crew gave him one of the best pit stops of the night, sending him back out into the lead.

The *lead.*

He might win.

The remaining laps felt like a dream, Lance shaking his head when he heard Terry say, "One to go."

Less than a minute later he crossed beneath the

checkered flag, his cry of exaltation so loud he nearly deafened himself.

"Wahoo! We did it," Lance cried as he pounded the steering wheel.

He'd won.

And Sarah had witnessed it.

SARAH RAN OUT of the transporter's lounge only to stop suddenly.

What was she doing heading for the winner's circle? She didn't even know where the darn thing was. Plus, she didn't belong.

But she wanted to see, even if it was just from the periphery. And so she slowly walked toward the winner's circle, stopping at least half a dozen times and turning back only to just as quickly face forward again. Just a peek. That's all she wanted.

The crowd let out a loud cheer, Sarah realizing why a second later. Lance stood atop his car, his arms held above his head, the joy on his face so great Sarah felt tears well up in her eyes, the same tears she'd felt when he'd crossed the start/finish line.

Oh, Lance.

He turned, and to her shock, their gazes met. He smiled, motioning her over. Sarah shook her head. He jumped down, heading for—no. He wasn't seriously coming for her, was he? She froze, people moving out of his way as he made his way toward her, scooping her up in his arms the moment they were close enough to touch.

"Did you see it?" he asked. "Did you?"

There was no holding back the tears. "I did," she said.

"We did it," he said, swinging her around.

Which made her laugh. And when Lance guided her toward the crowd inside the winner's circle, she didn't balk. The team welcomed her with open arms—literally—hugging her and smiling, more than one of them saying, "Can you believe it?"

And, no, she couldn't believe it. She couldn't believe she was standing in the winner's circle at a racetrack, thousands of fans looking down on her, with Lance Cooper, famous race-car driver standing next to her. She felt a nearly irresistible urge to mouth into the camera, "Hi, Mom," when it swung toward her. Even though she hadn't talked to her mom since the whole picture ordeal.

"Lance Cooper," she heard a reporter say. "It's been a year-long drought for you. How does it feel to break your losing streak?"

Sarah stepped away, not wanting to infringe on his moment of glory, but she couldn't move with the team crowded around her. Sarah tried not to feel too conspicuous. But she could see herself on a tiny TV screen mounted atop a camera that pointed toward the grandstand. Oh, geesh. She should have brushed her hair before dashing out. She still wore her white shirt, the same one from earlier, but it now had a splotch of catsup on it, compliments of the wiener dog she'd had for dinner. And was that catsup on her nose, too? She leaned forward as if looking in a mirror, realizing too late that she'd obstructed Lance for a moment. He glanced at her and she smiled lamely.

Sorry, she tried to tell him with her eyes, hoping he didn't see the catsup, too.

He smiled, smiled at her in an intimate way that had her toes curling inside her tennis shoes.

No, screamed a voice. *Don't let Mr. Ultra Sexy Race-Car Driver Who Just Won a Race turn your head.* Do not *let that happen.*

But it was happening. Every time he glanced at her through the minutes that followed, every time he pulled her back to his side whenever she tried to move away, she sank a little deeper.

So she stayed by his side, and the longer she stayed, the more he'd look for her. Courtney tried to lure him away to talk to some more print reporters, but Lance held up his hand, the garage all but deserted at this hour. The moment the race had ended the cars had been packed away and hauled off.

"I'm done," he drawled, his southern accent suddenly more pronounced, the floodlight above their head perfectly illuminating his features. Earlier he'd changed out of his firesuit and into his Star Oil polo shirt; his face above the ribbed collar was tired.

"Um, yeah," Courtney said, flicking her long blond hair over one shoulder. "Okay. But remember. You have to be on a plane by six tomorrow morning."

"Don't worry," Lance said, having never looked away. "I'll be there."

Sarah caught his eyes, feeling suddenly shy. For a moment she wondered if she might have forgotten to breathe during the past thirty seconds because suddenly she felt light-headed. And afraid.

Lance took her hand, his expression suddenly tender. "Thanks for hanging with me tonight."

"You're, um, you're welcome."

"Seriously, Sarah. You've been a big help."

She wanted to ask who, exactly, she'd helped, but she was feeling tongue-tied.

"Ready to leave?" he asked.

"Yes," she said softly.

"You want a ride back to your room?"

And there it was, the question she'd been both dreading and anticipating. But she knew by the look in his eyes that he was asking far more than if she wanted a ride.

Do you want to spend the night with me?

"I don't know," she admitted.

He moved in front of her, and, yes, she hadn't been wrong because his gaze had turned warm. He didn't touch her, but he moved as close to her as possible without physical contact.

"I don't know either," he admitted, one of his hands lifting to swipe a lock of hair out of her face. It was after midnight, his face looking gray beneath the giant lights. But she could see his eyes and they told her he felt just as much uncertainty as she did.

"I'm scared."

"I know," he said gently. "But if it's any consolation, I'm worried, too."

"What about?"

"That I should stay away from you. I don't need my head turned. I need to focus, but I can't—" His words trailed off, his hand dropping to his side.

"You can't?" she prompted.

He looked into her eyes again. "I can't stop thinking about you, about us, about how much I want to touch you and kiss you and—" he looked away for a moment "—to just hold you."

"Oh, Lance."

"I know you're worried about getting hurt, but I won't. I promise."

And still he didn't touch her, didn't kiss her or reach out to hold her hand. She realized in that moment that he was giving her the power. This was her decision, and whatever it was, he would go along with it.

She took his hand.

He sighed, his breath stirring the hairs around her face.

"Sarah," he said softly, bending down to kiss her, the moment seeming to flash in her mind, a mental picture taken of what it was like to feel his lips against her own—their masculine ridges, their surprising softness, the candy-sweet heat of his tongue when it slipped inside her mouth.

His hand lifted, skating up her side, pausing just beneath her breast. Memories of the last time he'd touched her there flooded her mind and so she was left wanting more as his thumb stroked her side.

They heard voices. Lance drew back. "Come with me."

Sarah looked into his eyes. In kindergarten they encouraged the children to enjoy the first day of school. It was nothing to worry about and once it was over they'd realize that all the fear, all the anxiety was for naught.

Lance made her feel like it was the first day of school.

"I'll go," she said.

Chicago

What a Difference a Race Makes
Q&A with Lance Cooper
By Rick Stevenson, Sports Editor

Some of you might remember that earlier this year I sat down with Lance Cooper. We talked about how much he's struggled in the past couple of years and how much he'd hoped to turn things around. Well, after this past week's win at Daytona, people are wondering: Is Lance Cooper back?

RS: Lance, what's your take on the situation? Are you back?

LC: Back. Definitely back.

RS: Good to know. But what turned it around for you this weekend?

LC: I think my head is back in the game. I'm working on some new prerace strategies that seem to be helping a lot.

RS: Rumor has it that prerace strategy involves cookies.

LC: [Laughs] Yeah, that's certainly part of it. Also, a friend of mine kind of put it in perspective when she reminded me of why it was I started racing in the first place—I love to race. If there were no fans, no sponsors, no year-end-championship, I would still want to race. I forgot that for a while.

RS: So is it safe to say you'll be keeping this woman around?

LC: I don't know. Depends of if she keeps making me sugar cookies.

RS: Sugar cookies?

LC: Yeah. She bakes the team cookies every week. We love them. And as far as if I'm going to keep her, I'm afraid the ball's in her court.

CHAPTER SEVENTEEN

IT WASN'T a dream.

When Sarah opened her eyes the next morning she remembered immediately what happened. There was no momentary horror. No remorse. Just a languid sense of satisfaction.

She'd slept with Lance Cooper.

And he really did wear purple underwear.

She smiled, rolling over in bed only to sit up a bit. Where was he? She wondered, looking around. The motor coach's bedroom door was open so she could see down the long aisle. And though the blinds might be drawn, and a sunshade stretched across the front windshield, she could see the kitchen and family room area perfectly. Empty.

Wait. Lance had had to leave early. It was…nine o'clock! Jeez, she'd slept late.

Likely because of your night of drunken debauchery.

She hadn't been drunk, but she felt sort of punchy right now.

Her cell phone rang. *Lance.* It had to be Lance

because nobody else had this number. She clutched the sheet around her, seeking out the location of her purse by cocking her head. It was like playing Marco Polo, but she found the darn thing in one of the cabinets where'd she stashed it for safekeeping.

"Hello?" she said, her every muscle buzzing with anticipation.

"Hello, Sarah?" said a voice, a feminine voice. "Sarah? That you?"

Oh, jeez, Sarah thought, wilting onto one of the couches. *Mom.*

"Hi," Sarah said automatically, clutching the sheet around her tighter as if her mom could see her state of dishevelment right through the phone.

"It *is* you," she said, her raspy voice sounding even more raspy at—what time was it on the West Coast?— six o'clock? "Sarah Tingle, you have no idea what a tough time I've had trying tracking you down!"

How had she gotten this number? How? She'd deliberately not given her mother any number but the one to her voice mail service.

"What if I'd dropped dead from a heart attack?" she lectured.

A distinct possibility, given her mom's addiction to cigarettes.

"You should never leave town without making sure I have a way to reach you."

But that was the whole thing. Sarah didn't want to talk to her mom. To say that they weren't close would be like claming Mars and Pluto weren't within walking distance of each other. "I'm sorry, Mom. I forgot to let you know where I was going."

"Forgot, huh?" There was suspicion in her mother's voice. Sarah winced. Long ago Sarah had realized that most of her problems, including her propensity to involve herself with the wrong man, stemmed from her mother.

"I did," Sarah proclaimed, perhaps a little too vehemently, a headache beginning to throb at her temples. "But I see you managed to find me."

"No thanks to you," said the woman who was the poster child for bad behavior. When they'd last talked Sarah had been shocked when her mom had taken the moralistic high road, plunging yet another knife in her back when she'd berated Sarah over the pictures. It wasn't that she was an abusive mom, but she'd made plenty of rotten choices for Sarah to emulate.

"Um, Mom? How *did* you find me?"

"The TV."

"The TV?"

"I saw you in the winner's circle last night."

"You watched the race last night?" Sarah asked, deadpan.

And suddenly her voice dripped so much honey Sarah wouldn't have been surprised to hear the drone of bees in the background. "Why sure I did, baby," she said. "I told you Hank was a huge

NASCAR fan. Imagine my surprise to look up and see my baby girl standing next to Lance Cooper."

Sarah hadn't been her "baby girl" since she'd kicked her out of her trailer at seventeen. Actually, probably even before that.

"Me? On TV?" Sarah said, trying to sound surprised. "Oh, Mom, you must be mistaken."

"Don't play with me, Sarah Ann Tingle. You forget I called you on a company phone. A Lance Cooper, Inc. company phone. I got the number from someone at the shop."

Doop. Busted.

"Look, Mom, I'm not sure why you called, given the way our last conversation ended..."

"Oh, now, honey—I hope you realize I didn't mean nothin' by that."

"You were rotten," Sarah felt bold enough to say.

"I was only telling you a few home truths for your own good. I may not be the best mom in the world, but I thought I raised you better than to take your clothes off for some man."

"But that's just it," Sarah practically yelled, shooting up from the couch before realizing all she wore was a sheet, the back end opening up so that cold air hit her backside. She sat back down again. "I didn't take my clothes off, Mom. Peter must have Photoshopped someone else's...things on me."

"Really, Sarah? And how can that be possible?"

her mother asked, Sarah dumbfounded that her mom still didn't believe her.

"It's possible," Sarah said. "And anyway, it's not like you're one to judge me."

"No, no. Don't you go there with me, missy. I did the best I could."

Sarah began mouthing the words along with her.

"I was a single mother, working at a convenience store, completely unprepared for the realities of motherhood."

"Mom," Sarah said.

"You're lucky I didn't give you up for adoption."

"Okay, that's enough," Sarah said, wondering why she even bothered to try.

"But all that's in the past now," her mother said, her voice turning sugary-sweet again, the kind of sweet that only ever attracted flies. "You're all grown up and dating a race-car driver."

Okay. So now she knew the purpose of the call. Her mom saw visions of garage passes dancing in her head. "Mom, I'm not dating him. I drive his motor coach."

"Well then, you'll be able to get us tickets to California."

Oh, jeez. Why hadn't she seen that coming? "I'll look into it for you."

"No need," she wheezed, sounding like a squeaky toy. "I already asked the nice girl at Sanders Racing to put me on their list."

"You did *what?*"

"She didn't mind. After I proved to her that I was your mother, she was only too willing to accommodate me."

The underlying message being, *unlike you.*

Sarah closed her eyes, thinking things couldn't get any worse.

"In fact, Hank and I were thinking of joining you in Chicago."

"Chicago!" Sarah cried, straightening so fast the sheet just about fell off. "Mom, you can't afford to do that."

"Hank's paying."

"But, Mom—"

"So I'm thinking we'll see you there on Thursday, honey," she interrupted. "If we end up making it, I'll give you a call so you can come pick us up at the airport."

"I can't pick you up—"

"Bye."

And that was that.

The connection was closed and Sarah was left hanging.

But really, there was nothing new about that. Her mom always did what she wanted to do without a care or a thought about how Sarah might feel. It was the story of her life. Her mom would move them from trailer park to trailer park, little caring that Sarah had made friends, or liked her old school.

She'd done as she pleased and when Sarah had turned seventeen, she'd booted her out.

As sad as it seemed, there were times when she'd wondered why her mom *hadn't* put her up for adoption, except she'd always had this horrible feeling that her mother had kept her around because as much as she might consider a daughter a pain in the you-know-what, Sarah had been a good cook and a whiz with a toilet brush; all the skills her mother had lacked. It was only when her mother's latest boyfriend objected to having a teenager around the place that Sarah had been kicked out.

Her phone beeped again. Sarah tried to see who was calling because if it was her mom, she wasn't answering again. But the odd thing was, it wasn't a cell phone ring, it was a beep.

Alert.

That's what the display screen said. Then she remembered. She pressed the button on the side, the phone chirping in response. "Hello," she said into the speaker.

"Are you up?" Lance asked.

She wanted to close her eyes, wanted to open her mouth and spill out all her angst-filled feelings for her mother. But despite their physical intimacy last night, she couldn't.

"Where are you?" she asked, realizing too late that she'd sounded almost accusatory.

Get it together, Sarah.

"I'm in Indiana. Testing."

And he said the words like she should have known where he was. Then she remembered that he *had* told her where he was going, but it'd been right after he'd…well, she'd had other things on her mind shortly thereafter.

"You're at the brick factory," she said, suddenly remembering the name.

"The Brickyard," Lance said with a smile in his voice.

"When I woke up and you were gone I just…" Felt abandoned, but maybe that was just the way she felt after her mom called. "Felt weird."

"I didn't want to wake you."

He'd told her that, too, she vaguely recalled. "I know. I remember now. I just forgot."

"Long night," he said, his voice low and sending shivers down her spine.

"Yeah, um, it was."

He chuckled, the sound raising an image in her head of Lance kissing her body, sinking lower and lower, a wicked little grin on his face…

Stop, she warned herself. Just stop.

"Lance, look, I've had some bad news."

"What's wrong?" And he sounded so instantly concerned that she felt like closing her eyes all over again and spilling her guts.

"Nothing," she said. "Well, not really *nothing.*

My mom called. She saw me on TV last night and now she's thinking of coming to Chicago."

"Terrific. I'll have Mandy arrange credentials—"

"No," Sarah interrupted. "You don't need to do that. She can purchase tickets if she comes."

"Sarah, don't be silly. I don't want your mom to think I'm some kind of jerk."

"That's just it," Sarah said. "She can't know that we're um, er, seeing each other. That would be a disaster."

"A disaster?"

"She's...she's..." Sarah tried to formulate the words. But how to explain what Sylvia Tingle was like? Now that her mother knew that Sarah was involved in the racing industry she'd never leave her alone. It was like that when she got hired as a full-time teacher at the prestigious private school. Her mother had somehow gleaned that the position had come with a healthy pay increase (well, and why wouldn't it considering she'd been driving for County Transit before that) and she'd called Sarah every week asking for money.

"She's what?" Lance prompted.

"She's horrible," Sarah said. "I'm not kidding, Lance, she's not a good person. There were days when I was growing up that I wished she'd just tie me to a lamppost and leave me. No, don't laugh. That was a serious fantasy of mine. She's not someone you want around."

"She can't be that bad."

"She's *that* bad," Sarah corrected.

"Well, then I'll have her banned from the track."

"Can you *do* that?"

"No," he said on a huff of laughter. "I can't do that. But honestly, Sarah, if she's as bad as all that, why don't you simply tell her not to come?"

"For the same reason I don't tell the moon not to rise and the sun to set. For the same reason I can't stop the Earth from turning and the stars from shining."

"I get the picture. I have a dad that sounds a lot like your mom."

"Terrific. We should put them in a room together and see who comes out first."

Silence. Sarah was just on the verge of feeling uncomfortable when he said, "I missed you this morning."

Boy, that was an abrupt change of subject. "Yeah?" she asked.

Had that sounded too needy? Did he think she was fishing for compliments?

"You were out cold when I left."

"I was pretty tired," she said.

"You look adorable when you sleep. Did you know that? And that you snore."

"I what?" she asked, having been momentarily distracted with thoughts of a raspy chin rubbing the sensitive parts of her body.

"You're adorable when you're sleeping. I could stare at you for hours."

She dropped her gaze as if he were standing in front of her. She wished he was standing in front of her because then she could see if he was feeding her a line or if he really meant it.

"Will you fly out to meet me Tuesday night?"

"What?"

"I'll send my jet for you."

"Lance," she said. "I can't do that. I'll be halfway to Chicago by then."

"Don't drive. I'll stay in a hotel."

She smiled, her mother forgotten as she thought about what it'd be like to jump on a plane and meet up with him.

No.

No, no, no, she told herself. It was very important that she maintain her own identity. This…affair with Lance was tentative at best. She shouldn't go rushing into something.

"Lance, I think it'd be best to meet up with you again in Chicago."

The line chirped instantly, Lance saying, "Chicago! That's too long."

"Well, I don't really think you have a choice. I have a job to do. I'm going to need all three days to get up north."

"Fine. You're fired."

"What?"

"You're fired. I'll find someone else to drive my bus. I can't wait three days to see you."

He was serious. "Lance," she said softly. "I don't want to rush into anything, 'kay. Please, let's just meet up again in Chicago. We can take it from there."

"Sarah—"

"You said you needed to focus, Lance. Having me around isn't going to help you do that."

A long pause. "What day are you going to get in to Chicago?"

"Probably Thursday morning."

"Fine. I'll see you then."

And when the phone chirped off a moment later Sarah wondered if she'd just blown it.

CHAPTER EIGHTEEN

SO SHE DROVE.

Driving always helped her focus on a problem. She could let her thoughts wander, although inevitably they always circled back to Lance and how other women enjoyed flings. And if Lance Cooper ended up being nothing more than a fling, so what? Why not have some fun?

Because she had a feeling Lance Cooper would slip beneath her defenses faster than a fly beneath a door. She'd be in love before she knew it, and falling in love with a professional driver was *not* a good idea. She was too insecure a person to deal with all the women who'd try to steal him away from her. Plus, she had a feeling the only reason he kept her around was because he thought she brought him luck. What kind of a sick relationship was that?

The next morning, Sarah decided it was time to renew her efforts at finding a job. A quick check of her voice mail at home revealed ten messages from her mom and five from her creepy ex—although she had no idea how he'd gotten her number. She'd just subscribed to the service and the number was too new to be listed.

Jerk.

She stopped at the first pay phone she could find—not to call her mom. No. That could wait. She dialed the number Peter had given her—a cell phone, she realized when it took forever to connect.

"Hello, Sarah," he said the moment he picked up.

"How the heck did you know it was me?"

"Because you're in Florida and I recognized the area code."

"How the heck do you know where I am?"

"It's not hard to figure out now that you're working for some race team."

Okay, that did it. "Peter, you know entirely too much about me and it's really starting to creep me out."

"I'm just trying to keep tabs on my girl."

"I'm not your girl. I haven't been for almost a year, which makes your behavior all the more disturbing."

"I miss you."

"You do not. You're just trying to get even with me for dumping you."

"No, Sarah. I really do miss you. I care for you."

"Oh, yeah? Then why'd you send those pictures to that magazine, huh? Why? *Why?*"

"That wasn't my fault. Someone stole the photos from my hard drive, Sarah. I called to apologize."

"How did you get them in the first place?"

"I bought them from the guy that took them. For safekeeping."

"And how'd you find him?"

"The same way I got your new number. I called your mom."

"My *mother?*"

"She told me you're working for a race team now. And that you're dating a race-car driver."

"I'm not *dating* him. I work for Mr. Cooper. That's all."

"Oh. Your mom made it sound like something more."

Her mom would.

"Look, Sarah," he said. "I'm really sorry about what happened with those pictures. A roommate stole them off my hard drive. I had nothing to do with what happened."

"You expect me to believe that?"

"It's true."

Maybe it was. And maybe it was exhaustion that caused her shoulders to droop. Suddenly the fight drained out of her.

"Your mom told me they caused you to break up with that guy you were dating, the one you left me for."

Sarah sighed. "Peter, I didn't leave you for him. I met him the week after you and I broke up."

"Yeah. I know. That's what you say," he said, sounding like he didn't believe her. "But I'm sorry just the same."

Was he sorry? Was he really? "Thanks, Peter," she said, figuring what the heck. He might be a creep, but she wouldn't throw an apology back in his face.

"Be careful, Sarah."

"What? Why should I be careful?"

"Because I know you really are dating that race-car driver. I saw you on TV the other night."

What? Had everybody seen that flippin' broadcast? "He's not my boyfriend."

"Well, I hope not, especially since he's off judging a topless contest right now."

"What?"

"When I Googled his name it came up."

"A topless contest?"

"Yeah," he said. "Some Bimbos thing."

No. Lance wouldn't do something so tawdry. He wouldn't go along with something like that. He wouldn't involve himself in something that exploited a woman's body.

"Well, even if it is true, it's none of my business. He's my boss."

Silence. And then, "Yeah. Okay."

"Look, Peter, I've got to run."

She hung up before he could say another word, her hands shaking as she stared at the pay phone, the silver and blue half booth providing little shelter from the sun.

What topless show? What the heck was Peter talking about?

The Bimbos Girl International Calendar Girl contest, that's what, she learned later.

Sarah read all about it that afternoon when she pulled into an Internet café to check—all right, snoop—on Lance. Again.

So it was true. He really was judging a contest, although the girls wouldn't be topless. Bimbos. The restaurant chain with the big-busted girls in tight yellow tops.

Why the heck hadn't he told her?

And why the heck was she upset? It wasn't as if they were boyfriend and girlfriend. Well, maybe. But doing stuff like this was part of Lance's job. It didn't mean anything. Plus, it'd probably been scheduled long before she'd met him.

But *why* hadn't he *told* her about it?

That's what upset her, she realized. He should have mentioned it to her. The fact that he hadn't seemed suspicious, but it sure explained why he hadn't wanted her to join him until Tuesday. She'd wondered about that.

Unfortunately, her stress level only went up from there. The motor coach popped a tire, scaring her to death, but it was ultimately more of an annoyance than anything else.

By the time she arrived at Chicagoland Speedway—hours later than expected, thanks to her blown tire—she was ready for a nap. It was a clear night, the sky an eggshell pink that faded to purple. Humid, too (big surprise), thick air hitting her when she went outside to hook everything up. And why, she wondered, was it humid everywhere race cars went? Even this late in the day moisture adhered to her cheeks like a spray-on tan. She missed California.

"Where *have* you been?"

Sarah yelped, the hose she'd just turned on spraying water all over the neighboring bus.

Her *mother*.

"What are you doing here?" Sarah cried, the hose wilting like a dead flower, which is how Sarah always felt around her mother.

"Turn that thing off," she ordered.

And in the dusky half-light Sarah could see that she'd splashed water all over her mother's shirt. And the reason she could tell *that* was because her mother wore a white blouse, one that tied around the middle. Now, Sarah didn't consider herself any sort of fashion diva, but she was reasonably certain middle-aged women should not, as a rule, wear tops that tied around the middle, especially if that middle happened to have more rolls than a Wonder Bread factory.

"Sorry," Sarah said, immediately turning toward the spigot and thinking this day just couldn't get any worse.

Oh, yeah?

"What do you mean what am *I* doing here? I told you I was coming."

Oh, damn.

"Uh, yeah," she said lamely. "That's right."

The flash of annoyance faded, but only a little. Sarah couldn't completely disguise the fact that she was less than thrilled to see her mother. But years of living with her had taught Sarah that the only time her mom was happy to see her was when Sarah was about to give her something she wanted.

"Aren't you glad I made it?"

No. "Uh, yeah."

"Good. Then come here and give your mother a big hug."

"Um, no, Mom. That's not a good idea. It was a long drive and I haven't had a shower in—"

Her mom stepped forward and before Sarah could stop her, wrapped her in a hug, the breasts that were abnormally large, and yet, perversely enough given all the *unnatural* things about her mother, totally real, pressing into Sarah.

"Hi, mom," she said, leaning forward with a minimum of contact. Her mom liked to use a lot of perfume, a lot of *cheap* perfume.

"Sarah," her mother said, drawing back and— was that a tear she saw in her left eye?

Oh, please.

"I've missed you so much," she sniffed. "You never call me anymore."

"Mom. Have you forgotten that not too long ago you called me an idiot and accused me of being a closet porn star?"

"Pssh," her mom said with a dismissive wave of her hand, the talons she called nails studded with rhinestones. "I was just worried about you is all," she said, dabbing at her eye.

"Careful, Mom. You'll smear yourself."

Her mom instantly dropped her hand, probably because she didn't have her Wagner power sprayer with her to put her makeup back on.

"Where's Hank?" Sarah asked.

If he's smart, running for the hills.

"I don't know. When I saw you pull in, I got excited. I dashed out of the rental car ahead of him."

"How'd you know it was Lance's bus?"

"The gal at Sanders Racing told me what it looked like."

Sarah was going to have a talk with "the gal."

"Where is Lance, by the way?" her mom asked. "Is he inside?"

Mmm-hmm. Just as Sarah thought. "Mom, Mr. Cooper doesn't drive from race to race. He has a jet. And he's at home or doing media appearances between races. I drive the motor coach so it's here waiting for him when he arrives."

"You mean he's not with you?"

"'Fraid not."

"But we've been waiting in that hot, stuffy car for hours." But then she leaked out a sigh of long-suffering resignation. "Well, I suppose we'll just have to meet him tomorrow."

"Mom. I'm not going to be here tomorrow. My job is to drive the bus to the track, then hang out at a hotel until the race is over."

"You can't be serious? You mean you don't cook for him? You don't do his laundry? You don't cater to his every whim?" The last was said with a smirk, one that left no doubt as to exactly what sort of whims her mother had in mind. Oh, brother.

"No, Mom. I don't—"

"Took you long enough," a masculine voice teased.

And Sarah wanted to groan. She wanted to plunge her head into the turf beneath her feet. What, was there a GPS on her rear end?

"I got a flat on the way here," Sarah said, refusing to look him in the eye, because if her mom caught even a hint of what Sarah was feeling whenever she looked at him—the jolt that had gone through her body upon hearing his voice, the anger she felt over the whole *Bimbos* thing, the way she had to fight her own anxiety upon realizing she'd have to talk to him about it because there was no way she could let it slide—she'd never hear the end of it from Sylvia.

"Are you okay?" Lance asked, concern coloring his blue eyes. He started to come toward her, but Sarah held up a hand. Lance stopped in his tracks, a puzzled look on his face.

Her mom had turned to gawk at him, but she

glanced back at Sarah with narrowed eyes. Sarah could tell she knew something had happened behind her back. But then her brow unfolded, her face smoothing into a look of welcome.

"She's fine," her mother said. "My little darling is just wonderful."

Her little darling? Sarah's jaw unhinged. She snapped it closed just as her mother turned back to her, a wide smile on her face. "Sarah, aren't you going to introduce us?"

No.

But she knew she'd never get away with saying that. "Mr. Cooper, this is my mother, Sylvia Tingle."

Lance smiled, reaching out and taking her mother's outstretched hand. You'd have thought Elvis was alive the way her mom's eyes went all gooey. She clasped Lance's hand like she might need it for support, fake eyelashes so wide they looked like Venus flytraps. And as Sarah watched her mother, she figured she should just have herself spayed and be done with the whole genetic line.

"Nice to meet you, Mrs. Tingle," he said with that All-American smile that girls all across the U.S. had sighed and cooed over.

"Mrs?" her mother said. "Don't be silly. I'm not married. Goodness, why would Sarah tell you such a thing?"

And here it came: The subtle digs. The inference

that Sarah was somehow in the wrong. Next she'd be insulting her appearance.

"Sarah didn't tell me that, Ms. Tingle. I just assumed that a woman as pretty as you had to have a husband."

Oh pul-leez, Sarah wanted to say. And when Lance looked in her direction and winked, she couldn't stop herself from rolling her eyes. What? Had he been picking up cheesy lines at *Bimbos?*

"Pretty?" her mom said. "Why, you sly dog. I'm old enough to be your moth—sister," she quickly corrected. "But you're very sweet to notice how I take care of myself. I keep telling Sarah she should do the same, but she just won't listen."

And there it was. Insult number three and they hadn't been conversing more than a minute. Her mom was on a roll.

"But Sarah doesn't need to take care of herself," Lance said with a wide grin. "She's one of those women with a natural beauty no amount of cosmetics could ever enhance." It was such a subtle dig that Sarah doubted her mother even realized it.

"Well, of course she's beautiful. The apple doesn't fall far from the tree, you know."

That did it. "Mom. I'm sure Mr. Cooper would like to settle in for the night. And since you're here, maybe you could give me a ride to my hotel."

"You mean you're not staying with Lance?"

Scotty, beam me up.

"Mom, I told you, I only *drive* for Mr. Cooper. That's all. Just drive." Jeez. What was wrong with her?

"Oh, honey, don't be silly," she said, nudging her in the side. "I'm your *mother.* There's no need to keep secrets from *me.*"

"Mom, it's not like that—"

"Sarah," Lance interrupted. "I think we can be honest with her."

No, Sarah tried to tell him with her eyes. *No, no, no. Don't do it.*

"You're right, Ms. Tingle. Sarah *does* do more than drive for me. She bakes me cookies during race week, too."

"What?" her mom asked.

"Bakes me animal cookies. Well, not just me—the whole team. She's a real part of the crew and I don't know what me and the boys would do without her."

It was apparent her mother didn't know how to take that. It was equally obvious that her mother didn't know if she should believe him or not.

"Look, Mom," Sarah said with a silent sigh of relief. When she caught Lance's eye he winked at her again. She ignored him. "Why don't you go find Hank? By the time you get back I should have most of my chores done here. I'm sure Mr. Cooper wants to get to bed."

With you, he silently mouthed, then grinned as she blushed.

"But Hank wanted to meet Mr. Cooper, too."

"He can meet him tomorrow," Sarah said firmly. "Seriously, Mom. Go. Find Hank. I have stuff to do here."

"I'll help you set up," Lance said to Sarah before turning to her mom. "And when you find Hank, you can introduce him to me."

Which made her mother's face light up. "I'd be delighted to introduce you, even though, you know, Hank's more of a friend."

"Really? I'm surprised he hasn't snapped you up," Lance said with another one of his patented smiles. It occurred to Sarah that this was a side of Lance she'd never seen. Wait. That wasn't true. She *had* seen it before—at the Super Tools autographing. But she hadn't seen it since then because the Lance she knew had never smiled at her with such insincerity in his eyes.

But he could keep secrets from her.

"Ooo," her mother all but cooed. "You're such a sweetie." She stepped up to Lance and pressed herself against him in a way that seemed faintly suggestive, which, knowing her mother, it likely was. This time Sarah's face filled with color.

"I'll see you in a bit," Sarah said, turning back to the hose and connecting it to the water system. She heard her mother walk away, knew Lance stood over her a second later; Sarah was almost afraid to turn and face him.

"Lance," she said when she finally gained the courage to stand.

He kissed her.

CHAPTER NINETEEN

HE'D BEEN WANTING to do that since the moment he'd first seen her.

"Lance," she said, pushing him away far too soon. "You can't do that."

"Why not?" he asked. "She's gone."

"That's not the point," Sarah said. "We shouldn't be out here in public."

"Why not? Most people haven't even arrived yet."

"Yeah, but even if one person sees us it'll start rumors flying," she said firmly, the pink-and-purple sky above them turning her eyes a shimmering amber. She had amazing eyes, Lance thought, wondering yet again how her mother could ever think her daughter wasn't beautiful. Must be blinded by all that makeup she wore.

"Sarah, I think most people have figured out we're a couple."

"We're not a couple," she said. "We just happened to have...to have slept together," she added, her eyes sliding away from him.

Lance tried to hide a smile. He'd known she'd

react this way the first time they came face-to-face. She wasn't the type of woman who'd ever be comfortable trading sexual sallies. It was one of the things he loved about her. She was almost, but not quite, shy. Ladylike, he realized.

Unlike her mother.

And those women who'd tried to come on to him Monday night.

"Well, I don't know about you, but I don't make a habit of sleeping with someone unless I like them."

"You don't?" she asked, meeting his eyes at last, her curly hair all springy and somehow happy-looking. "And do you make a habit of judging calendar girl contests when you're dating someone?"

He winced. "You know about that?"

"I know."

She didn't say anything, just crossed her arms. *Uh-oh.*

"Sarah, it was nothing. Something that's been on my schedule for months."

"Why didn't you tell me about it?"

"Because I knew you'd get upset," he admitted. "And because I was sort of hoping to just get it done and then forget about it."

"Did you have a good time?"

"I would have had a better time if you'd been there," he said, stepping forward and trying to pull her into his arms. "I missed you."

"Then why didn't you invite me?" she said, trying to wiggle away.

"Because I knew you wouldn't come." She tried to wiggle away again, but he held her firmly saying, "Wait. Be quiet."

She went still suddenly, eyes swinging around as if she expected her mother. "What?" she asked.

"Do you hear that?" he asked.

Her brow scrunched as she cocked her head and listened. "Hear what?"

"That sound."

"What sound?" she asked suspiciously.

"That tiny little thud," he said softly, his whole body relaxing as he stared down at her. "That was the sound my heart made when it fell for you."

"Wha—" And then her face fell, and that was *not* the reaction he'd been hoping for. "Oh, Lance," she said softly. "That's the corniest line I've ever heard."

It felt like he'd hit the wall at 180 mph. *Blam.*

"It wasn't corny. I meant it."

She just rolled her eyes. He bit back an oath of frustration.

"Look," he said. "Can we go inside? I don't really want to talk about this out here."

"There's nothing to talk about," she said, and he saw sorrow in her eyes; it made him feel ill. "Lance, we can't do this."

"Why not?" he asked. "Because from where I sit, this relationship is totally doable."

"But not from where I sit," she said, finally wiggling out of his arms. She stepped back from him, crossing her arms to guard against him tugging her into his arms again. "From where I sit this relationship is anything *but* doable."

"Not this again," he said. "Don't tell me it's the whole race-car driver thing."

"That's part of it," she admitted, her eyes so brown and so serious Lance realized he would have done anything in that moment to put a smile back on her face. "But it's also what being a race-car driver entails. Mad dashes across the country to go test a car, or to judge a calendar girl contest, or do something else."

"I told you, the calendar girl contest was nothing."

"And I believe you. But it's *not* just that," she said.

"What?" he asked, crossing his own arms in front of him because no matter how much he fought it, he still felt an almost irresistible urge to pull her into his arms. "What is it that keeps you from seeing me? Because to me, Sarah, this seems like a no-brainer."

"To *you*, Lance," she said softly. "To me it's a *bad* idea."

"I'm not going to hurt you."

"That's what you tell me, Lance, but I don't believe it."

"Sarah—"

"No," she interrupted, holding up a hand. "I know what you're going to say. You're going to tell me how much you care for me. How you would no sooner hurt me than you would hurt yourself, but believe me, Lance, I've heard it before. And while I've been known to stare down a room full of unruly kindergartners, the truth is that I'm a coward."

"You're *not* a coward."

"Yes, I am, Lance. I'm a lily-livered, blue-bellied coward. I'm terrified of getting involved with you. Just the thought of going out in public with you makes me want to toss my cookies. I can't compete with the beautiful women who'll make a play for you at calendar girl contests and other places and I'll make myself sick giving it a try."

"Toss your cookies?" he said, trying not to feel insulted.

"Not toss my cookies," she quickly corrected. "Well, maybe just a little bit. Or—gosh. I don't know," she said, obviously agitated. "All I know is that I'm not very good at dating ordinary men. I can't imagine what it'd be like dating an extraordinary man."

"But I am ordinary," he said. "I'm an ordinary man who happens to have an extraordinary job. Don't confuse Lance the race-car driver with Lance the man."

"But you see," she said, brown eyes unblinking. "I'd be afraid to date Lance the ordinary man, too." She shook her head, looking away for a moment.

"Why?" he said softly, uncrossing his arms, wanting to touch her but knowing that wouldn't be a good idea. "I don't understand why you'd walk away from this."

"Lance, in school we don't give children long division when the most they can do is add and subtract. You're the square root of pi."

"Huh?" he asked. She wasn't making sense.

But she looked determined to make him understand. "I had my heart tossed down and stomped on by someone I thought I could trust. Because I thought—I truly thought—that man was *the one*. Only he wasn't and I don't trust my judgment anymore and so even though you tell me you won't break my heart, I can't date you on blind faith alone, not when the odds are so stacked against me. I'm not physically capable of that, just as students who can barely add and subtract aren't ready for geometry."

And finally he understood. He really did. What was more, her bruised soul lingered in her eyes, and it hurt him, too, to see the humiliation and the disappointment in her eyes. It tore at Lance's heart. He wanted to ram his fist down the throat of all the bastards who'd hurt her. No, he wanted to ram his fist into the side of his bus. Damn it. Now what? How could he fix this?

Maybe he couldn't.

"So this is it?" he said. "You don't want to see me again?"

She nodded sharply.

"Well, okay then," he said stepping back from her.

She tried to follow him, her hand outstretched. "Lance. Wait—"

"No," he said. "If you want to end it, you want to end it," he said. But the anger disappeared as quickly as it'd come, his shoulders sinking with disappointment. "I refuse to pressure you. You're the type of woman that'll bolt if I do that. So I'm just going to walk away and hope that one day you'll change your mind."

His answer surprised her, he could see. Well, good. Maybe if she realized he wasn't the same type of jerk as those other men she'd dated, she'd come back to him. Maybe.

"Thanks," she said softly, looking down.

He wanted to go to her. Wanted to hug her. To tell her that everything would be all right. But he couldn't touch her because if he did that, he'd never let her go.

"Goodbye, Sarah. I'll see you around."

"Bye, Lance. I'll, um… I'll text message you when I'm done setting up here."

"Don't bother," he said. "I'll come back later and do it all."

And when he turned around, he almost bumped into Sarah's mother.

AND JUST LIKE THAT it was over.

"*You* are the biggest fool that ever walked the earth," her mother said, the two of them watching as Lance disappeared between a row of parked buses.

He walked away from her with understanding in his eyes and nary a show of temper, and Sarah wasn't sure what to think about that.

"Have you *any* idea what you just gave up?"

"Where's Hank?" Sarah asked, wondering what she should do now. Should she go ahead and finish setting things up? Or should she find a ride to the hotel? And what about later? Did she keep on working for Lance? How could she keep doing that after what had happened between them?

"Who cares where Hank is? *You're* the one that needs a serious tongue-lashing."

"Mom. Not now," Sarah said, walking to the back of the bus and then bending down to open a side compartment. A massive generator hid inside. She flipped a few switches, and the thing roared to life. Maybe it'd muffle her mother.

"Don't tell me not now," her mother said, having followed her. "Not only did you *lie* to me about your relationship with that man, but you let him get away."

Sarah straightened, taking a deep breath before facing her.

"You let a man who makes millions of dollars a year get away!" she said, her eyes wide and filled with outrage.

"So?" Sarah said.

"So! Have I taught you nothing? Who cares if he might break your heart? Enjoy the ride while it lasts, Sarah, because with your looks it isn't going to last forever."

It should hurt, Sarah realized. Her mother's awful words should really hurt. But they didn't. She was so used to her mother's thoughtless remarks that they barely even fazed her anymore. Besides, Sarah agreed with her on that score.

"I'm sorry for lying to you, Mom, but right now I have a job to do and I'm not, repeat, *not* going to discuss what just happened between me and Lance Cooper. Not."

"Well. What are you going to do?" her mother called after her.

"I'm going to get the bus ready for Lance to occupy and then I'm going back to my hotel," where she'd draft a letter of resignation, one she'd fax to Sal tomorrow.

"Can I see the inside?" her mother asked, having followed her.

And that was the way it was with her mom. She pushed and pushed until Sarah pushed back and then, like most bullies, she gave up. Just like that.

"Sure," Sarah said, wondering why she humored her.

Because she's your mother.

Yeah, well, cockroaches were mothers, too, but that didn't stop them from eating their young.

Pocono

Elvis Has Left the Building
Q&A with Lance Cooper
By Rick Stevenson, Sports Editor

Or has he? With Lance Cooper fresh from a victory at Daytona International Speedway, perhaps it's a bit too early to predict his demise. But the naysayers are quick to claim Cooper's recent win was just a fluke, especially after this week's poor practice times at Chicago. Was it a fluke?

RS: Well, Lance, was it?

LC: Well, Rick, I think it's a bit early to be stabbing the stake into my heart.

RS: But you've got to admit, after your stellar performance in Daytona, this week's been a bit of a disappointment. Tell us what you think the problem is.

LC: Simple. I didn't get my weekly batch of animal cookies.

RS: No animal cookies? What's the world

coming to? But, seriously, how do you think you're going to do this weekend? And tell us honestly if you're worried.

LC: I hope I can keep my focus, but it might be kind of hard. I'm dealing with some personal issues and that's got me a little distracted, so I guess we'll just have to wait and see.

RS: Personal issues? Anything we should know about?

LC: Nope.

RS: Nope it's no big deal? Or nope, you're not going to talk about it?

LC: I'm not going to talk about it.

RS: I see. Well, good luck qualifying and good luck this weekend. We'll catch up with you again after New Hampshire.

CHAPTER TWENTY

SARAH DIDN'T SEE HIM the rest of the week, although she listened to the race on the radio. But before the broadcast, she'd watched qualifying on TV, Sarah admitting to herself that for a woman who'd just broken up with a man, she was pretty obsessed with him.

He didn't do so well.

And her heart went out to him despite her unwillingness to get involved. She saw him on TV, his face tense as he climbed into his car and she knew just by looking at him that his times wouldn't be good.

Because of her?

As much as she'd like to take credit for Lance's recent spate of success, she had a feeling it had less to do with her and more to do with Lance sorting out his own mental game. Too bad he appeared to have lost concentration again.

Because of her?

Stop it, she warned herself. She shouldn't feel responsible for Lance's performance. So what if he didn't have her cookies to eat? Cookies did not a race-car driver make.

So why did she wince when he bobbled his warm-up lap? And why did she cover her face when his first lap wasn't the greatest? And why, oh why, did she feel the urge to call him when he ended up twenty-fifth?

This was bad. This was really, really bad.

And she didn't fax off her resignation. She told herself she didn't do it because she had no place to stay, no other job lined up, no nothing. In the past two weeks she'd earned just enough to pay off some bills, and she didn't even want to think about what she would do about her car which, she was told, should be all fixed by the end of the week. How would she pay for that? She was stuck working for Lance, no doubt about it.

Her mother didn't help matters. She and her boyfriend, Hank—a man Sarah despised instantly with his Fu Manchu mustache, leather vest and silver necklace—were so completely starstruck by Lance that Sarah had to endure daily phone calls (because she refused to go out to the track) detailing what a great guy Lance was, and how wonderful he was to Hank (probably because Lance was afraid of Hank), and most of all, how much Sarah had blown it by breaking up with him.

So, when she arrived at the track to pick up the motor coach late Sunday night, Sarah wasn't in the best of moods. She'd watched the race and it'd been almost painful to see Lance struggle the entire day.

Plus, she was almost certain Lance would be there. Wait, that wasn't quite right. She wasn't *certain* he'd be out there, she just secretly *hoped* he'd be out there. Yes, that's right, hoped, because no matter how much she told herself not to, she really missed talking to Lance.

He wasn't there. She stood outside his bus waiting for him to answer a knock and when he didn't appear she felt the urge to cry. Stupid, stupid, stupid.

It was worse when she went inside. She smelled him. There were signs that he'd been there—tiny crumbs on the counter, indents on the couch, reverse patterns on the carpet in his bedroom. His bedroom. The place where they'd—

She shut the bedroom door, turning away and making sure all the other doors were closed, too— the cabinets, the overhead hatches, the drawers. And when she was finished she started the big bus and drove away.

SHE EXPECTED TO FEEL BETTER in a day or two, but she didn't. And the reason she felt worse was because despite being the one to break things off, she'd been hoping Lance would call her. He didn't, the man having the gall to respect her wishes and leave her alone.

Of course, that should make her happy, not mad, she admitted. But for some ridiculous reason she actually felt hurt that he was respecting her wishes.

She'd lost her mind.

Such were her thoughts as she pushed a cart of groceries toward Lance's bus that Tuesday. Part of her duties included keeping the bus supplied, although Sarah had a briefly malicious thought that she should leave the toilet paper behind. But as quickly as the thought had come, she dismissed it. It wasn't his fault that he hadn't called. She'd been the one to break it off. Frankly, the ball was in her court.

If he'd take her back.

"You a Lance Cooper fan?" a woman asked.

She'd parked the bus far away from other shoppers and so the words startled Sarah. "I beg your pardon?" Sarah asked, turning toward a woman with stringy black hair and a painful-looking hoop sticking out of her eyebrow.

"Are you a Lance Cooper fan?" she asked with a smile that exposed a few missing teeth.

"Uh, no," Sarah said. "The owner of the bus is— I'm just the driver."

"Really?" the woman said. "What an interesting job."

"Um, yeah," Sarah said, smiling before she started pushing the groceries again.

"Do you like driving his bus?"

That caught Sarah's attention. "Whose bus?" she asked after stopping again.

"Lance Cooper's."

Uh-oh. Sarah eyed the number of vacant parking

spaces between her and the motor coach, wondering if she could make a dash for it.

"Actually, no. He doesn't own the bus," Sarah lied, pushing the groceries forward again, only faster this time, the wheels clink-clinking in such a way as to make steering difficult.

"Is he inside?" the woman asked, coming up alongside of her.

"What makes you think Lance Cooper owns this bus?" Sarah asked, stepping along even faster.

"It was on a TV show."

"Not this bus," Sarah said. She was almost to the door.

"Can I go inside?"

"Can you—" Sarah let the cart roll to a stop, ducking around the side of it to open up the door. "No, you cannot go inside. And Lance Cooper does not own this bus."

"Yes, he does. And you're his girlfriend. I recognized you inside." She thumbed toward the single-story supermarket behind them. "You stood next to him in the winner's circle at Daytona."

Okay, that did it. Sarah opened the door, darted up the steps, leaving the groceries outside.

"Wait," the woman called. "Don't go. I just want his autograph."

"I'm not his girlfriend," Sarah called, feeling better now that she'd locked the door. "And Lance Cooper does not own this bus."

"Yes, he does," the woman yelled back. "Those are his sunglasses on the dash."

Oh, jeez. This was unbelievable. Now what did she do? A peek outside the window revealed that the woman hadn't moved. She stared up at the door of the bus as if she expected Lance Cooper to emerge at any moment, the hopeful look on her face confirming that Sarah's out-and-out lies hadn't dissuaded her one bit.

"Okay, look," Sarah said through the door. "If I hand you some signed race cards, will you go away?"

"I knew this was his bus," the woman said. "I *knew* it. Is he in there?" she asked again.

"No, he is not in here. And I would really appreciate it if you would leave me alone."

"I don't believe you. I think he's in there."

Well, considering the fact that she'd lied about it being Lance's bus, she could hardly blame the woman for thinking that.

"I'm really going to have to insist you leave. If you don't, I'll have to call the police."

And when Sarah peeked out the window again, it was to find the woman digging into a twelve-pack of toilet paper. "Hey," Sarah said, banging on the window. "Don't do that."

"This is for Lance, isn't it?"

"I don't believe this," Sarah murmured. "I just don't *believe* this." But with nothing else to do, she picked up her cell phone and called 911.

"I'm calling 911," Sarah said, but the woman outside just kept on rifling through Lance's groceries. Sarah was flabbergasted that she didn't seem the least bit concerned that the police were on their way.

Of course, it was a little hard to explain why it was an emergency when all she had to complain about was that someone had stolen her toilet paper (and maybe some potato chips). But oddly enough, the moment Sarah explained that the woman outside was a race fan convinced her favorite driver was inside the bus Sarah drove, the operator seemed to understand. She was, Sarah learned later, a 911 operator who happened to love stock car racing.

Her hands were shaking by the time the police had the woman in custody and Sarah felt safe enough to open the bus door again.

"You okay?" a burly state trooper asked, mirrored glasses turning her reflection into tiny crescent moons.

"I think so," Sarah said. And then she caught sight of the remnants of her groceries. "What the—" She clutched her head. "Jeez oh peets. What? Did she take one of everything?"

"Race fan, ma'am," the cop said, as if that explained everything, which, Sarah realized, it did.

"Yeah, I sort of got that."

"This Lance Cooper's tour bus?"

"Yes," Sarah said, glancing at the brown and gold police car. The woman sat in the back of the car, legs hanging out, arms cuffed behind her, her eyes still staring in the bus's direction as if she *still* expected Lance to finally come out.

"You have any race cards on hand?"

"Do I have any what?" Sarah asked.

"Race cards?" the man asked. "The woman told me you had some. And I'm actually more of a Dan Harris fan, but I don't mind Lance Cooper."

Sarah wanted to sink down on the bus's steps. Was there no end to this madness? But it only served to remind her of yet another reason she should steer clear of Lance Cooper and his crazy job.

But dealing with Stalker Girl happened to be the least of her problems that day because when she tried to drive away after the police had left (Stalker Girl in custody), the bus wouldn't start. At first she thought she might have let the battery drain down, but it didn't sound like a drained battery. And so, for the second time in as many weeks, she was forced to call the emergency repair service. And since she was out in the sticks, it took forever for someone to come out. And once someone finally *did* come, it was to tell her something truly shocking.

The bus had been sabotaged. Someone had dumped sugar into the diesel tank.

TWO HOURS LATER Sarah learned that the motor coach's engine was ruined, that it would take at least a week to get a replacement, and that the only place capable of repairing a bus was a truck stop nearly sixty miles away. The final bummer was that the only place that could tow a bus happened to be closed for the night. Oh, and that the nearest hotel was thirty miles away and so she'd be forced to stay in the motor coach.

Sarah wanted to cry.

She didn't want to stay in the motor coach and so she called Sal. Sal sounded concerned, told her to hang tight while he arranged for a rental car to be brought to her, and to not worry about a thing.

Easy for him to say.

He wasn't stuck in Nowhereville, Illinois with Stalker Fan on the loose. Well, okay, maybe the woman was still in jail, but you never knew. Worse, with the bus being stuck where it was, and darkness quickly approaching, Stalker Fan would know exactly where to find her. And what if she came back with friends? What if those friends brought guns? What if bullets started flying?

An hour passed, Sarah retreating to the Piggly Wiggly where she befriended the manager. And still her cell phone didn't ring. A call back to Sal and she got his voice mail. Terrific. Now what?

One of the grocery store clerks offered to drive her to the nearest bus depot. When another hour passed, and then another, Sarah decided to take the woman up on the offer, returning to the bus one last time to leave a note for the rental car people and

collect the suitcase she'd bought the week before—
not that she expected the rental car people to show.
Obviously, they'd realized she was out in the middle
of nowhere and decided to leave her there.

The bus was hot inside, despite the fact that the
sun had long since sunk below the horizon, and
mosquitoes followed her across the deserted
parking lot. Sarah quickly wrote a note, thinking it'd
be just her luck if Stalker Fan returned when she
was inside the bus.

Bam.

Sarah screamed, turned. Someone had banged on
the back window—it still reverberated from the
contact. She crept toward the bedroom, peeking out
the window, but whoever had done it had fled, or so
Sarah presumed because she couldn't see anybody.

Now what?

Was it Stalker Fan again? And if so, did she leave?
Should she go outside and check? But wouldn't that
be dumb? Like those movies where the heroine went
outside when you just knew she shouldn't.

She almost called the police again, but right as
she picked up the phone someone knocked on the
Prevost's door, causing Sarah to scream yet again.

"Sarah?" a voice called in concern.

And Sarah knew. It wasn't Stalker Fan. It was
Lance.

CHAPTER TWENTY-ONE

"LANCE, THANK GOD you're here," Sarah said, standing inside the bus on the steps above him.

The words were music to his ears; too bad she didn't say them because she was happy to see him, because she'd missed him. She said them because she was very obviously terrified.

"Are you okay?"

"Was that you who banged on the back window a moment ago?"

"No."

"Shoot," she said, looking, in a word, frazzled and all he wanted to do was pull her into his arms and hug her. Only he couldn't. He'd told her he'd give her space and space he would give her.

"Someone banged on the back window?"

"Yeah. I don't know who. Scared me to death."

"You shouldn't have been hanging out here. You should have gone someplace safe," he said, ducking into the bus before she had time to protest. "Not hung out here."

"I *was* someplace safe. Up until two minutes ago

I was hanging inside the Piggly Wiggly, which, by the way, smells like old shoes and Pine Sol."

"Why'd you come back then?"

"To write the stupid rental car people a note," she said, holding up a piece of paper. "They never showed."

"They didn't show because I'm here to get you."

"And if that isn't the dumbest thing I've ever heard of, I don't know what is."

"What do you mean?" Lance said, feeling confused. "I just flew a few hundred miles to come get you."

"And you didn't need to. I could have taken care of myself, which was exactly what I was about to do. One of the ladies who works at the Piggly Wiggly was going to give me a ride to the bus depot."

"You were going to get on a bus?"

"Why not? It's better than waiting around here and maybe bumping into Stalker Fan again. And speaking of Stalker Fan, you're in deep doo-doo if she catches sight of you."

"Stalker *who?*"

"The woman who poured sugar down your bus's engine."

"It was a *woman?*"

"Yeah. Didn't Sal tell you?"

Lance shook his head. "He said someone had vandalized the bus and tried to steal some things."

"She poured sugar down the tank, the police think as a way of keeping *you* here," Sarah said, her look turning to one of accusation—again. "When I told her you weren't around, she decided to help herself to your supplies, I can only assume because she wanted to be able to wipe *her* butt with the same toilet paper you wipe *your* butt with."

And just like that, Lance wanted to laugh. It amazed him how quickly Sarah could make him do that. "Sarah, you say the damndest things."

"Well, I'm glad I can be your personal comedian."

He wanted her to be a lot more than that. "C'mon," he said. "We're going home."

"What about the bus?"

"Someone will come and haul it away tomorrow. Sal's made all the arrangements."

She looked about ready to protest again, but then turned and collected her luggage, a tiny black suitcase that he'd seen before. "I can't believe you flew all the way up here to pick me up in your jet."

"I thought you'd be happy to go home."

"In case you've forgotten," she said, brushing by him as she exited the bus, the suitcase bumping down the steps with a thud-thud-thud. "I don't have a place to stay."

"I've taken care of that," Lance said, resisting the urge to inhale her scent.

"I'm not staying with you."

Lance had nearly bumped into her at the bottom of the steps, not having realized she'd stopped. "No. You're staying with the Sanderses," he said, squeezing by her. Crickets chirped in the distance, the parking lot's fluorescent lights buzzing. Or maybe that was insect wings he heard. That sure was the sound of their bodies colliding with the streetlight's plastic cover.

"Blain and Cece Sanders?" she asked, her russet brows lifted, brown eyes looking almost black.

"That's them."

"But they don't even know me."

"The other option is to stay with me."

"No," she said quickly.

Lance had figured that would get her to change her mind. Damn. He'd been hoping their separation might have softened her up a bit. Apparently not.

"That's what I thought," he said.

"But I'd rather stay at a hotel."

"Another place that rents rooms by the hour?"

"I was not renting a room by the hour," she said, closing the trunk on her suitcase and then sliding inside the rental.

He went around to the other side, getting in and starting the car. "I saw the place where you were staying, and those rooms were *definitely* available by the hour."

"It was the best I could afford," he heard her mumble, crossing her arms again. But then she straightened. "Wait," she said. "I need to tell that nice woman inside that I won't be needing a ride."

"I'll drive you over there," Lance said.

"I can walk."

"No," Lance said firmly, trying not to lose patience. "It's too far. And it's too dark."

"Fine," she said. Lance thought she sounded as surly as the kids she used to teach.

"And why the heck did you park so far away from the store, anyway?"

"In case you hadn't noticed, you own a big bus and it doesn't exactly fit in the compact spots. Plus, when I got here earlier, there were a lot of people. The place was packed."

"Next time do your shopping in a major city."

"Yes, sir," she said, saluting him just before she hopped out of the car.

Lance watched her go, thinking he'd never met a woman that could so quickly amuse and then exasperate him. Granted, he was being something of an ass, but he'd been worried sick about her the whole flight into Ohio. And when he'd discovered just how Podunk a town it was that she'd broken down in, he'd been even more worried. What the heck had she been thinking to pull off the Interstate and select this Piggly Wiggly out of all the Piggly Wigglies in the country?

Unbelievable.

"Oh my gosh, it really is Lance Cooper."

Lance froze behind the wheel, catching sight of Sarah's false smile right before she opened her door and said, "Lance, this is Mary Ann and she's a big fan."

Soon a whole crowd of people surrounded the car, all Piggly Wiggly employees, and all sporting scraps of paper for him to sign. When he caught Sarah's eyes, she smirked and Lance almost smiled. Obviously, this was her way of paying him back for giving her such a hard time.

"I'll just wait in the car," she said, sliding inside while he dealt with the masses.

And yet again, Lance found himself chuckling. Score one for her.

HE DIDN'T LOOK MAD. He didn't look perturbed. In fact, he didn't look anything at all. Considering they were about to board a private jet—one that he owned—that seemed pretty remarkable. Then again, this was old hat to him.

Not so her. *She* had butterflies.

It was nearing midnight and yet their pilot greeted them with a wide smile at the top of the ramp, saying, "Made it," as Lance led her inside.

"I found her," Lance said. "She was in a Piggly Wiggly parking lot, but I found her."

"Gotta watch out for those Piggly Wigglies," the pilot said, meeting her gaze. "You never know what kind of crazed people you might run into there. Here, I'll take that," he said, taking her suitcase.

Terrific, so the whole world knew of her encounter with Stalker Fan. But then Sarah caught her first glimpse of the inside of the jet and she almost halted next to the pilot.

Whoa.

Plush ivory carpet spread from wall to wall, padded leather seats and elegant wall sconces that seemed to ooze ambient light making the interior look more like something out of *Fine Homebuilding* rather than a plane. And as she stood there, her gaze darting around, small niggles of dismay passed through her. Okay, so fine, she could admit it: for a moment she found herself thinking she'd been a fool to break things off with Lance. The least thing she could have done was let him fly her cross-country for a few dates before throwing him over.

"Take a seat anyplace," Lance said, motioning to the eight or so seats that were all empty. He sat in the front row, flipping open his phone the moment he leaned back and then he…ignored her.

Sarah watched, trying not to feel even more dismayed. To be honest, he'd been pretty much ignoring her from the moment he'd climbed back into the car at the Piggly Wiggly. At first she'd thought he might be mad at her for siccing the fans on him (but it'd been worth it). But then he'd politely asked if she was comfortable, adjusting the heat when she'd said she was a bit cold before going back to ignoring her.

He was only doing as she asked—leaving her alone. A part of her recognized this, but it still felt wrong somehow, she thought, listening to him drawl into the phone (and who was he talking to this time of night, anyway?). And all right, maybe she hadn't *dumped* him, that sounded so harsh, but she'd certainly been the one to call things off and in her experience, men didn't normally take that very well.

Lance certainly didn't have a problem with it, although there'd been a moment when she'd first opened the bus's door, just a brief second, when she'd thought he might pull her into his arms. And since she was being Mother Teresa honest, if she were *completely* truthful, she could admit to *wanting* him to pull her into his arms. Gosh, how she'd wanted to wrap her arms around him and tell him how tired and afraid she felt.

Only she couldn't, and she didn't. And apparently, she'd imagined the look in his eyes.

"We should be back in North Carolina in an hour or so," his pilot yelled out to them from the cockpit after closing the main cabin door (so much for a PA system). Sarah glanced toward the front of the plane, realizing it must have been a copilot that had greeted her. There were two bodies up there.

"Um, excuse me."

Lance turned around. One of the pilots looked back.

"Do I have to wear my seat belt?"

"Always a good idea to buckle up," the pilot said.

"Although I promise not to report you to the FAA if you don't."

She caught Lance's eye. He lifted a brow, then went back to his conversation. New girlfriend? He was talking so damn low that she could barely hear him over the jet's suddenly high-pitched whine.

She didn't care who he was talking to, Sarah reminded herself.

Liar, liar, pants on fire.

THEY LANDED about one in the morning, Sarah thinking that the Sanderses couldn't be happy to have an unwanted guest arrive in the wee hours of the morning. Sarah tried to insist on a hotel again, but Lance wouldn't hear of it. He didn't think hotels were safe.

What did that say about his feelings toward her? She mentally yelled at herself. *Stop. It.*

So he dropped her off at Blain and Cece Sanders' house, Sarah a little bit relieved to learn that it was actually a guest house, one to which Lance just happened to have the key.

"They just built it," Lance said. "It's for the nanny, when they hire one, but so far Cece's resisted."

"Okay," Sarah said, eyeing the Spanish-style bungalow to the left of the house. Lance's headlights had swept the property when they arrived. Sarah tried not to gawk at the stunning two-story home less than a hundred yards from the shore of Lake Norman.

"She'll come by in the morning and introduce herself, by the way."

"Lance, are you certain this isn't a problem? I mean, I don't know that I'd want a perfect stranger to camp out in my nanny quarters. And I really don't mind—"

"You're staying here," he said. His parking lights were on and the only light came from the display on the dash, but she could see the intensity in his eyes when he said, "You'll be safe here."

And suddenly she felt—she tried to put a name to it—*aware*. Aware like a person who knows they're being watched in a way that's so elemental it gives them goose bumps.

He wasn't as immune to her as he pretended.

She smiled. She couldn't help herself. The joy she felt upon realizing he hadn't completely dismissed her from his mind was so unmistakable it should have sent off claxons in her head. It didn't.

"Thanks, Lance," she said softly.

He looked away. Sarah watched as his hands clenched the steering wheel. "Do you need me to bring your luggage inside for you?"

The goose pimples turned into fire because she knew what he was really asking. Did she want him to come in?

Did she?

The answer was, yes. But just as suddenly as she knew the answer, she knew she couldn't indulge herself in the pleasure of Lance's touch. Not now. Not ever.

That way be dragons.

"No thanks," she said, opening the car door before she changed her mind. But her heart pounded against her chest like they'd just engaged in the most passionate of kisses, her skin so flushed it was as if he'd touched her with his hands.

That way be dragons.

She wished she had the courage to slay them.

CHAPTER TWENTY-TWO

SHE SLEPT like the dead.

It was probably the best sleep she'd had in weeks. In fact, she slept so peacefully, her sleep shirt didn't ride up her middle and her matching dark-blue pants hadn't twisted themselves around the back. And as she stretched her arms, yawning, Sarah admitted that she and hotels didn't get along. The bed she'd slept in was heavenly (not hard), the room was gorgeous (and the windows actually opened) and as she lay there, muted sunlight drifting in through a window to her right, it was nice to know nobody would be knocking on her door yelling "Housekeeping!"

A child giggled.

It was such a familiar sound, one so dearly missed in recent weeks, that Sarah padded to the nearest window, pulling aside a gauzy floral curtain in time to hear a black-haired little boy laugh again. The child played on the grass between the nanny quarters and the house, a cocker spaniel licking his face like he was a boy-flavored dog treat.

Sarah smiled. It was such a perfectly beautiful scene to wake up to after the hustle and bustle of the racetrack that she could have stared at the boy and his dog all day.

"Stop it," she heard the boy giggle, hands and legs flailing as he tried to ward off the dog. "Stop it."

"He's happy to see you," a woman said, amusement tingeing her words.

Sarah changed the angle of her head, spying a woman who stood near the home's elegant front door, arms crossed, blond hair pulled back in a ponytail.

"Mommy," said the boy. "Help."

Which made the woman laugh and then clap her hands and call out, "Clifford," as she walked toward her son.

Sarah drew back from the window too late—the woman caught Sarah's eyes. "Hey there," she called out, bending down and picking up the silky-coated dog. "Good morning."

Sarah smiled, horribly embarrassed that she'd been caught snooping on her hostess and her son.

"Come on up from the grass, Randy," the woman said, helping her son to stand, the cocker spaniel still trying its darnedest to lick the boy's face, pink tongue fully extended in the child's direction.

"But, Mommy. Want to play with Fifford."

"Clifford will be here when you get back. You've woken up our guest and we should let her get some sleep."

"Oh, no," Sarah called, going to the door and opening it before she checked her appearance.

Smart, Sarah, you probably look like a bag lady. Way to make a first impression.

But to be honest, she was more worried about Cece Sanders thinking she'd woken her.

"I was already up," Sarah said, tugging down her sleep shirt just in case. "I was just lying in bed."

"Randy didn't wake you?"

Sarah could see now that Cecelia Sanders was one of those stunningly gorgeous women that didn't need makeup to help her be pretty. Even with her hair pulled back tightly and wearing a pink T-shirt and plain old blue jeans she looked good; like one of those high fashion models posed to look "casual" although there was probably nothing "casual" about the price of her clothes.

"No," Sarah said, trying not to feel envious. If God had wanted her to be a skinny blonde, she'd have been born skinny and blond. Wasn't much point in being jealous of the woman in front of her, especially not when she smiled in such a warm and friendly way, and when she had a squirming dog in one hand (who'd transferred his attention to *her* face by now) and a writhing child by the other hand, writhing because the little boy had spotted *her* now and it was obvious he wanted to go see the new stranger.

"Mama, go," he said, reaching his arms out to Sarah.

"It's okay," Sarah said. "I love children."

The blonde held her eyes for a second, Sarah getting the impression that she'd just been scanned as thoroughly as a pack of Twinkies at a checkout counter. The woman let the little boy go, and Randy raced toward her as if they'd known each other their entire lives.

"Hey, little guy," Sarah said, kneeling down so she could greet him at eye-level. Oh, how she missed her kindergartners.

"Hair," the little boy said, pointing.

Sarah laughed. "Lots of hair," she said, going nose to nose with the boy. "And you have biiiig eyes."

It was the child's turn to laugh. Sarah glanced up again. Cecelia had a slight smile on her face, her head tilted as she watched the two of them.

"Do you mind if I pick him up?" Sarah asked.

"No. Go ahead."

So Sarah scooped Randy up, balancing him on her hip and little minding that her hair appeared to be Randy's latest pull toy.

"Careful," his mom said.

"No, it's okay," Sarah replied. "I'm used to it." She spun Randy around, the little boy smiling when she stopped.

Cecelia watched her, saying, "You're good with kids," after a few more spins.

"I used to be a kindergarten teacher."

"Really?"

"Yeah," Sarah admitted, and no doubt Cece Sanders could see the sadness in her eyes. "I miss it."

"I bet you do," the woman said.

IT TURNED OUT that Cece (as she liked to be called) was on her way to drop off Clifford (so named in honor of the big red dog) at the groomer's and then do some shopping and Sarah didn't know who was more surprised, Cece or Sarah, when an offer was extended for Sarah to join them.

"I know it might seem kind of strange," Cece said. "We just met, but Randy seems to like you and I could sure use the help. He's a handful and my back can get sore from time to time."

"Your back?"

"I was injured a few years ago," she said. "And it still hurts every so often."

Sarah felt like a fool. She'd known that Cece Sanders had been an FBI agent before marrying Blain. Sarah had read about how she'd been injured in the line of duty. Actually, she'd been injured at the track. Sarah had just forgotten.

"Well, okay then," Sarah said. "Sure, I'd love to go. I really appreciate you letting me stay here and so *any* time I can help you out, you just let me know."

Cece smiled, her gaze so warm Sarah found herself thinking she must have a kind soul. Generosity of spirit all but poured from her eyes.

"Thanks," she said. "I may take you up on that."

So a half hour later they set off, Sarah trying not to gawk at the banana-yellow Hummer Cece Sanders drove. "Safest vehicle on the road," she said, backing out of a palatial garage. "And this one has armor plating."

"Seriously?" Sarah asked.

"Seriously," Cece said with a smile.

They lapsed into silence. Sarah found herself wondering how she'd gotten from teaching kindergarten in California to driving through some of the prettiest country Sarah had ever seen while inside a banana-yellow Hummer. It seemed a bit surreal, actually, and yet...nice.

"So you're Lance's girlfriend," Cece said, darting Randy, who was sitting in his car seat behind them, a glance in the rearview mirror.

"Who told you that?" Sarah asked.

"Becca."

Ah. Well, that explained that. "I'm not his girlfriend."

"You're not?" Cece asked. "Randy, don't put your thumb in your mouth, baby, it'll give you crooked teeth."

"I'm not," Sarah said. "I never really was."

"Never *really?* What does that mean?"

And just like that the story came pouring out. Well, most of the story, anyway. She left out the part about her and Lance spending the night together, but Cece seemed to know.

"And so I was surprised when he showed up yesterday. I thought Sal was arranging for a rental car."

"I'm not surprised he showed up," Cece said. "Lance is that way. I've never met a man with a bigger heart. Well, aside from my husband, Blain."

"Your husband seems like a nice man."

"He is," Cece said. "I think men who've had it tough as a child either end up as total jerks or total princes."

"Did Lance and Blain have it tough?"

"Yeah, but in totally different ways. Blain grew up with a silver spoon in his mouth, but that spoon was provided by a workaholic father who was never around. Lance grew up in a home where his father was *always* around—because he was always drunk."

"You're kidding."

Cece shook her head. "Nope. Lance went to work at fourteen in order to help the family make ends meet."

"You're kidding."

"Yup. Local auto mechanic gave him a job sweeping floors. The guy had a son that raced quarter midgets, but he grew out of them. One day he decided to put Lance in one of his kid's old cars and the rest, as they say, is history."

Lance had grown up poor. Sarah had no idea why the realization left her reeling.

"He's worked hard to get to where he is today, and everybody at my husband's shop knows it.

That's why it was great to see him win that race. I understand we have you to thank for that, too. Special cookies or something?"

Was there nothing the woman didn't know? Sarah found herself laughing nonetheless. "That's what Lance claims, but I'm not convinced my secret voodoo cookies had anything to do with his winning."

"Well, you and *I* know that, but the men won't think that. They get weird about things like that."

"So I've heard."

"So why don't you bake Lance a batch of cookies for the race this weekend and I'll take them to him?"

"Are you going?"

"Yeah. I usually attend the races that are on the east coast. It's not a long flight and so if Randy gets fussy it's usually not a problem. Except Randy was sick weekend before last, so I stayed home from Daytona."

That explained why Sarah hadn't seen her before Chicago.

"So," Cece said as she flicked on her blinkers and made a right-hand turn. "Will you do it? Will you bake the team cookies?"

Sarah smiled and then shook her head. "I'll do it." But, she sternly told herself, she was doing it for the Sanderses, *not* Lance.

CHAPTER TWENTY-THREE

HE CAME IN SECOND.

Sarah watched the race from the nanny quarters after refusing Cece's offer of a ride to the track—she didn't have the courage to face Lance. Besides, the motor coach was still broken and so she could legitimately claim she had no business being at the track, although Cece didn't appear to buy it.

Cece and Blain got back right as the sun set, the Carolina sky fading from purple to blue to gray.

"Can you believe it?" Cece asked. Sarah felt touched and surprised that Cece had come to see her before going inside her own home, Blain holding Randy in his arms. And even after her plane flight and long day, Cece looked more glamorous than Sarah could ever hope to look in rhinestone encrusted jeans and a gauzy silk top that exactly matched the green in Cece's eyes.

"Your cookies worked."

"Worked," Randy echoed enthusiastically, trying to wiggle out of his father's arms.

"It's okay. You can let 'er rip," Sarah told Blain.

They'd been gone three days, Sarah taking over household duties, something they'd offered to pay her for but that Sarah refused. Oddly enough, Lance was still paying her.

"Sair-ah," Randy said, reaching for her with his arms.

"I swear," Cece said. "I wish you'd quit working for Lance and come be our nanny." It was an idea that had been mentioned before. "Blain and I talked about it again and since you refused us the last time, we've decided we'd offer you double whatever Lance is paying you, plus we'll provide room and board."

"Oh my gosh," Sarah said, giving Randy an exaggerated look of surprise which made him laugh, although inside she was doing anything but laughing. She should jump on the offer, she really should.

But she didn't.

"I don't know. I'll have to think about it."

"Don't think too long," Blain said. "We'd really love to have you. Cece says you've been a big help."

Sarah caught Cece's eyes. Blain's wife studied her closely; too closely.

"You think about it," the woman said. "And in the meantime, you keep baking those cookies." She lifted her hands in the air, doing a little dance. "We came in second, came in second, sec-ond."

Sarah smiled as well. How could she not? She'd felt a spurt of elation, too, when she'd watched

Lance cross the start/finish line. Second. It wasn't a win, but it was close enough.

"Oh, and before I forget," Cece said. "Tomorrow is Little Racer Day at the Huntersville Mall. I'd really love for you to go because it's a special event held just for kids and it's so much fun watching them meet the drivers. Their joy is contagious. Lance will be there, too," she said before Sarah could ask. "I know things might be awkward between you, but you have to face him sooner or later. Heck, you're still technically employed by him."

Face Lance? Tomorrow?

Sooner or later it would have to happen, she admitted, but after watching Lance grin into the camera that afternoon, she wasn't so certain she was ready. She'd been unable to tear her eyes away from him, unable to stop herself from feeling elated and happy and overjoyed that he'd come in second. But most of all, she'd had to squelch a nearly irresistible urge to pick up the phone and call him.

"I'll go," she said, even though a little voice inside her head told her it was more than likely, a bad, *bad* idea.

"Great," Cece said. "I'm so glad. So, we'll see you tomorrow then?"

"Yeah," Cece said. "Sure."

It would all be over tomorrow. She knew deep in

her heart that she had to accept the Sanderses' offer of a job. Working for Lance had to come to an end.

Especially since she'd started to fall in love with him.

THE NEXT DAY WAS so overcast and gray, and the air so thick and warm, that Sarah knew thunderstorms were on their way. The central coast of California was arid and dry, so it still surprised her to hear the distant boom of thunder, cumulus clouds with atomic-looking tops mushrooming into the upper atmosphere. It was, Sarah decided, the perfect day to quit a job.

Cece drove, Randy strapped in the back seat, and Sarah was treated to a blow-by-blow account of the race, something that she knew she'd be forced to listen to time and again. Of course, her job with Cece might be temporary, too, something Sarah had already made clear. Teaching was her first love. Life in the fast lane had only ever been a temporary pit stop—she gave herself a mental pat on the back for that appropriate metaphor.

The mall was packed, at least judging by the parking lot. Of course, that might be because the mall was always packed, but Sarah somehow doubted it. There were an awful lot of vehicles sporting their favorite driver's car number, the surest sign of a race fan.

"Ready?" Cece asked after they'd transferred Randy to a stroller, a middle-aged man doing a double take when he caught sight of her. That was to be expected given that Sarah felt like a gawky teenager next to the prom queen. But when someone else did a double take near the entrance to the mall, Sarah started to doubt that it was just Cece's looks. She had a feeling Cece Sanders had been recognized.

"Is Blain coming?"

"He said he'd meet us here," Cece said, smiling at someone who called out her name as if they knew her. Cece waved.

"Do you know that person?" Sarah asked.

"No."

They were stopped every ten feet, perfect strangers and their children chitchatting with Cece as if they'd known her her entire life. Cece just took it all in stride, slowly making her way toward the center court where the Little Racers event was being held.

There were hundreds, literally *hundreds* of children around, their parents holding their hands or pushing them in strollers. It was a single-story mall with brightly lit neon signs reflecting off the polished floor. The center court was actually an atrium nestled between four major department stores. Lush plants spread their foliage toward a glass ceiling, the air thick with humanity and the dark chocolate smell of freshly watered plants. When they finally made it through the thick crowd, Sarah realized this wasn't an autographing like she'd thought it would be. This was more like a schoolroom.

Numerous awnings had been erected over craft tables, and children were sitting around with their favorite drivers while they made cutout cars with construction paper, or decorated T-shirts with paint pens. Parents stood around the perimeter observing, huge smiles on their faces as they watched their children laugh and interact with some of the world's most famous stock car drivers.

It made Sarah misty-eyed. She was just so touched that not one, not two, but at least twenty drivers had taken the time out of their busy schedules to do this. Or maybe it was the way joy seemed to emanate from the food court, like a happy cloud that hovered over the place. Or maybe it was the sight of Lance, tongue tucked between his teeth, as he tried—not very successfully—to thread a bead, a small girl staring up at him with an unblinking stare, hero worship in her eyes.

"Kind of gets you right here," Cece said, thumping her chest with her fist.

"Yeah, it kinda does."

"And there's Rebecca," Cece said, waving to the redhead who was as chicly dressed as Cece. "C'mon. Let's go on in and help."

"Wait. Is that okay? I mean, I'm not anyone famous."

"Pssh," Cece scoffed. "Who said you need to be famous to make some kid's day? C'mon."

So they entered, a security guard letting them through once he recognized Cece. Hundreds of eyes watched their progress between craft booths, Sarah telling herself to ignore Lance, but like Lot's wife, unable to stop herself from taking a peek—just one little peek.

He stared at her. Sarah felt as if she'd been painted red, a bright, neon cerise that she was certain everyone around the perimeter could see. The little girl who'd been watching him tugged at his arm and he looked away, but not before he nodded at Sarah as if to say, "Hey."

With the ice broken, Sarah began to relax. Cece put Sarah to work, although not in the way Sarah had anticipated, that being to watch Randy. No, Cece put her to work painting wooden cars, with Todd Peters her "driver," and six little kids helping out. Sarah had met Todd only a few times before, so she was flattered when he said, "Hey, Sarah. Bring any cookies?"

With a laugh and a shake of her head, Sarah helped kids decorate toy stock cars. Boys and girls alike visited Todd's table, although the girls tended to glue sparkly beads on their cars rather than stick with traditional paint schemes. By the time the event was almost over, Sarah knew she had just about as much paint on her skin as the little cars had on their bodies.

"And so then what'd you do?" a little boy asked her, dipping his brush in the black paint so he could put the finishing touches on his tires. Todd was off signing autographs for the kids who hadn't gotten the chance to visit his table and so Sarah was all alone with her "kids," each of whom had her autograph and Todd's on the bottom of his toy.

"I closed my eyes," she said, concentrating on her own car, which she was painting pink. "I couldn't watch. It was too scary."

"So then how'd you see what happened?" a little girl asked. Her car was pink, too—Sarah had been touched.

"Well," Sarah said, remembering back to that long-ago day in Lance's motor coach when she'd watched him qualify. "I only closed them for a moment. And when I opened them back up again, the car was okay. Lance had brought it under control."

"And you think it was the cookies that helped?" another boy asked.

"Oh, I know it was the cookies," Sarah said, "because Lance told me afterward that after he bobbled that lap, he flipped up his visor, reached for one of my famous cookies and popped it in his mouth. And you know what happened then?"

"What?" asked another little girl, gray eyes wide, awe in her voice.

"He drove his fastest lap ever at that track."

"Wow," someone said, Sarah wasn't sure who. She was concentrating on painting a tiny number twenty-six on the side of her car.

"Lance told me he plans to grind some of those cookies up and put them in his fuel. You know, he got second last weekend. I haven't talked to him about it, but I wonder if that's what he did and that's why his car went so fast."

"My dad says Lance Cooper is all washed up."

Sarah looked up, a child of about eight years meeting her gaze with all the seriousness of a twenty-year-old race fan.

"He's a big Todd Peters fan," the child explained.

"Oh," Sarah said. "I see. Well, you tell your father that Lance Cooper is not washed up. You tell your father that I've seen Lance Cooper do things with a race car that would make Dale Earnhardt envious." Well, okay, maybe that was a bit of an exaggeration since she'd never even seen the famous Earnhardt drive. "You tell your father that Lance Cooper is going to blow the socks off the competition in the coming weeks, and not just because of my cookies, either, but because he's one of the best drivers out there, not to mention one of the nicest men on Earth."

Silence greeted her words. Well, okay, maybe not silence, one little girl with blond pigtails let out a few, "Ah hums," that were supposed to sound like coughs.

Then Sarah knew. She just knew.

"He's standing behind me, isn't he?" she asked *sotto voce*.

The little girl with the fake cough nodded.

"That's what I thought."

"Well, don't let me stop you," Lance said, coming around to stand next to her. "I want to hear more about how great I am."

Which made all the kids laugh and Sarah want to sink beneath the table. But then Lance bent down, Sarah's eyes all but bugging when he swiped a bit of paint off her nose, drawing back just a bit when he'd finished to stare into her eyes.

"Hey, Sarah," he said softly.

She was a goner. No doubt about it. As she stared into his eyes, her heart went as gooey as the acrylic ringing the sticky paint bottles.

"Hey, Lance," she said.

"Are you his girlfriend?" one of the little girls asked.

"I'm—"

"Yes," Lance said, cutting her off. "And since Todd has abandoned you, I thought I'd come on over and join you guys."

"Cool," said the girl with pigtails. "You can sign my car, too."

"I don't know," Lance said. "If I sign it after Todd's signed it, the car might combust."

"But your girlfriend signed it, too, and so I'm sure it'll be all right."

Which made Lance and Sarah both laugh.

From that point on, Sarah could only watch as Lance interacted with the kids at the table. Their gazes would meet from time to time, Sarah's whole body going still. She felt all funny inside, like she'd just gotten off a Disneyland ride, one that made her disoriented and unable to determine which way to the exit.

"Well," Cece said, Randy in her arms and clutching a string of beads that Sarah now realized was the lanyard portion of a credential holder. "Are you ready to go?" she asked Sarah, giving Lance a quick wink.

"Well, I—"

"I'll take her home," Lance said.

Sarah felt her breath catch. She knew instantly that if she didn't want things to go forward with Lance, now was the time to say something.

She kept quiet.

Blain Sanders came up behind Cece, putting his arms around Cece's waist. "'Bout time you two got back together. I was about ready to ask one of the other drivers to start flirting with Sarah just to get you off your you-know-what," he said with a smile.

"Yeah, well," Lance said, looking slightly embarrassed. "I was trying to give Sarah time to realize what a great guy I am, which, you two should be glad to hear, she does. She just told a bunch of kids what a great guy I am."

"Really?" Blain said. "Then you really do have her fooled."

"Blain," Cece said, elbowing her husband.

"Just kidding, just kidding," Blain said with a smile.

TWO MINUTES LATER, Lance took her hand and led her away, Sarah feeling suddenly shy.

"You do realize, don't you, that you're covered in paint?"

"I do," she said with a glance down at herself.

"But I don't care," he said, stopping suddenly and pulling her into her arms.

"Lance—" she started to protest.

"I missed you," he said.

"Did you?" she asked, looking up in time to catch his eyes.

"You have no idea," he said earnestly. "When I picked you up in Illinois all I wanted to do was touch you. But I was afraid of scaring you off. I worried that if I pushed you, you'd shut me down."

"I thought you'd moved on," she admitted.

His big hands reached up to cup her face, his head lowering as he whispered the words, "How could I move on after I'd fallen in love with you?"

Her breath hitched.

"You're it for me, Sarah. You have been from the moment I first set eyes on you. Or did you think I slept with all my motor coach drivers?"

"I wasn't sure," she said softly, sudden tears making her vision blur. "I just wasn't sure."

"Well, you should have been sure. I'm not into men and even if I was, Frank, my old driver, really never turned me on."

"Oh, Lance," she said.

And then he kissed her, Sarah's laughter fading as he softly and gently pressed his lips against her own.

"Get a room," someone yelled.

They broke apart. Todd Peters passed by.

"You're just jealous," Lance said, putting his arm around Sarah and pulling her, if possible, even closer.

"Jealous?" Todd said. "Of you? When I can whip your ass on the track? Not hardly."

"Jealous that I snagged Sarah and you didn't."

Todd looked contrite. "Well, all right. I'll give you that. But if you ever change your mind, Sarah…"

Sarah laughed, knowing he was joking, but flattered nonetheless. "I'll keep that in mind."

"Are you kidding?" Lance asked. "She ain't gonna want nobody after having me, are you Sarah?" Lance asked, his southern drawl more pronounced whenever he put on that fake leer of his.

"Well, I don't know—" she teased.

He kissed her. Again. Only this time he pushed her into a little alcove she hadn't noticed before, Lance lifting his head long enough to say, "See ya," to Todd Peters before he went back to kissing her between two public phones.

"Lance," she hissed, embarrassed. "People are staring."

"So," he whispered back. "I don't care who sees me kissing you, Sarah. Not now. Not ever. They better get used to it, just as you better get used to *being* kissed."

As his lips covered her own, Sarah thought there were worse things to have to endure.

A lot worse.

CHAPTER TWENTY-FOUR

LANCE FELT on top of the world.

After his second-place finish the previous weekend, he'd ended up on the pole at Pocono. Not because he'd suddenly mastered a track that had always eluded him in the past, but because of Sarah. Once again she'd managed to completely put things in perspective for him by reminding him that this one race would not make or break his career—and that (and this had made him smile) some kids repeated grades. He would be able to repeat Pocono next year if he failed to make the grade this year.

He just loved her teaching analogies.

But it had helped. She was right. Whatever happened, there was always next weekend—and next year. And so as he sat in his car waiting to lead the field out onto the track, he felt more relaxed than he could remember being in a long, long time.

Too bad Sarah didn't look that way.

"You're nervous," Lance said as he reached for his helmet, getting ready to strap it on, his words nearly drowned out by the thousands of people who'd come to watch the race, and who all looked down on him and his car while they were lined up on pit road. Sarah stood near the driver's side window, her eyes having never looked away from his own since the moment he'd crawled inside.

"I keep thinking this is a really small track," she said, looking up and at the grandstands, her brown eyes shielded by the bill of a Star Oil hat, brown hair poking out of the back like a horse's tail. He'd managed to get her into a Star Oil polo shirt, too, the orange star on her shirt pocket matching the one on her white hat.

"Nah," he said, giving her a reassuring smile. "It's not that small. Bristol, now that's small."

"I suppose so," she said, still pensive.

"Hey," he said, motioning for her to lean down next to him.

"What?" she said, red-brown brows lifting beneath the ball cap.

"Whatcha gonna give me if I win this race?"

She drew back, but only a bit, her lips pressing together just before she shot him one of her Naughty Boy looks. "I'll give you another 'I told you so,'" she said.

He shook his head, motioning her to lean closer. She tried to appear stern, but he could see the way her lips twitched a bit.

"How about a kiss?" he asked.

"*That* I'll give you even if you *don't* win the race."

He smiled just before she leaned down and gave him a kiss, Lance thinking that it was really true: she didn't care. She wasn't hung up on his winning the championship, or about his fame—or anything to do with racing, except for him.

"Time to break it up, you two," Allen, his crew chief said.

Lance pulled back, wondering why it was that some drivers preferred not to say much to their girlfriends or wives on race day. Frankly, he counted on Sarah to calm him down.

"Let's blow this taco stand," Lance said, smiling up at Sarah one last time before putting in his earpieces and donning his helmet.

But before they put up the window net he tapped the side of his car, catching Sarah's attention. She turned back, clasping the hand he held out, Lance giving her a squeeze. She smiled and squeezed back.

And that, Lance decided as he started the car, was the way he wanted to start every race of his career. And by God, just as soon as this race was over, he would make sure that's exactly what happened.

JUST ANOTHER DAY at the track.

That's what Sarah kept telling herself. It was just another day at the track with Lance doing what he loved to do most in the world, the forty-three car field just then rounding turn four sounding like a swarm of angry locusts.

Just another day of biting her nails and praying he came home safe.

"He'll be just fine," her mother said after catching up with her near pit road. Sarah resisted the urge to shield her eyes whenever she glanced in her mother's direction. There were so many rhinestones sewn onto her mom's shirt, she looked like a walking explosion. Typical Sylvia attire. And typical of her to crash yet another race. Sarah mentally winced at the word "crash."

"I know he'll be fine," Sarah said, something clenching in the pit of her stomach as she said the words. Fear? It sure felt like that. "I'm just in a hurry to get back to the motor coach. I don't want to miss the start of the race."

"Why don't you watch it with Hank and me in the pits?" her mother asked, her penciled brows lifting.

"Because I don't want to be in the way."

"Then get up on top of the pit box. Lance told you that'd be okay—"

"Mom," Sarah said, stopping to turn and face her. "I don't want to watch the race from pit road," she said. "Now, you can either come back to the motor coach with me—" please, God, no "—or, you can stay here. But whatever you decide, I'm going back to the coach."

"Fine, I'll watch it with Hank," her mother said, sounding petulant. "If you change your mind, you know where to find us."

As if she would ever seek her mother out.

Sarah! She mentally chastised herself. She is your *mom*.

Yeah, but she didn't have to advertise that fact.

"I'll see you after the race," her mother said.

"Yeah," Sarah said. "After."

"From the winner's circle," Sylvia called.

"I hope," Sarah muttered.

She very nearly missed the start. Sarah arrived back at the motor coach just in time to see the green flag drop. Lance fell back immediately, which Sarah knew by now was all right. There was plenty of time to fix whatever might be wrong with the car, though she was disappointed for Lance's sake as he sank back in the field.

"Damn," she said into the empty motor coach, back in service after Stalker Fan's sabotage. "Just relax, Lance," she told him, reaching for the scanner that sat on the kitchen counter and flipping it on.

"It's looser than Sarah after she's had a few drinks," Lance was saying.

"Hey," Sarah said, wishing she had a headset with her so she could counter that remark. But her boyfriend knew well and good she was watching…and listening.

Boyfriend.

For a moment she allowed herself a moment of

wonder that she'd somehow managed to catch the eye of a race-car driver, one who claimed to be in love with her.

Claimed?

Well, all right, after the past few days, she was pretty certain they were both head over heels. The things he'd said to her…the things he'd done to her…her cheeks lit up like an OPEN sign, no doubt as red as her mother's lipstick.

Outside, she could hear the cars picking up speed again as they exited turn three.

"We'll try and get a handle on the problem during the first pit stop," Allen said, "Just sit tight for now, driver."

"Tight is what I wished I was," Lance said. "I'm telling you, Allen. This thing is bad loose. I'm gonna have to back it off some more."

And on the TV, Sarah watched, her anxiety mounting, as Lance faded back a couple more spots. The further back in the field you were, the more likely you were to get caught up in something, and her stomach clenched again, Sarah wondered if she were coming down with something. It wasn't like her to feel sick while watching Lance race.

"Outside," came the spotter's voice.

On TV Sarah watched as a brightly painted car passed Lance on the outside.

"Damn," he said. "Maybe I should pop the floorboard and stick my feet out like Fred Flintstone. Might help."

"Just be patient, driver," Allen said. "We'll get her fixed."

Another lap passed. Then another and another, Sarah wishing they'd show more of the entire field so she could watch Lance's car in action. But there was no need to see what was going on; the live leader board showed Lance falling farther and farther back.

"Something's really wrong now," he said a moment later. "Vibrating like crazy."

Vibrating? What would make a car vibrate?

And then there he was on TV, or rather, there his car was, Lance's helmet nothing more than a fuzzy blur behind the windshield. The television announcers were talking about Lance's handling issues, and how close he'd come to wrecking a few times, and that he might have a problem.

As if the announcer's words were a portent of things to come, Sarah watched in horror as the back end of Lance's car began to spin around. One of the cars behind him checked up, but it was too little, too late. Unable to stop his forward momentum, the driver plowed into the side of Lance's car.

"OH SHIT."

Lance knew it wouldn't be good the moment

he felt the ass end lift. Years of racing had given him an intuitive sense for what would happen next and sure enough, he felt his car roll sideways, flipping into the air like a kite whose string had been cut.

Boom.

It was all he heard, all he felt, the crash jarring every bone in his body and straining the helmet harness. Then he flipped again. And again, through the windshield loomed blue sky and then grass, blue sky and then grass and then…grass.

And then silence.

SHE WANTED TO VOMIT, except she couldn't—she had to run.

He'd wrecked.

Sarah had known it could happen, but watching his car flip over and over and over again, and then waiting to see if he would climb out… She truly felt sick as she ran toward the garage.

By the time she found the Star Oil hauler, she could barely speak. "Where is he?" Sarah asked the first person she could find. A tire changer named Tony, she thought.

"At the Infield Care Center," the burly man answered.

"Where's that?"

"Over by the Media Center."

"And where is *that?*" Sarah replied, her hands

shaking so bad she could barely swipe away a lock of hair that had fallen out of her ball cap on her mad dash over.

"C'mon," a soft voice said. "I'll take you."

Sarah turned. Cece Sanders.

"Thank God," Sarah said in a rush. "I don't know what to do or where to go, I'm so worried. Is he okay? Do you know? What did the paramedics say?"

"He's fine, Sarah. Got into the ambulance by himself and walked into the Infield Care Center." She frowned, blond brows drawing together. "The question is—are *you* okay?"

"No, I'm not okay. Seeing my boyfriend roll his car makes me most definitely *not* all right. And how can he be okay after crashing like that—"

"Sarah," Cece said, grabbing her by the shoulders, giving a squeeze that was meant to be reassuring. "He's fine. Really. He climbed out of the car and walked to the ambulance all on his own. Scout's honor."

"Are you sure?"

Cece gave her a stern look. "Yes. I'm sure."

Sarah wilted then, her shoulders sagging like wet paper towels. Actually, she could use some paper towels right now because suddenly she was crying so hard she could barely stand.

"I was so scared," she sobbed.

"You shouldn't have been. You'll see in a moment that he's fine."

THEY WERE ALMOST THE exact same words Sarah heard Lance say the moment they entered the single story Infield Care Center, a blast of cool air hitting her square in the face when she paused near the entrance of the off-white room.

"Sarah," he said in relief when he spied her standing next to Cece and Blain, Lance giving them a welcoming smile, too.

"Lance," she echoed softly, her eyes darting over him. No cuts. No bumps. No bruises. At least none that she could see.

Maybe he really *was* all right.

"Are you okay?"

"I'm fine," he said. And then, "Come here," when he must have seen how hard she fought to hold back tears. "You look worse than me."

"I was so scared," she murmured as he crossed the linoleum floor and drew her into his arms.

"I'm fine," he repeated softly. "Despite what the doctor says."

She drew back. "And what, exactly, *does* the doctor say?"

"That he appears fine on the outside," said an older man who stood near the middle of a room with two curtained cubicles that were obviously used for exams. A row of white cabinets stretched along the wall behind him. "But he's severely dehydrated. He's complaining of dizziness."

"I just need to drink some water," Lance said. "It was hotter inside that car than the fire Cece started on Thanksgiving Day."

"Hey," Cece said. "That turkey ended up being just fine."

"That's what we let you *think*," Lance said, turning to Cece and giving her a teasing smile.

His boss's wife came forward, opening her arms so that she could give Lance a reassuring hug, too. "Yeah, right," Cece said, saying in a softer voice. "But I'm glad you're okay."

"Thanks."

Blain came forward then, slapping Lance on the back. "Good to see you up and about."

"Are you kidding me? Takes more than a roll down the backstretch to keep me off my feet. Now, a roll in the hay—"

"Hey. Excuse me. I think you guys are missing the point," Sarah said, slipping between the two of them and directing the conversation back to where it should be: Lance. "He's not okay. I can tell by the look in his eyes that something's wrong. And the doctor says he's dehydrated." She turned to the fatherly-looking man. "Does he need to go to a hospital?"

"Yes, he does. He needs fluids. Right away."

"See," she said, turning back to Lance. "So you're going to the hospital. Now."

"Sarah, wait," he said, bending down and placing a kiss on her forehead, Sarah almost positive he wobbled a bit when he straightened. "There's no need to go tearing off. If it was serious, Doc here would have me airlifted out."

"That's a possibility," the doctor grumbled, the words obviously a threat.

"Don't fight it, Lance," Sarah said. "You're going and that's that."

"That's the pot calling the kettle black," he said with a weak smile. "Not long ago it was *you* refusing medical care."

"That was different. I didn't have a doctor standing over me."

"He's not ordering."

"Actually, I am," the doctor said. "You have no choice here, Mr. Cooper. You need to go."

"See," Sarah said, glancing at Blain and Cece so they could add their insistence. "Doctor's orders."

"You know the rules, Lance," Blain said. "If you're ordered to go, you need to go."

"This is ridiculous," Lance said, glancing between the four of them. "I'm just a little dehydrated. It'll go away." He turned to the cabinet, motioning for the water bottle that sat on top of it. "Here. Hand me that water. I'll take a big swig just to make you happy."

"Lance," the doctor said sternly, not even glancing at the bottle in question. "That's not going to do it."

"Sure it will." He took a step. Except…

He never made it.

The moment he turned, he tipped to the side. And then he started to fall.

"Lance!" Sarah cried in panic, dashing forward as he collapsed, his big body making a sickening thud when he hit the floor.

"Oh my gosh!" Sarah cried, reaching him a split second before the doctor. *"Oh my gosh."*

"Lance," the doctor said loudly. "Lance, can you hear me?"

No answer.

"Lance?" he asked again.

Lance shifted slowly. "Don't move," the doctor ordered.

"Fine," Lance mumbled, turning onto his side, "'m just fine."

But when he rolled onto his back, his pupils so dilated his eyes looked black, it was apparent to everyone that Lance Cooper was *far* from fine.

"HE'LL BE OKAY," Cece said over and over again, rubbing Sarah's back as they sat in Penn State-Geisinger's lobby an hour later.

"How can he be all right?" Sarah asked. "You saw him fall down. And then the whole way to the hospital he barely said a word—"

"But the doctor told you he might have a concussion now, thanks to his fall. That, combined with his dehydration, messed him up. But it's nothing serious. Well, it is, but he didn't even really pass out and so I'm sure it's nothing. Try not to think the worst."

Easy for her to say, Sarah thought. Cece hadn't ridden in the back of an ambulance for the half hour it'd taken to get to the hospital. When they'd arrived and wheeled Lance away, it was all Sarah could do not to burst into tears.

"Any word?" Courtney asked when she arrived a few minutes later.

"No," Sarah said in a small voice, a part of her so detached by everything that had occurred it felt like she was in a dream. "We're still waiting for word."

"Good," Courtney said. "That gives me time to make some calls."

Good? Lance had just passed out and all Courtney could think about was making phone calls? Sarah despised the woman then, she really did. She even opened her mouth to take her to task, but the receptionist called out her name right at that exact moment.

"Here!" Sarah said, darting up so fast Cece's hands fell away.

"You Lance Cooper's wife?" The woman asked with a lift of her brows, her hair so severely drawn back that it must have made raising them hard to do.

"No," Sarah said. "I'm his girlfriend. He doesn't have any family."

"Oh?" she asked. "Well, that's probably a good thing because the way he's cracking bad jokes back there—" she motioned to the E.R. behind her

"—he might have just driven away any family he had."

Sarah stared at the woman for a moment, trying to absorb her words, but when she flashed blinding white teeth, what she said finally sank in.

"He's cracking jokes?" she asked.

"Yup. Bad ones, too. Think maybe there really is something wrong with that head of his the way he keeps coming up with them."

Cece, who'd come up behind Sarah, exchanged a look with her, and smiled as if to say, "See. Everything's going to be fine."

"Was he just dehydrated?" Sarah asked, still thinking the receptionist wasn't telling her something.

"Won't know for sure until he returns from his CAT scan, but the IV the paramedics started seems to be doing the trick. We're just doing the scan as a precaution after his nasty fall. I'll call you when he's back in his room."

Sarah nodded, stepping back from the counter. Her mother arrived then with Hank in tow, the dark-haired man glowering at Sarah as if this was all her fault. Right behind them were Allen and a few crew members. The media arrived next, Courtney working a deal so that they'd leave them alone until more about Lance's condition was known.

But the biggest shock of the day was when Sarah's mother pulled her into an embrace. Large, comforting arms tried to shelter her, Sarah trying to pull away, but her mother wouldn't let her go. Eventually, Sarah began to relax, began to think that her mother truly *did* care. Sure, there was a side of her that wondered if Sylvia's worry had more to do with Lance than any type of maternal instinct, but when she drew back and looked into her mother's brown eyes, she saw genuine concern there, and compassion.

Sarah was humbled, floored, and really, truly touched.

And then came the moment Sarah had been waiting for, though it came what seemed like hours later. The big woman behind the counter was discreet, waving Sarah over in such a way so that no one else saw.

"He's back in his room," she said softly. "And he's asking for you. Through the door and to the right. Bed six."

"Is he going to be all right?"

"Doctor will fill you in."

Sarah turned toward the door.

"I'll come with you," her mother said, Sarah shocked to realize she'd followed her to the counter.

"Only one person allowed at a time," the receptionist said, the look she shot Sylvia one Sarah instantly recognized, having used such looks on her students before. "You can go in later."

Her mother sank back down on the couch,

Sarah taking a deep breath as she was buzzed inside to bed six.

Inside the E.R., there were curtained-off rooms, each with a gurney in them, some empty, some filled with people in various stages of care. She looked around, trying to find a number to identify the beds, but only the "real" rooms had numbers on the outside, and no bed six.

"I hear he has a girlfriend," a nurse was saying as she passed by.

"Yeah, but I hear she's not much to look at."

Sarah halted in her tracks.

"How do you know that?" the first woman asked another blonde.

"Dr. Lungren's a huge race fan."

"Doc Lungren? The obstetrician? Go figure. Lungren's single, too, though, so she would know. And she's a barracuda. Probably has her sights set on him."

"Can I help you?" Someone came up behind her, tapping her on the shoulder.

Sarah turned, but she glanced back at the two nurses who'd gone quiet.

Something snapped inside her then, something that probably had to do with her scare today, a death-defying ride in an ambulance, and her crazy mother in the waiting room. "I'm looking for Lance Cooper," she said, and then smiled at the two nurses. "I'm the girlfriend who's not much to look at."

Their mouths dropped open, which on the plump blonde wasn't all that attractive—gave her a second chin.

"Um, yeah, sure," said the person who'd tapped her on the shoulder, a woman with dark hair who Sarah hoped was the female obstetrician. "He's right over here."

Sarah straightened her shoulders like she'd watched Rebecca Newman do just before giving an interview, and fixed a look of aloof superiority on her face—she hoped—as she turned away.

Take that. And your catty comments, too.

But she forgot all about the nurses when the curtain to Lance's room was pulled back. He rested in a reclining bed, looking rumpled and yet no less handsome in his hospital gown.

"Sarah," he said.

That was all he said, just her name, but the look in his eyes made her breath catch. There was such a burst of happiness in his eyes, so much relief and sorrow. When he held his arms open, she went right to him, clutching and holding and inhaling him as she tried with all her might not to cry.

"It's okay," he said softly, rubbing her back. "I'm fine. Just a little dehydration mixed with a concussion. That's all."

"You passed out," she said, her whole body beginning to tremble. "That's not fine—"

"Shh," he soothed, pushing her back so she could look in his eyes. "It was the dehydration that made me pass out. The CAT scan was just a precaution. And the technician told me I'm fine, even though he also told me that technically he can't tell me that—we have to wait for a doctor, but I'm fine. Trust me."

The tears came then, pouring out of Sarah's eyes as if a darn spigot had been turned on.

"Hey," he said, cupping her face and wiping her tears away with his thumbs. "This is just a part of racing. It happens sometimes."

"I know," she said, swallowing what felt like a gulp of air. "I know. It's just that the doctor told you something was wrong. And then you refused to go to the hospital, and so when they did your CAT scan, I was worried they'd discover you had no brain because only a brainless idiot would be so pig-headed, and if you had no brain, what would I tell the press?"

He blinked once, twice, then slowly smiled, a laugh escaping as he drew her to him, nestling his chin into her hair, wrapping his big arms around her shoulders. "Sarah, sweet Sarah," he murmured. "I love you so much."

"I love you, too," she said, hugging him back. "I didn't realize how much until I saw your car flip over for what looked like a million times."

He gently pushed her back again, his face suddenly serious. "Do you?" he asked gently.

"Do I what?"

"Love me?" he asked.

Her face softened, tears coming to her eyes for a whole other reason. "I do, Lance. I really, really do."

He smiled, a grin so blinding she was certain the ceiling reflected its glow—a glow that warmed her heart and her soul.

"Good," he said. "Because that makes wrecking my car worth it."

CHAPTER TWENTY-FIVE

THEY RELEASED HIM that day.

Sarah and Lance flew back that evening; Sarah was never more relieved than when she caught sight of Lance's home and the sparkling lake behind.

"You know, Lance," she said. "I'd be really happy if you never wrecked again."

"'Fraid that's not possible," he said, giving her a reassuring grin as he helped her out of the car.

"I know," she said, sinking into his arms. "I just don't know if I'm cut out for this."

He drew back, looking suddenly serious. "You better be," he said, half joking, half serious. "Wrecking comes with the territory."

"I know," she said, pasting on a brave smile. "I'm just teasing."

But was she? To be honest, the whole thing had thrown her for a loop. Not only had the TV cameras thrust in her face surprised her, but so had their questions as they were leaving the hospital. On the way back to the track they'd listened to the race on the radio, Sarah blown away when she'd heard herself quoted.

"Welcome to fame," he'd said, smiling at her.

Welcome to fame.

"Yo, Mr. Lance," Rosa all but screamed as they opened up the front door; she came tearing toward them so fast Sarah worried she would knock Lance off his feet. "You scare me to death!" she cried, wrapping him in her huge arms.

"Rosa," he said, giving her an affectionate smile. "You know it takes more than a few little rolls to knock some sense into my head."

"It no the sense I'm worried about. It you," she said, Sarah surprised to see tears in the woman's eyes. "Cece tell me you okay, but I no believe it until I see with my own eyes. You okay?" she asked, clutching "Mr. Lance" by the face so hard she scrunched his cheeks.

"I'm othay," he said between squished lips.

She released him. And to her surprise, Rosa turned toward Sarah next. "And you?" she asked. "You doin' okay?"

"I'm fine," she said.

Rosa smiled widely. "Good. I no like you wrecking, Mr. Lance, but it part of you job." She wagged a finger at him. "Just don't you be doin' it again, *sì*?"

"See," Lance said, smiling.

And that was that.

Except…that wasn't that. The phone began to ring

practically the moment they stepped into the house, and Sarah's hope to have Lance to herself—all right, to have Lance *in bed* to herself—faded away. All the motor sports reporters in the world wanted to talk, and Lance had insisted to Courtney that he take the calls himself. Sarah wasn't sure what to do with herself. It didn't help matters that they were still so new to their relationship that she wasn't really sure if she was living with him or not. Most of her stuff was still over at the Sanderses', and Lance hadn't mentioned anything, which meant he might want a night to himself…

"Whatcha thinking?" he asked, startling Sarah, who had moved to the patio. She sat in a lounge chair staring out at the lake. The afternoon sun sparkled off the water, making it glow as if liquid fireplace embers covered its surface, causing Sarah's vision to spot when she glanced up at Lance.

"I'm wondering if I should leave," she said, her gaze lowering to the rock patio. "You know, let you get some rest?"

"Are you kidding?" he asked her, drawing her up and wrapping her in his arms. "You're never leaving my side."

"Do you mean that, Lance?" she asked, meeting his gaze. "Or are you just being flip?"

"I'm not being flip, Sarah. I want you here."

It was such a relief to hear those words, very nearly a physical release, the tension in her shoulders easing suddenly. Sarah realized in an instant how stressed she'd been. Sure, they'd said they loved each other, and sure she was reasonably certain he'd meant those words, but still…she'd known men in the past who had said that and then thrown her over a few months later.

Don't do that to me, Lance. Please, please, please, she thought, nestling her head in the crook of his shoulder.

"I want to take you upstairs," he whispered in her ear.

She tingled, her whole body coming alive at the words. "I want to go upstairs with you," she whispered back.

"Then let's go," he said, tipping his head down to give her a warm-up kiss, but his lips quickly made her want more.

"I want you," he said, kissing her ear, his tongue swirling around the inside and making her shiver.

"I want…" But she couldn't speak for a minute because he'd stopped kissing her ear and moved down her neck, nipping her sensitive skin, his head sinking lower and lower.

She moaned, tipping her head back and staring up at the half-moon above.

"Lance," she moaned, his teeth nipping her through her shirt.

"I love you," he said, lifting his head.

"I love you, too," she said, her whole body buzzing from his touch. God help her, she wished it could be like this always. Just the two of them.

But it would never be that way. Life with Lance

would be a whirlwind, always. And though later he touched her soul in ways no man had ever touched her before, thoughts kept intruding, niggling doubts and worries that she tried to shove firmly aside. She couldn't shake a feeling that sooner or later, the other shoe would drop.

She just wasn't expecting it to drop quite so soon.

SARAH MOVED INTO Lance's house the next week. And while she appreciated his palatial estate after living most of her life in places so small and run-down, they made homeless shelters look like presidential suites, she still wasn't used to living a life of luxury. She couldn't get used to Rosa being around all the time, cooking for her and cleaning up after her. She couldn't get used to her every desire being just a phone call away. And she couldn't get used to doing nothing all day. She still wanted to teach and so she busied herself with sending out résumés—but to no avail. Lance told her she could still drive the bus for him, but she was happy to hand that job over to someone else.

Rebecca and Cece came over sometimes, which was a good thing because often Lance was off doing things—autographings, appearances (though no more calendar girl contests—thankfully), testing his race car—and she was left pretty much to herself.

On that particular day, the day that would ulti-mately change her life forever, Sarah kissed Lance goodbye early in the morning and then promptly went back to sleep.

A knock woke her.

That wasn't all that unusual. Rosa would sometimes knock if she thought Sarah might be up. But this wasn't her usual, tentative, are-you-awake-or-sleeping knock? This was a, "Get up, you lazy slug, I have something to tell you."

Sarah sat up, shoving her loose hair off her face and then quickly scrambling out of bed and diving for the floor to look for her purple night shirt and matching pants.

"Thank God you are awake," Rosa said, swinging open the door right as Sarah pulled her pants up over her waist.

"Well, actually, I wasn't—"

"You must see this," Rosa said, holding out what looked to be a newspaper.

Sarah stared at it. She didn't want to look. She didn't want to see whatever it was that Rosa had woken her up for because sure as the sun was rising, it wouldn't be good news. All it took was one look at Rosa's pale face. The woman wore so much dark brown foundation that with her skin so white, Sarah could see where she'd missed spots.

"What is it?" Sarah asked.

"Look," she said, waving the paper.

Sarah's own face stared back at her from the

cover of the *TATTLER*, her mouth tipped up in a smile that was supposed to look sensuous, but that had always looked uncomfortable to Sarah, likely because that was exactly the way she'd felt when she taken the photo.

"Oh dear Lord, no," she murmured.

But sure enough, there she was, leaning back on red satin pillows, black bars in the spot where her bathing suit top and bottoms were supposed to be, black bars because once again she wore someone else's…parts.

"SARAH, CALM DOWN," Lance said over the phone from pit road at Phoenix International Speedway where they were testing a few cars for the November race. "I'm sure it's not as bad as you think."

"Not as bad as I think?" Sarah said. "Lance, I'm wearing Pamela Anderson's breasts and God knows who else's you-know-what, and on a nationally distributed magazine that's next to every grocery store register in the country. Women the world over are catching sight of that photo and wondering a) who's the bimbo with the bars across her private parts and b) why is she on the cover of the *TATTLER*? But, see, they won't be wondering for long because right above my picture is the headline Lance Cooper's Latest Squeeze Revealed."

"Sarah," he said. "Nobody reads the *TATTLER*."

"Hey, Lance," Brad, his tire changer, said, "you seen the *TATTLER* this week?"

"Shh," Lance hissed.

"I think you'll like the cover," Brad said.

"What was that?" Sarah asked. "What did he say?"

"Nothing," Lance said, giving Brad a glare.

"He said you'd like the cover, didn't he?"

"No. He said…" *Think, Lance, think.* "…he said *Hot Rod* magazine has a nice cover this month. There's a '69 convertible on it."

Silence.

She didn't buy it.

"The only thing that has its top down," she said in a low, obviously irritated voice, "is me." And then, "Son of a *bitch.*" The word was said with relish. Obviously Sarah was enjoying her brief flirtation with cussing. "How the *hell* did this happen? How? *How?* And why would they put me on the cover of that magazine? Me? The girlfriend of some obscure race-car driver."

"Obscure!"

Silence again. "I didn't mean that the way that sounded."

Lance wasn't so sure, but he wasn't about to call her on it now. "Sarah, calm down," he said again. "This'll blow over in a couple of weeks. In the meantime we can call the *TATTLER* and tell them that those are not your private parts. We'll get them to print a retraction."

"A retraction?" she said. "A retraction? And just how many people do you think will actually see a retraction printed in the back of the *TATTLER*, likely written in the tiniest of print, buried beneath an article about alien autopsies or something? How many, Lance? How? Just take a guess."

"I don't know," he said lamely.

"None," she said. "Nobody will see a retraction, if they even print one. Nope. I'm ruined. Any teaching job I hoped to get in this town is shot. The whole industry will have heard about this in a matter of days. Word will spread. Nobody's going to hire a kindergarten teacher who's been 'revealed' to every mom in the county, not to mention their husbands."

"So. Don't teach. Come work for me. You can do something at the shop for the team."

More silence, and then, "Lance, I don't want to work for the team."

"Lance," Allen said. "We need to get started."

"I'm coming," Lance said. "Look, Sarah, I'll be home tomorrow night. Don't stress out. We'll figure something out. I promise."

"How, Lance?" she asked. "How can we fix this?"

"I don't know—"

"Never mind," she said. "I'll fix it myself."

And the line went dead. Lance realized she'd hung up on him.

Crap. This he did not need, not when he was about to get behind the wheel.

"Lance?" Blain asked. "You okay?"

They were camped out on pit road, the back of

the hauler open, his crew in the shade beneath the
car ramp. To the left, next to a stack of tires, the
team's engineers sat behind a folding table, computer open, everyone waiting for him to climb in the
car and go do some laps.

Shit.

"Lance?" Blain asked, black brows aloft.

"It's Sarah," Lance answered, hating to drag Blain
into this. "Apparently, a few doctored-up photos of
Sarah are on the cover of the *TATTLER*."

"The *TATTLER*? And what do you mean 'doctored
up'?"

Lance shook his head, "They were taken years
ago, by an ex-boyfriend. But then someone else
fiddled with them because Sarah swears she's never
posed nude."

Blain looked momentarily skeptical, but it faded
quickly, turning into concern. "Sounds like a
lawsuit to me."

"Yeah, but she's pretty upset."

"I can understand why. Sarah's not used to things
like this. She's never been in the national spotlight,
Lance. It's got to be pretty humiliating."

"Yeah," Lance said. "I'm sure it is." He turned
away for a second, only to face Blain again. "Shit.
I don't know what to do."

"You want to go home?"

Home? He couldn't do that? But Lance glanced

at the brightly painted big rig, at the empty grand-stands and the suites in turn one nonetheless.

"No," he said. "I'll call her later. She'll be okay until then."

SARAH DID SOMETHING she swore she'd never do again, something she'd promised herself that she'd only ever do if she were dangling over a pool of crocodiles and the only choice left was to cut the rope and end her own life or pull out her cell phone and dial her mom.

She dialed her mom.

"Sarah," she said immediately. "Thank God. Lance has called here at least a thousand times—"

"Mom—" Sarah tried to interject.

"Where are you? What the hell is going on? Lance told me some photos were published of you. Those weren't the same photos—"

"Mom," Sarah tried again, louder.

"Because if they were," her mother was saying, "I really think you ought to sue the man that took them. He can't keep on doing this without your permission—"

"MOM," Sarah yelled, covering her eyes with her hand even though it was pitch-black outside. The only light that made it through her splayed fingers was from a giant Best Western sign that hung overhead.

"And Lance is so worried about you. He said

you're not answering your cell phone and that Rosa said you left the house."

Sarah didn't say anything. It was true. She'd been ignoring Lance's calls—all ten of them.

Finally, *finally,* her mom stopped speaking. "Sarah?" she asked, as if afraid Sarah had hung up on her, a legitimate concern given how many times she'd done that in the past.

"Mom, I'm on my way back to California."

"You're *what?*"

"I'm on my way back. I needed some time away from Lance, somewhere far away from Mooresville and the whole racing community. So I'm headed back to California."

Silence.

"I know this seems sudden." *There you go, Sarah, trying to explain things to your mom. Will you never learn?* "But it's not really sudden. I've been a little weirded out since his wreck. I mean, who wouldn't be after watching their boyfriend flip a car at a hundred and sixty miles per hour? But it's not just that. I mean, I've always known Lance could get hurt. It's the whole fame thing. The media circus. The constant attention. I just—"

Stop trying to justify this, Sarah.

"I just don't know if I'm cut out for this kind of life."

More silence, the only sound the roar of the nearby freeway and a car door slamming in the hotel parking lot. *Okay. Here it comes.*

Sarah braced herself for the inevitable lecture, and for the inevitable barbed comments that would make her feel as low as chicken poop on the bottom of her mother's heel.

To her surprise all she said was, "Where are you?"

"Kentucky."

"Are you stopped for the night?"

"I am. But, Mom, please don't tell Lance where I am. Please, please, please. Just tell him I need some time away."

"Don't you think *you* should be the one to do that?"

"I will," she said into her cell phone.

Oh, yeah? When?

"Just not right now."

"When?"

"In a few days."

"Over the phone?"

"No, I—"

Oh, jeez. What was she doing? What was she *doing?*

"I just need some time," she mumbled. "I'll see you in a few days."

To her surprise, all her mother said was, "Drive careful," something that made Sarah immediately suspicious. Cripes. Her mother was probably dialing Lance right now, telling him where she was.

Her cell phone rang.

She looked down on the display.

Okay, maybe not talking to Lance because that

was him. Sarah stared at the number for a full five seconds before looking away.

There were tears in her eyes when she shut off her phone.

"ON HER WAY to California?" Lance said.

"She says she needs some time," Sarah's mother explained. "That she's not certain she's cut out for life with a famous race-car driver. Or words to that effect."

Not sure she's cut out…?

"That's ridiculous," he said. "I love Sarah. She knows that. All the rest of it—" he waved his hand, staring out the window of his home office "—all the rest of it doesn't mean a thing. It's just BS that you have to put up with."

But Lance could practically see Sarah's mom shaking her head on the other end. "It's not BS for Sarah," she said. "She's not the sort of person that's comfortable in the spotlight. When she was ten her teacher signed her up to play a part in the school play. The day before the play opened, she got hives so bad her eyes swelled shut."

Great, he thought, his hand clenching around the cordless phone. Just great. And he was only learning this *now.*

"Look, Lance, she'll be here in a few days," Sylvia said, her voice sounding calm, certainly more calm than Lance felt. "I'll call you then."

"Call me every night. I want to make sure she's all right."

He thought he heard a sigh, knew for a fact he heard her mom take a deep breath. "You really do love her, don't you?"

"I do," he said, shaking his head again. "And I can't believe she's let those pictures get to her so much."

"Hives," Sylvia Tingle reminded him. "Huge, gigantic boils. She didn't go to school for days."

Shit. He had a race this weekend. And he was going to drive like crap. He just knew it. He needed Sarah. She was his dojo master. His rock. His cookie maker.

And he loved her.

"I'll call you when she gets here," her mom said.

"Thanks, Mrs. T. And when you do, would you tell her that I love her?"

"I'll tell her," Sylvia said softly.

CHAPTER TWENTY-SIX

BUT IT WASN'T until later that week that Sarah arrived in California, and she was *not* in the mood for her mother's lectures. So when she pulled up in front of her mother's double-wide trailer, Sarah slipped out of her Bug, holding up her hand to stall the inevitable lecture that Sarah was certain her mother was waiting to unleash on her.

"Mom, I don't want to talk about it."

"I know. I know you don't, but I have something to say to you before you go inside."

And suddenly Sarah knew. She knew beyond a shadow of a doubt that Lance Cooper was inside her mom's trailer.

"Mom, you didn't."

"I didn't what?"

"You didn't tell Lance I was supposed to arrive today."

The guilty look on her mom's face said it all. "He loves you, Sarah."

"I don't believe it."

But why shouldn't she believe it? It was Saturday.

Lance didn't race until Sunday, and that race happened to be on the West Coast not more than two hours from here. She should have known this might happen. But she'd been so careful in keeping her arrival date vague.

"He's been here since last night. Someone else practiced his car today. Sarah, do you know how hard it was to arrange that? But he did it. For you."

She wanted to cover her face. She wanted to get back in her car and drive away. She wanted to run and hide.

But she couldn't hide. Not anymore. It was time to face the music.

"Wait out here," Sarah said.

"Sarah, stop." Her mom stopped her. "Before you go I have something else to tell you."

What? What more could she possibly say?

"It was Hank that tipped off the *TATTLER*. I found out after someone from the magazine called and when I confronted Hank, he didn't deny it."

Hank? Had tipped... Why, that no-good—

"I feel so bad," her mother said. "I know how much it hurt you, and how much trouble this caused and I'm so sorry. I kicked him out the moment he confirmed the truth. I may not have been a good mother in the past but I hope you know I'd never want to hurt you." She shook her head. "Jeez, I have such horrible taste in men. I don't know what's the matter with me. Why I pick such—" She stopped, straightened when she looked Sarah in the eye. "But that's not what I'm trying to say. What I'm trying to say is that I might not have such great taste in men, but I think *you* do. Lance is a winner, and I don't mean in a car, I mean with you. He *loves* you. I would give anything to have a man love me like that."

And despite herself, Sarah felt herself tearing up.

"Please, Sarah," her mom said. "Give him a chance."

Sarah held her gaze for a moment, but she didn't nod. Didn't agree or disagree. Instead she moved toward the trailer, but she hesitated near the front door until, with a deep breath and a stiffening of her spine, she opened it and went inside. The smell of the place enveloped her instantly: mac 'n' cheese and salami—what it always smelled like.

"Hello, Sarah."

Okay, why was she already crying? All he'd done was say hello.

"Hello, Lance," she said, finally gaining the courage to lift her head.

He looked good. And damn happy to see her. And so damn gorgeous. Lord, she couldn't believe a man like him actually claimed to love her.

"You left," he said, not moving toward her, something that took Sarah by surprise. She'd expected him to do what he always did—give her that boyish smile, maybe crack a joke or two, and then pull her into his arms. He didn't.

"I left," she echoed because, really, what more was there to say? She'd left and now she had to admit what a coward she was.

"Was it because of the pictures, because if it was, I've already got someone on that."

"It wasn't the pictures," Sarah said.

"Then why? Why'd you do it?"

"Because."

"Because what?"

"Because of everything, Lance. Because of the fact that I'm newsworthy enough to publish photos like that. Because of the fact that when I needed you, you were off testing cars."

"Sarah, that's my job—"

"I know that's your job," she interrupted. "I know that, Lance, and I understand," she said, sucking in a deep breath so she wouldn't cry. "And that's just it. Your job. It's so, so—" she searched for the right word "—amazing. You have this amazing job. This amazing life. This amazing everything and I'm such an ordinary woman."

"No, you're not," he said, coming toward her at last. "You're far from ordinary."

Sarah braced herself, trying not to flinch—or fling herself into his arms—when he touched her. She wore a T-shirt, but it felt like she wore nothing when his hand touched her flesh, every memory of those same fingers stroking her in different ways flooding into her mind.

"You shouldn't love me."

"Yes, I should. You're amazing, too. Beautiful, but you don't even know it," he said gently. "And your snores. Jeesh, I've never heard anything so amazing. And there's your rendition of 'Wheels on the Bus,' too." He smiled crookedly. "And I want you to sing that song to *our* children."

She wanted that, too. God, if he only knew how much. She wanted all that and so much more. And yet... "How will that be possible, Lance? How, when this thing you do for a living takes up so much of your time?"

"I don't know, Sarah. But we'll make it work. Other couples do."

"But we're not one of those other couples, Lance. I'm not one of those *other* women," she said. "I hate that women stare at you like they want you to be the father of their children, although come to think of it, they probably do. I hate that when they look at me they make me feel so inferior. I hate that I'm so damn insecure that whenever they get that glint in their eyes I want to run. But if I run, I worry that one of them will make a play for you, and when they do, if you're going to be strong enough to resist them."

"I would never cheat on you," he said emphatically, sternly, his eyes having gone hard.

"That's what you say, Lance. That's what every man says, and then something happens and before you know it, you're in bed with someone else and I'm at home wondering why you're working so late."

"But, Sarah, that kind of thing can happen in any marriage."

"But most marriages don't have to deal with trophy girls. Or, or helmet lickers. Or pit lizards. Or whatever else they're called in the garage. You should see what some of those women say about you online."

"Online?"

"Yeah," she admitted. "I've been lurking for weeks now and you should see what some of those women say about me. How I'm not pretty. How I'm fat. How frizzy my hair is. It's horrible and embarrassing and it hurts my feelings every time."

"Then don't *read* that crap."

"It's too late," she said. "I already have. The damage has been done and the truth is that I know myself well enough to know I'm not strong enough to deal with it. I may love you. I may love you more than I've loved any man in my life," she said. "But I'm not strong enough to *be* with you, to trust that you'll be my Sir Lancelot. Just the thought of trying to make this work, of all the worries and fears I'll carry with me. And now there's these…these *pictures* to deal with and just the thought of going to the racetrack makes me sick. I can't deal with it, I just can't deal with any of it. And I'm so sorry, Lance," she said, her voice clogging with tears. "I'm so darn sorry that I'm not strong enough for you."

"Sarah—" he said, trying to pull her into his arms.

She wouldn't let him, used her forearms to block him. "No," she said, shaking her head. "No," she said again. "Don't do that. Don't make this harder on me."

His arms dropped to his sides and she knew...she knew right then that he finally understood. That he was finally starting to get the message.

She looked down at her mother's seventies-orange carpet, at the numerous stains and missing patches, trying hard not to cry.

"Can I call you later?" he asked.

"No," she said. "Don't call. It'll only make things worse."

"So this is it then? This is goodbye?"

She still stared at the carpet. "It has to be."

"No, it doesn't," he said, the anger she heard in his voice causing her to lift her head. "It doesn't have to be this way and I can't believe you're ready to just walk away from this, from *us*."

But she'd expected his anger. She expected him to be stubborn, too. He hadn't gotten to be one of America's top race-car drivers by simply giving up.

"I'm sorry, Lance," she said, moving to her mother's front door, opening it, still not meeting his eyes.

"No," he said. "No. You look at me and tell me you want me to leave, Sarah Tingle. Look at me right now and say the words 'Leave, Lance Cooper.'"

She closed her eyes for a second, inhaling deeply,

praying for the strength. "Leave," she said, meeting his gaze and nearly crumpling to the ground at the pain and anguish that appeared in his eyes. "Leave, Lance Cooper."

"Sarah…"

"Fine. Then I will," she said because she couldn't, she just couldn't stand there another second. Couldn't continue to hurt him.

"Sarah—" he called out.

She brushed by him and then a second later, her mom, wiping tears from her eyes as she headed for her car.

"Sarah!" he called again.

But he didn't reach for her as she climbed into her car. Didn't try to open the door after she'd closed it. He stood by the driver's side and stared down at her as she started her car, Sarah feeling his gaze, hearing his calls as she backed out of her mom's gravel carport and drove away.

She drove away. But it wasn't just his heart that was breaking as she did it—it was hers, too.

CHAPTER TWENTY-SEVEN

"GIVE HER SOME TIME," Sylvia Tingle said as Lance watched her go, a pain in his stomach so great it made him feel ill.

Or was that his heart?

"I'm not sure that will help," Lance said, thinking he might puke.

"It'll help," her mother said, placing a hand on his arm. "She's smarter than me. Always has been. You just need to give her time so she can see the forest through the trees."

"I don't think she sees a forest," Lance said, his eyes on the spot where Sarah's VW had disappeared from view. "I think she sees a jungle, one with tigers and crocodiles."

"Then it'll be your job to cut through that jungle," she said. "Give her a glimpse of the paradise beyond."

"Kind of hard to do when she won't return my calls."

"Lance Cooper," Sylvia Tingle said. "You're a professional athlete. You telling me you're gonna walk away?"

And he almost smiled—almost, because the truth of the matter was, he might be a professional athlete, but even pros knew when to throw in the towel.

"I guess not," he said, but the words were more for Sylvia's sake than anything else. He'd seen the look in Sarah's eyes. It was over. She wanted him to leave her alone.

It was long past time that he did exactly that.

IT WAS FUNNY, really, because after Sarah drove away, she got mad.

Really, really mad.

So far, every man she'd ever met had messed her up. Okay, so Lance was the one notable exception, but everyone else had messed her up to the point that now she was such a basket case she was afraid of her own shadow.

It pissed her off.

Yes, *pissed,* she told herself, feeling yet another surge of emotion at the use of the vulgar word. Pissed, pissed, pissed.

She found the bar where her mother hung out, Cowtown Bar, same place she'd been coming to for years. Hank was right where she'd known he would be—sitting at the bar, his back to the door, black leather vest immediately marking him. There were other people in the bar, too, mostly locals. The bartender gave her a glance as she entered.

"You're a total piece of crap," Sarah said, coming up behind Hank and pushing him on the shoulder.

"Hey," he said, his eyes meeting hers for a second. And then his face lit up. "Sarah," he said.

His face lit up. As if he hadn't done anything. "Hey, nothing, you low-down piece of horse manure."

His gaze lifted, looking behind her. "Is Lance here?"

"No," she said. "And you better be grateful that he isn't because if he was, he'd sock you in the face." And at his look of surprise she said, "I know about the pictures, Hank. My mom told me what you did. But what I want to know is where you got copies of the photos."

"Hey look, Sarah. No need to get mad at me. Your ex-boyfriend Peter told me he was going to publish the photos. I just hooked him up with the *TATTLER*."

Peter had been going to publish the photos? "Peter? Are you sure it was *Peter?*"

"Yeah. He called looking for you and when you weren't around he told me what he was going to do. Just so happened I have this friend who works at the *TATTLER* and so I hooked him up."

And Sarah didn't know what shocked her more—that Peter had lied to her or that Hank seemed to think there'd been nothing wrong with "hooking him up."

"Why didn't you try and stop him?"

Hank shrugged, his complete lack of remorse

causing Sarah's temper to flare again. "Needed the money," he said when he finally noticed her outrage.

Still, it took Sarah a second or two before she could speak again. "You're a real piece of work, you know that? Don't you ever come near me again, you hear? Ever. If you so much as go to a NASCAR race, I'll make sure you get booted out."

"You can't do that," he sneered.

"Yes," she said. Never mind that she herself was through with the racing industry. It sounded good. "I can."

"Yeah, right," Hank scoffed. "You'll be lucky if NASCAR lets you back in the garage. Then again, maybe they don't mind a bimbo or two parading around."

Something snapped, something Sarah had no clue was within her. She clocked him, right in the face, and oh, how good it felt—and oh, how much it hurt. She gasped in pain at the same time he roared in anger and clutched his head. "My nose," he said. "You broke my fuckin' nose."

It felt like she'd broken a finger or two herself, but Sarah didn't care. "I'm going to break a lot more than that if you ever, and I do mean *ever* call a woman a bimbo again. Got it?" she asked, pushing against his shoulders and sending him reeling back over the bar. "You're a total piece of crap and you didn't deserve my mother."

And then she turned and left because to be

honest, she was a bit worried he'd retaliate. And her hand hurt so much that she had tears in her eyes.

All right, maybe she had tears in her eyes for another reason because suddenly she was so tired, so damn tired of feeling like everyone else's punching bag. Lance might have been one of the kindest, sweetest men she'd ever met, but those people who called themselves his fans, those women who lusted after him, they were cruel. As were the media, the article that had accompanied her photo so demeaning and sick she'd run to the bathroom and almost thrown up after she read it.

Life wasn't fair. But she wished with all her heart that it was.

Which was probably why she started to cry. She started her car, drove a half mile down the road, then had to pull over because the tears had started to come so fast and so thick that she couldn't see.

It wasn't fair.

She wanted Lance. She wanted him like she'd never wanted another man in her life. But she couldn't have him. She was too battered, too bruised to trust that things would work out between them. Best to end things now because if she were to trust Lance and something were to happen she wouldn't be able to survive.

Ah, heck, she thought, scrubbing at her wet cheeks. Who was she trying to kid? She was barely surviving right now. Obviously this was one of those cases where the cure might be worse than the disease. But she had to cure herself of Lance. She'd have to, because there was one thing she refused to do and that was to end up like her mother, bruised and beaten down by life and the men she'd dated.

CHAPTER TWENTY-EIGHT

THE NEXT WEEK Lance fingered a battered sandwich bag, the crumbs inside turning the plastic a powder-gray.

The last cookie.

It was dumb, really. He should have tossed the thing out. But for the same reason he wore purple underwear on race day, he couldn't bring himself to throw the cookie out even though by now it was nothing but crumbs.

Ah, hell, who was he kidding? He couldn't toss it out because it's the only thing he had to remind him of Sarah.

"Lance," Blain said, peeking his head in the lounge's door. "Practice starts in fifteen minutes."

Lance nodded, not looking up. He felt, rather than saw, Blain standing in the doorway.

"Did you get through to her?"

"No," Lance said.

His friend came in, placing a hand on his shoulder. "She'll come around. Look what I had to go through for Cece."

"Yeah, well, at least Cece understood racing. Sarah can't stand it."

"Then maybe she's not the right woman for you."

But as Lance stared at that bag, his eyes suddenly burned. "No," he said. "She was perfect for me."

And now she's gone.

"Cheer up," Blain said. "At least you won the race last weekend."

Yeah, but only because he'd been so furious, so mad, that he hadn't cared what happened out on that track. As a result he'd made a new enemy out of Dan Harris when he'd bump drafted the man out of the way. And later, he'd caused a ten-car pileup when he'd moved around the forty-eight.

NASCAR had *not* been pleased.

"And if we keep this up, you might just make The Chase."

But for some reason making The Chase didn't matter any more.

"C'mon," Blain said. "Let's go racing."

SARAH HEARD the announcer's voice coming from the black-and-white set in her mom's tiny family room. She rolled her eyes at the sound being turned up so that she could hear every word.

Rick Stevenson, sometime print reporter, sometime TV journalist, was talking to someone.

"How does it feel to be so close to making The

Chase when you started out the season so poorly?" he was asking someone.

"It feels good."

Sarah ducked her head, trying to cover her ears with her hands.

"Surprising, but good," he added, the sound so loud now Sarah could hear every word. Her mom had turned it up.

"I see you've got your cookie with you," Rick asked.

Cookie?

Sarah's head popped up.

"Yeah. It's a little battered, but I still have it."

"Think you need to get your girlfriend to make you some new ones?"

"I've been trying," Lance said. "But she won't return my calls."

"Did you hear that, ladies?" Rick said. "Lance Cooper appears to be single again."

That did it. Sarah shot up from her chair, the paper where she'd been circling Help Wanted ads falling to the ground.

"Where are you going?" her mother asked.

"Out," Sarah snapped.

Her mom shot up from her chair, stepping in front of the door before she could escape. "He still loves you," she said.

And Sarah realized something. Since she'd moved back home not one cross word, not one snide comment, not one derogatory remark had passed her mother's lips. Not only that, but she was wearing her hair differently, too. Less poofy. And less makeup. And looser-fitting clothes.

"Mom," Sarah said. "What's happened? You look…different."

"You're just noticing now?" her mom asked, swiping a lock of dark-blond hair off her face—a more natural blond.

"What happened?" Sarah asked again.

"Well, it was kind of funny, actually. I was watching a rebroadcast of a race we attended and I saw myself on TV, only at first I thought 'who's that fat woman on TV and why doesn't she do something with her hair?'"

Sarah's mouth dropped open.

"I know. Horrible. But, see, I didn't realize it was me and when I did, well, whew, talk about an eye-opener. And then I noticed something else," her mom said, her eyes peering into Sarah's, something floating in their depths—regret, sadness, maybe even sorrow. "I saw myself lean toward you, say something in your ear. It took me a moment to remember what it was I'd said, something about how you needed to dress better or something. But the thing was, you looked away, and when you did I could see the hurt was on your face—"

And to Sarah's total and complete shock, she spotted tears forming in her mother's eyes.

"I saw the hurt on your face and how your whole body seemed to wilt. I knew right then I'd done something stupid. My thoughtless words had hurt you and I'm so sorry, Sarah," she said, clasping her by the upper arms. "I'm so, so sorry for taking the joy away from you."

Tears were falling down Sarah's face by now, too.

"I say things sometimes. Stupid things. I don't mean to hurt you, but I guess that I do." She straightened. "Anyway. I decided then and there to make more of an effort at being nice. And to change the way I dress." Her hand fell back to her side. "For God's sake, Sarah, why didn't you tell me I looked like that?"

And Sarah laughed. She couldn't help it. Her mother looked so outraged that Sarah had let her traipse around looking like a paintball dummy that Sarah could only laugh and shake her head.

"Mom," she said. "You're too much sometimes."

And then her mother's gaze softened. "I know," she said. "But I love you."

Sarah did something totally unexpected then. She leaned forward and gave her mom a hug. "And I love you, too," she admitted.

"Thanks for not holding what happened with Hank against me."

"You're welcome," Sarah said, smiling. "But you sure do know how to pick them."

"Hopefully, that's going to change," her mom

said, laughing. "Maybe I can find myself a crew chief or something."

They both laughed then, Sarah realizing in that moment that, miracle of miracles, she and her mom might just end up as friends.

And if God could heal those wounds, maybe, just maybe he could heal others, too.

IT STARTED OUT as a nebulous idea, one that floated into Sarah's mind when she'd been talking to her mother. But it had taken shape in the ensuing weeks.

Men had been pretty miserable to her in the past—particularly the photo-faking Peter—and if she were ever going to take charge of her life, if she were ever to stop slinking away from problems, she needed to start standing up for herself. And so a few weeks after her heart-to-heart with Lance, she decided to do exactly that. Maybe it would make her feel better, since dodging Lance's calls sure hadn't done the job.

Peter Parsons lived four hours away, near San Jose State where Sarah had earned her BA. She really didn't expect him to live in the same place he always had—after all, it'd been a while since she'd last seen him—but when she'd called his old number, she'd been surprised to hear the same voice mail message he'd had for what seemed forever. Of course, he could have moved and had his number forwarded, but she doubted it.

Sarah drove to San Jose, figuring that at worst she could ask the neighboring tenant if he'd moved.

But he hadn't.

She knew the moment she spotted the dried-up and long-dead potted plants that still sat on the rail of his second-story apartment building. It was probably one of San Jose's oldest tenements, the narrow stairwell to the second story definitely not ADA approved. Two doors stood at the top of the landing, one to the left and one to the right. Peter's was the one to the right.

Well, now or never.

She took the first step, then another and then another, pushing the lighted doorbell button without giving herself time to catch her breath.

He opened the door.

That was a shock, because she hadn't really expected him to be home. She'd been prepared to wait for him out in her car. So when he opened the door it took her a moment to realize nothing had changed about his scrawny physique and narrow face. He looked like a little squirrel, right down to the gap between his teeth. Oddly enough, he didn't look all that surprised to see her.

"I saw you park your car."

"Good for you."

"It's the same one you've been driving for years. I recognized the sound."

She straightened, launching into her prepared speech that started with, "Give me the photos, Peter."

"What photos?" he asked.

"Put a cork in it, Peter Pan. I don't believe your whole roommate story. It was *you* who sold the photos to that magazine. I called and asked. I want those photos back, including the originals where I'm actually *wearing* something."

"Well surprise, surprise. So you actually figured it out."

"Yeah. I'm only surprised at how stupid I've been, believing your lies."

"No more stupid than I was about you. You cheated on me, Sarah."

She huffed in disbelief. "Is that what this is about? Revenge? Besides, I never cheated on you."

He didn't answer her, just said, "I'm not giving them back to you."

"Fine. Then my boyfriend and I are going to take you to court."

"You don't have a boyfriend."

"I do, too," she lied. "And he's famous. And he has lots of money."

"You and Lance Cooper broke up last weekend."

Okay, this was starting to get really creepy. "How do you know that?"

"I know a lot of things about you," he said.

Now she was *really* starting to get creeped out.

"Have you turned into a race fan?" she asked, trying to reassure herself. Maybe that's how come he knew about her and Lance. But a peek into his apartment revealed no lampshades with car numbers on them or throw rugs in a race team's colors. "How the heck do you know we broke up?"

"You want to come in?" he asked, sweeping his arm wide.

"Are you kidding me? I'm not going inside your apartment! Obviously, you're a total whack job. Jeez, I can't believe I didn't realize it before—"

He jerked her inside. Sarah yelped, pulled off balance by his sudden move. The door closed behind her and Sarah told herself not to freak out. Peter was a punk. She probably weighed more than he did. He wasn't going to do anything but try to bully her with words.

"You left me for Ron," he said.

But still, she eyed the door, knowing from experience that the only way out was that or the window.

"I know I left you, you little creep, and for obvious reasons. You're sick."

Okay, maybe insulting him wasn't a smart idea, but she'd had it. Just had it. He might be a pasty-faced geek, but he was still a bully.

"Give me the photos, Peter. If you don't, I'll tell the phone company about how you like to hack into their phone records in your spare time."

"And I'll delete my files so you'll have no evidence."

"I'm serious," she said, holding out her hand and wagging her fingers, her heart pounding so loud it boom-boom-boomed in her ears. "Give me the photos. All of them—the originals *and* the ones you stole the boobs from."

"You think I'm going to do that when I'm having so much fun seeing them displayed in public?"

"You little jerk," she said, lifting a hand.

He didn't move. She realized then that he wanted her to hit him, that if she did, it would give him power over her. He might be able to claim assault or something and then she'd never be rid of him.

Her hand dropped.

"Fine," she said. "My attorneys will be in touch."

He stepped in front of her, blocking her exit. "You don't have an attorney. You don't have anything. I made sure of that."

"Congratulations," she said. "I hope you feel like a *big* man at last." And she eyed his crotch in a derogatory way, telling him without words what she thought of his masculinity—just like she had the day she'd left him.

"I'll show you what a big man I am."

"Yeah, right," she said, trying to step around him.

He pushed her up against the wall and the funny thing was, she wasn't scared. Not really. She knew she should have been, but like an out-of-body experience, she wasn't.

"What's the matter?" she said. "Internet porn not doing it for you anymore?"

"Why stare at pictures when you can have the real thing?"

"Yeah, right."

He tried to kiss her.

Unbelievable. She shoved him away. But he took her by surprise, wrestling her to the ground.

That was when she realized just how dangerous a situation this might turn out to be.

"Let me go," she ordered, her hands held by his hand, his weight pressing into her so that she couldn't move. Yeah, he was small in stature, but he was still taller than she was.

"No."

"I'll scream."

"Like you did when I slapped the window while you were in the bus?"

"What?"

"I've had such fun following you from race to race."

"You were in Illinois?"

"Yeah. And it was fun. Pouring sugar down that engine. Putting ether in a few tires. Even tried to get you to rear-end someone, but that didn't work."

She struggled to free her hand and throw him off, but Peter just shoved her into the floor even harder.

"And it worked, too." He was starting to pant. "Look who's here."

He tried to kiss her again, but to be honest, Sarah had had enough. Using a move Cece had taught her shortly after the Stalker Fan incident, Sarah bucked her body, bringing one of her legs around and in between Peter's, then twisting her own body so she was on top.

Pete cried out in shock.

And before Sarah could stop herself, she drew back her fist and punched him in the nose.

CHAPTER TWENTY-NINE

HE WAS HAVING a shitty race.

Things had gone to hell right from the get-go, Lance cutting a tire on the tenth lap. He'd been a lap down until he'd gotten the free pass a few laps later. That had put him back on the lead lap, but his car was looser than a three-wheeled go-kart and he was having a hell of a time holding on.

"We need a pit stop," he told Allen.

"I know, I know," Allen said. "I keep praying to the pit stop gods, but they ain't listening."

"Well then break out the anti-crash fairy dust because at this rate, *I* might wreck."

They rounded turn two, Talladega's Union 76 sign flashing by. Dan Harris was coming up behind him, Lance glad he wasn't the only one having a shitty day. But Dan was still holding a grudge, and so as he came up on his rear, he tensed up.

Bam!

Oh, shit. Payback was a bitch.

The car began to lift. Through the grace of God and maybe a few caution fairies, he didn't go slideways. Dan whipped around him, Lance catching a wave out of the corner of his eye.

Okay, so now they were even. The death of Dan's best super speedway car had been avenged.

"May I now pronounce you man and wife," Lance murmured, because now the two of them could go back to being buddies on and off the track.

"Excuse me," a voice said inside his head. "You cheatin' on me out there?"

Lance shook his head a bit, thinking he'd really lost it. That had sounded like Sarah.

"I mean really, Lance. If you were having an affair with another driver, you should have told me."

He almost slammed on the brakes. He almost wrecked his car. Again. Instead he held on for dear life, watching the entrance to pit road zoom by and turning his head a bit to see if he could catch a glimpse of—

"Sarah?" he asked.

"What's the matter? My hair not big enough for you to spot from inside that car?"

He almost laughed. Hell, maybe he did laugh. He didn't know. All he knew was that suddenly he felt as if he were on top of the world.

"Hell, honey. I thought maybe you'd like a threesome."

"Nah," she said. "I don't do boy-boy-girl."

"Ahem," Allen said. "Might I remind the two of you that we're being scanned by NASCAR?"

"Ah hell, Allen," Terry, Lance's spotter said. "Don't make 'em be quiet. It was just getting good. Now. What were you saying about girl-girl-boy?"

"Actually," Sarah said. "I was about to tell Lance that there's only one man for me."

Resisting the urge to pull his car down pit road, get out, and snatch her up in his arms, Lance gripped the steering wheel.

"What did you say?" he asked.

There was a momentary pause and then, "I love you," she said softly. "And I'm sorry."

He closed his eyes, only to snap them open a half second later because Terry was yelling something in his ears.

"Caution, caution, caution," he was saying. "Go high, Lance. High and stay in the groove."

A cloud of smoke loomed before him. Lance could briefly see spinning cars, debris and flames. And then he was clear. He banged the steering wheel.

"Now," he said to Sarah, and also as a way of letting his team know he'd made it through. "What were you saying?"

"She said she's not saying anything else unless you win this race," Allen said. "And since I hate to disappoint a lady, we're putting a pound of air in the right rear. A round in the back and half pound of pressure out of the front left. Copy that everyone?"

Echoes of "copy that" rang out.

"Well, since Sarah's not talking to me anymore

maybe you can send her back to the hauler to get the kitchen sink? Couldn't hurt."

"Copy that," Allen said although laughter tinged her voice. "She's on her way."

"Thirty-two hundred RPMs, Lance," his spotter said. "We're right after the number seventy-two car."

"Copy that," Lance said, growing tense as he entered pit road.

But then he saw her. She stood near the front of his pit box, out of everyone's way and yet close enough to the wall that he could glimpse her smiling face. Heck, she even waved.

"Go, go, go," Allen said less than fourteen seconds later. And then, "Good stop, guys. Great job. Lance, let me know how she feels."

"Hey now, Allen," Lance said. "You know I never kiss and tell."

Silence. Lance thought maybe Allen wouldn't play along. But then he said. "Sorry. I was talking to Sarah. She told me she'll kiss and tell, and that you like it hard on the outside and soft on the inside—"

"Hey," Lance said.

"With icing on top," Allen finished, laughter in his voice. "But not the dot sprinkles. You like the little hot-dog-shaped ones."

Lance knew that anyone who was listening in was no doubt laughing, and that put a smile on his face, too. Damn. He hadn't felt this good in a race car since…well, since the last time Sarah was around.

"Getting ready to go green," Terry said. "Stand by."

Lance stomped on it the moment he heard, "Green, green, green," the rear tires biting down on the track and launching forward like a bat out of hell. He knew he had bottom end. That had never been the problem. The problem was when he got to the top end of speed, he couldn't hold on to it.

Until now.

He knew going into that first turn that things were better. His back end didn't break free for the first time in what felt like fifty laps (and probably was). And when he threw it deep into the corner, he was able to hold on to it.

"Better or worse?" Allen asked.

"Better," Lance replied when he came out of turn two. "Much, *much* better."

"Let me know if it stays better," Allen said.

And that was the next test. Would the setup go away? Or would the car only get better?

By turn four he figured he was just a bit tight, the front end of his car wanting to head straight for the wall. But it wasn't bad-tight, and he had a feeling as his tires wore down that tightness would loosen up and in the meantime he was passing cars.

"Damn," Lance said, the smile on his face so big, he knew his cheeks would hurt by the end of the race.

"What's the matter?" Allen asked, sounding grave.

"Nothing," Lance said. "I'm just having fun."

"Ten-four," Allen said, and Lance could hear the smile in his voice.

But the best moment for Lance came when he was able to pass Todd as if he were standing still. They raced each other cleanly, as they always did, Lance taking the top line even though he knew Todd might drift up and into him. He didn't, and when Lance ended up in front, he lifted his hand and gave a wave.

"Uh, Lance?" Allen said a few minutes later after he'd managed to pick off a couple more cars. "NASCAR wants to know if you put some of Sarah's cookies in the fuel tank."

"Tell them no, but that that's a good idea. I'll be sure and do that next weekend."

They pitted one more time under a green flag but by then Allen knew which direction they needed to go. When Lance shot off pit road, he knew he had a rocket.

One. Two. Three laps and he was sitting in the top five with forty laps to go.

Suddenly, a win looked possible.

A caution with twenty laps to go helped him pick off another few cars. His crew got him out so fast, he was second off pit road.

Second.

A win might be only a few laps away.

"Hey, Lance," Sarah said, Lance swinging his car back and forth to warm up the tires.

"Ee-yesss?" he drawled, thinking that he really didn't care if he won the race or not. All right, maybe he did, but the truth was he already felt like a winner.

He had Sarah atop his pit box.

"You know those cookies you love so much?"

"Ee-yess," he said.

"Well, if you don't pass that car, you'll never bite into one of them again."

"That sounds suspiciously like a threat."

"It is," she said, deadpan.

Lance laughed. "Well alrighty, then."

Two minutes later they waved the green flag, Lance putting the number twelve car in his sights. "So sorry to do this," he said as he came up on the car's back end. "But I'm left with no choice."

They went into the turn, Lance swinging up as if he were taking the high groove, only to fake left at the last moment, his fresh tires shooting him past the twelve car as if he were standing still.

"Now that's more like it," Sarah said.

Lance was still grinning as he took the checkered flag, but he didn't burn the tires in front of the grandstands. Oh, no, he went straight to the winner's circle, just about beating his crew and the network TV cameras and...Sarah.

She was there, hanging back a bit as if afraid to join the crowd. So he dropped the window net, disconnected his steering wheel and slid out of the car.

People screamed and cheered—the fans, his crew, perfect strangers. Lance didn't really hear them. All he heard was the beating of his own heart as he pulled her to him, inhaling her vanilla scent and burying his face in the crook of her neck. Cookies. She always smelled like cookies.

"You're here," he said.

"I'm here," she echoed. "Thanks to a Sanders Racing helicopter ride and a terrifying trip in Courtney's rental car."

"And you're shaking like a leaf."

"Must have been the drive over." But they both knew that wasn't why.

"There's no need to be scared."

"I know that," she said, meeting his eyes. "I was just so afraid you'd be mad at me. I've been dodging your calls for so many weeks."

"But you're here now."

"I should have been here weeks ago. I've been such a fool," she admitted. "All this time I've been preaching about how you can't be afraid of losing and suddenly I realized I needed to heed my own advice."

Lance's hands squeezed her shoulders, emotions nearly overcoming him: relief, gratitude and most of all, joy.

"Does this mean you're through running away?"

"It does."

"Thank God."

He pulled her to him. Someone began to shower the two of them with something. Sarah cried out. Lance laughed, the two of them hiding in each other's arms.

"Careful of my cookie," he said, pulling out a bedraggled bag from his firesuit pocket.

"What the heck is that?" Sarah asked, having to yell over the sound of applause.

"It's one of the first cookies," he said. "I was worried you wouldn't bake me any more, so I kept this one on hand."

"Oh, Lance," she said, smiling and laughing. "You can toss that thing away. I'll bake you new ones later."

"Not going to cut it," he teased, pulling her toward him again. "I'm going to want these puppies every week."

"Every week, then," she said, having to swallow rapidly.

"For the rest of our lives," he added.

And there went the tears, falling down her cheeks despite Sarah's best effort. "For the rest of our lives," she echoed.

"And a weekly performance of 'Wheels on the Bus,'" he said.

Laughter bubbled up, forcing its ways past her tear-clogged throat. "Well, now, that might be a deal breaker—"

"Oh?"

"Yeah," she said. Sarah knew that hundreds of people were probably watching them, but she didn't care. At that moment she realized they could be watched by hundreds of thousands of people and it wouldn't matter, because it felt like they were the only two people in the world.

"Then what are we going to do?" he asked.

"Kiss me," she said, "and maybe I'll change my mind."

One of the network TV cameras swung toward them right then. Sarah didn't care. She hoped the whole world saw Lance Cooper bend down and do something she hoped he did every day for the rest of their lives—kiss her senseless.

AND AT HOME, a hundred miles away, Sylvia Tingle clapped and cried. "Atta girl, Sarah. Show all those hussies at home that Lance Cooper is officially off the market. O-F-F."

And then she collapsed back into her chair, breaking out into sobs the moment her rear connected with the worn and tattered fabric. "She's gonna live happily ever after," she told the empty room. "My baby's gonna have the fairy tale."

And as it turned out…she did.

EPILOGUE

IT WAS A SPARKLING WINTER DAY in Manhattan, one of those rare days when blue sky could be seen between the uneven tops of skyscrapers. But Lance didn't notice—he was too busy pacing until he wore a path in the red carpet between the living area and the bedroom. He checked his watch, anxious because Cece and Becca had promised to have Sarah back in plenty of time to get downstairs before the awards ceremony started. And while he knew "dolling someone up" could take time, in his opinion, Sarah didn't need any dolling.

He went back to the bedroom and paused before the tall window, only to hear the click of the door that sent him spinning on his heels and going back to the main room.

Cece came in first, elegant as always in a sparkly off-white gown, a huge smile spreading across her face when she caught sight of him. Becca came next, shooting into the room like a car on nitrous oxide, making motions with her hands for him to stay put. She, too, smiled.

"Close your eyes," she said.

What had they done?

He closed his eyes as instructed, thinking to himself how nice it was to see Rebecca Newman smiling again.

"Don't peek," Cece warned in a singsong voice.

"I won't," Lance said. "But you guys better hurry. We're going to be late."

He heard dresses rustling, heard a couple of girlish giggles, then more rustling.

"Okay. Open," Cece called out.

A vision stood before him.

"Well?" she asked as the door closed behind her. Cece and Becca had left them alone.

"You look…" He tried to put it into words, eyeing the strapless gown with gauzy swishes of green netting that crisscrossed over her breasts and wrapped around her back. They'd swept her hair atop her head, her shoulders, usually so pale, a sun-bronzed brown that combined with the strands of red in her brown hair, made her look… "Breathtaking."

"Really?" she asked, her smile suddenly so bright, he couldn't help but smile back. "I wasn't sure about the dress." She glanced down at the floor-length gown that was such a perfect color of green, it made her eyes look like jade. "Cece said it makes my boobs look bigger—"

"It does," he said. "But you didn't need any help there." To hell with it. He wanted to touch her and so he did, his palm cupping her jaw, tipping her face up. "You look perfect. You *are* perfect."

"I just know how much tonight means to you."

He lowered his face toward hers, making sure she looked him in the eyes. "It would mean *nothing* if you weren't here by my side."

He watched as her eyes softened.

"I love you," he said, pulling her to him, thankful that she was here, in his arms. And that he hadn't lost her all those months ago. That she'd fought off the psycho ex who'd tried to rape her—and handily, too. At least he was no longer a threat. They'd found so many back door access codes on his computer that the Feds would be able to put him away for a very long time.

"What's this?" Sarah asking, bringing him back to the present. Her hand went to his breast pocket

Oh, damn.

"Lance Cooper," she said, drawing back. "What the heck do you have in your pocket?"

He reached inside, pulling out the bedraggled and opaque plastic bag.

"It's the cookie," he said.

Her mouth dropped open, her eyes snapping up to meet his. "You still have that thing?"

"Of course I do. It's special."

And then her eyes must have caught the flash of red inside the bag. "What's that?" she asked.

"Nothing," he lied, folding up the bag and trying

to put it back in his pocket before she became even more curious.

"Don't tell me that's nothing," she said, snatching the thing back from him. "It looks like—"

A velvet pouch.

Sarah felt her whole body still, felt her heart stumble against the wall of her chest, only to resume beating at a furious rate.

It was a velvet bag and inside she could just feel the contours of—

She looked up at Lance.

He'd taken the bag back from her suddenly numb fingers, opening it up and fishing in the crumbs to pull out the tiny jewelry bag inside. "I thought it was somehow appropriate to keep it here. Your cookie dust is pretty potent, and since I'm short on fairy dust, I thought this would do in a pinch."

Finely ground particles filled the air as he pulled the bag open, a ring spilling into his fingers, a flawless diamond set in platinum, the band molded to look like—Sarah leaned closer—like animals: a bear, a little elephant, a prancing horse.

She started to cry.

"I don't know how to bake cookies," he said, "but I do know how to draw. The hard part was finding a jeweler to take on the task of making them look like animal cookies."

"Oh, Lance," she said in a whisper, pressing a hand to her chest.

"Okay," he said, leaning back. "Let's see if I can do this right."

He got down on one knee. Sarah's hands moved to her cheeks.

"Sarah Tingle," he said, looking up at her, his blue eyes so steady Sarah couldn't look away. "Will you marry me?"

Yes.

The word nearly spilled out, but something stopped her, something made her straighten up, pretend to have to consider. "Well, I don't know," she said. "I'm not really sure I want to be the Mrs. Fields of the racing community. I mean, cookies every week until we're old and gray is an awful lot to ask."

"How about if you break it up every now and then with cupcakes?"

"Cupcakes? Are you kidding? Cupcakes are way less potent than cookies."

"Well then, what do you suggest?" he asked.

"I suggest you put that ring on my finger before I change my mind about this whole deal."

Which made him smile and chuckle. Some of his laughter faded, however, as he slipped the ring on her finger.

"Will you marry me?" he asked gently.

"Yes," she whispered, tears coming to her eyes, tears that she knew would ruin her makeup, but that didn't matter. "Yes," she said again, sliding into his arms. "Oh, yes."

"Good, 'cause I'm never going to let you slip away again."

Her smiled faded a bit, too. "Don't worry. I'm not going anywhere. I've learned my lesson."

"And what lesson is that?"

"That sometimes you have to risk it all in order to have everything."

"And do we have everything?"

"Yes," she said. "We have each other."

And they did, and they always would, along with one slightly strange housekeeper, several really good friends and one very different mother.

But they wouldn't have it any other way.

I Tip My Hat
By Rick Stevenson, Sports Editor

Many of my normal readers might be surprised to learn this column isn't going to be about racing. It's not going to be about Lance Cooper, either, and how he won the year-end championship in what has to be the greatest comeback story of the year. It's not going to be about how a team came together and created magic, won three of the last ten races and then led a chase for the championship that was truly memorable. This column is going to be about something different.

It's going to be about love.

I'll admit that might seem like an odd topic for a veteran sports reporter, a reporter who's covered racing through its ups and downs, its controversies and its commercialism. But this grizzled newsman shed more than a few tears at a recent wedding and, well, I feel compelled to write about it.

On December 10th Lance Cooper tied the knot with his girlfriend, Sarah Tingle. Those of us in the racing world watched as Lance met, courted and eventually wooed the spunky kindergarten teacher from California, a woman who didn't know a thing about stock car racing until meeting Lance. We all watched as little by little, she helped Lance Cooper overcome the worst slump of his career. We all watched as she taught him that it's not about the fame, it's not about the glory, it's about loving what you do for a living.

So this column is dedicated to Lance and Sarah Cooper. May your love be a shining example to others involved in our sport.

By the way, those were pretty darn good wedding cookies.

HQN™

We *are* romance™

From the author of *The Pleasure Slave*
and *The Stone Prince*

gena showalter

comes a sexy new title!

The fabled Jewel of Dunamis is said to hold the power to overcome any enemy. And it's OBI—Otherworld Bureau of Investigation— agent Grayson James's job to find and destroy it before it falls into the wrong hands. But when he finds the precious Jewel, only to learn that it is a woman and not a stone, destroying her is the last thing on his mind! Soon, both discover that they need each other to save the world of Atlantis, and need blossoms into passionate love—until a prophecy states that their newfound bond could destroy them both.

Jewel of Atlantis

His love could save her life—or destroy them both....
Available in stores in February.

www.HQNBooks.com

PHGS096

HQN™

We *are* romance™

USA TODAY bestselling author

SUSAN MALLERY

turns up the heat with the first novel
in her new Buchanan family saga.

At long last, Penny Jackson is on her way to becoming
a top name in the Seattle culinary scene. So when her
ex-husband, Cal Buchanan, offers her the chance to be
an executive chef at one of the best restaurants in town,
it's impossible to refuse. And before she knows it, the
heat between them is on…building from a low simmer
to full boil! But is it worth risking her heart for a little
taste of heaven…all over again?

Delicious

Being served in bookstores this February.

www.HQNBooks.com

PHSM056

HQN™

We *are* romance™

Fan favorite award-winning author

MARGARET MOORE

pens a new historical that will
sweep you off your feet!

In this sequel to *The Unwilling Bride*, handsome knight
Sir Henry defies the warnings of his family to assist
Lady Mathilde resist the efforts of her enemy—her nefarious
cousin Roald. Amidst dangerous political intrigue and shifting
loyalties, both cannot deny their forbidden attraction to each
other, and what began as a simple bargain leads to something
neither could ever have hoped for.

Hers to Command

Available in stores in February.

www.HQNBooks.com

PHMM095

An international crisis is about to
explode—unless a desperate trap
to catch a thief succeeds.
And one woman is the key....

TELL ME NO LIES

by ELIZABETH LOWELL

On Sale February 2006.

In a maze of
intrigue where
each deadly
twist and turn
leads deeper into
deception and
forbidden desire,
friends can be
enemies. Truth
may be lies.

*On sale wherever
trade paperbacks
are sold.*

HQN™

We *are* romance™

www.HQNBooks.com

PHEL125

Three classic tales from
New York Times bestselling author

JOAN JOHNSTON

Hawk's Way Brides

On Sale February 2006.

Three best-loved
favorites from the
popular family saga—
The Unforgiving Bride,
The Headstrong Bride
and *The Disobedient
Bride*—available in
this limited-edition
hardcover.

*On sale wherever
books are sold.*

HQN™
We *are* romance™

www.HQNBooks.com   PHJJ150

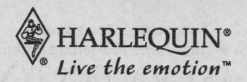
HARLEQUIN®
Live the emotion™

Upbeat,
All-American Romances

Romantic Comedy

 Harlequin Historicals®
Historical,
Romantic Adventure

HARLEQUIN®
INTRIGUE
Romantic Suspense

The essence of
modern romance

Seduction and passion
guaranteed

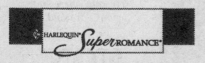
Emotional,
Exciting, Unexpected

Temptation
Sassy, Sexy, Seductive!

www.eHarlequin.com   HDIR204

HQN™

We *are* romance™

Don't miss the return of this classic romance novel
by *New York Times* bestselling author

CHARLOTTE HUGHES

Marilee Abernathy's life is a mess. Everyone knows about her
husband's affair with the town floozy. And when her dignified
farewell goes awry, perhaps a better way to cope might just be
with a new attitude. At least that's what her sexy neighbor
Sam Brewer thinks. Soon, Marilee's new attitude goes a long way,
reminding Sam of some of his own long-forgotten dreams. Now
he just needs to convince Marilee to turn
some of that sparkle his way....

A New Attitude

Available in stores in February.

www.HQNBooks.com

PHCH158

pamela britton

77035   DANGEROUS CURVES   ___ $6.50 U.S. ___ $7.99 CAN.

(limited quantities available)

TOTAL AMOUNT $ _____
POSTAGE & HANDLING $ _____
($1.00 FOR 1 BOOK, 50¢ for each additional)
APPLICABLE TAXES* $ _____
TOTAL PAYABLE $ _____

(check or money order—please do not send cash)

To order, complete this form and send it, along with a check or money order for the total above, payable to HQN Books, to: **In the U.S.:** 3010 Walden Avenue, P.O. Box 9077, Buffalo, NY 14269-9077; **In Canada:** P.O. Box 636, Fort Erie, Ontario, L2A 5X3.

Name: _____
Address: _____ City: _____
State/Prov.: _____ Zip/Postal Code: _____
Account Number (if applicable): _____

075 CSAS

*New York residents remit applicable sales taxes.
*Canadian residents remit applicable GST and provincial taxes.

HQN™

We *are* romance™

www.HQNBooks.com

PHPB0206BL